The Mildenhall Legacy

The Mildenhall Legacy

Albert Sipes

To order additional copies of this book, contact:
Xlibris
844-714-8691
www.Xlibris.com
Orders@Xlibris.com
840641

Contents

Acknowledgments

Thank you, Cathy Sipes, my wife, reader, and confidante.

Thank you, Mike Sipes, for your aircraft maintenance knowledge.

Thank you, Lynn T. Baca, my content editor, SFC Joshua W. Krueger, for your rudimentary understanding of the US military, Corbin and Jenifer Schon, for your IT expertise, Marlene Sipes Sweeney and Richard Al Gaskill for your help in the production of this novel.

List of new characters per chapter,
minor to the significant influence that moves the story along.

X X X

Chapter 1

RESTLESS SPIRITS

February 2015

Alfred felt the brisk, cold wind coming out of the north whip through his clothes and into his bones. It stirred the ponderosas to a frenzy. Cones dropped as trees waved to the Colorado sky. Brown pine needles fluttered and spread over the rocky ground. A morning trek to retrieve the newspaper was an uphill stagger against the wind. It bit into his face and cheeks. 'Another fine windy day,' he thought. Cleansed air washed over him, riffling through the light jacket and thin jeans. The wind ruffled open the newspaper to the headline, 'Denver Broncos Win Super Bowl 50.' He noticed the sounds of the pebbles clicking together as they swirled in circular swarms pushed by the wind. Their home was modest but offered safe refuge for over 20 years.

"Paper's in," he said to Katie. Entering the kitchen, he drew her near and pecked her lips with a modest kiss.

"We got a phone call while you were out," she said, "Our grandniece wants to come and stay with us for a while." Silence ensued as he hung his thin jacket near the door.

Wondering who she was talking about, he asked, "Which grandniece?"

"Kim Chamber's 20-year-old daughter, Eve, she's dropping by tomorrow, bag and baggage."

Offering safe harbor was something the couple provided now and then. The part about bag and baggage sounded like Eve wanted to stay on for a while. Katie and Alfred's life was simple since they had retired, living within their means, not prone to extravagance. In the foothills of the Rockies, their log home sat adjacent to a few neighbors, end of the roaders, a class distinction in itself. They could have been a safe house for the witness protection program. They would listen and not interrupt when friends dropped by with an agenda. It was part of being civil. Alfred always maintained that people were better than the sum of their parts. You had to take them warts and all; see them in all their moods. "We all have character flaws," he would say on occasion.

Alfred said to Katie, "I guess we'll see what happens tomorrow."

*   *   *

Several weeks earlier, Eve's trials had begun. Her main flaw was getting in too deep and not having an exit strategy. She cursed her own poor decisions and was determined to change. Old habits of codependence had dogged her through late adolescence. This latest encounter with a fellow housemate was a lulu! It involved degenerates below her pay grade. She needed to run, and she needed to hide. She grabbed her cell phone and a small backpack and quietly left the two-story house where she had been living for three months. There was enough daylight that Eve could safely reach the interstate on foot. In northern New Mexico, Eve would catch her second ride. Her first had come at the on-ramp from Mulberry to southbound I-25. She had joined an older man and his young nephew traveling to Raton, New Mexico.

Hitchhiking through mountainous terrain, Eve stood thumbing a ride just north of Las Vegas, New Mexico. Trucker Jill Clayborne had finished her load call with dispatch and was highballing toward Albuquerque. Once there, she would take on a load of window frames. Eve, carrying her backpack, wasn't desperate but determined to hitch a ride before dark. Seeing an 18-wheeler bearing down from the north with a female driver, she thumbed vigorously. The driver looked petit and had delicate features. Jill geared down and hit the jakes slowing the truck to a halt. Shifting to neutral, setting the air brakes and four-way flashers, she sidled over to the passenger side and rolled down the window. Slightly winded, Eve caught up to the passenger door.

"Where you headed?" Jill shouted over the idling diesel.

"Wherever you're going," shouted Eve from the ground.

Jill gave Eve a once-over with elevator eyes, not considering the woman a risk.

"What's in the backpack?" she asked.

"Nothing scary," said Eve. "Hair spray and clothes."

"Climb in and lock the door," said the driver; "I'm Jill Clayborne, and you?" Eve climbed aboard, settling into the seat, and hit the door lock.

Offering her hand, "Eve Chambers," she answered. Checking her driver-side mirrors, the two women remained quiet while Jill eased her rig back onto the interstate and geared up through the nine-speed transmission.

"So, anywhere, huh?" said Jill.

Eve formulated an answer before saying," Bad break-up!"

Two miles down the road, Jill offered another ice-breaker. "I'm empty now, but I'll be picking up a load in Albuquerque, then heading on to the L.A. basin." She said this with a wry smile, not pushing, only offering some assurance of a long ride. Eve nodded.

"I fueled at Loveland, and my next fuel stop is at the Petro in Milan, in a couple of hundred miles. I have to sleep in Albuquerque; I'm running a log book." Her passenger was noncommittal but nodded approval.

*   *   *

At their Carter Lake home, Katie and Alfred sat down to have an early brunch. They joined hands and offered a prayer of thanks before enjoying an omelet, V8 juice, and strong coffee. It was their morning ritual. They read their sections of the paper quietly; her section, the national news, and his section, the sports stories that never really interested his wife.

"ISIS militants executed more captives," Katie said, not looking up.

Alfred's response was to nod and take another bite of his food. "Um, there's always something," he finally offered.

Their lifestyle was one of seclusion, now that they were retired. The couple ventured out to the grocery shop and gas up the car when necessary. Alfred would wander out to his woodshop and Katie to her sewing room. It kept them out of crowds and away from the Flu bug. In their seventies, they had seen a lot of dysfunction on both national and local levels.

Now, into their quiet life of seclusion, a young relative was being inserted. Alfred didn't remember for sure who this girl was. Why was she even coming? The notion of a young relative coming to visit piqued their interest.

"Katie, I think I remember that girl, your sister's granddaughter. Didn't she take off from Fort Collins a couple of months ago?" It didn't hit him forcefully, but there it was, out in the open.

"You're right," said Katie, "She's my grandniece, Kim Chamber's daughter in Florida." Katie rolled her eyes and smiled. "I hope heaven will help us," she added. Two years earlier, Eve had come to attend Colorado State University with a friend, and now she was out running around like a little lost soul.

*   *   *

Two months earlier, Jill and Eve traveled south from Santa Fe at seventy miles per hour. Jill had picked Eve up as she was hitchhiking. The lights of Albuquerque came into view. Jill downshifted and applied a bit of trailer brake as traffic swelled.

"I'll find the place I'm to deliver on the map after we settle in at the Travel America truck stop on I-25 and 40," Jill said this more to herself than to Eve.

"I won't be loading until tomorrow. My appointment is at 8:30. You can take the top bunk. First, we can freshen up and get something to eat."

Jill aligned an empty hole on the T.A. truck lot on the third row. She rolled the Freightliner abreast of other idling tractors on either side. A Swift driver in his cab was bringing his logbooks up to date on the left. On their right was a driver couple dragging a canvas-covered flatbed.

"Grab your bag and come inside," said Jill. "I don't know about you, but I have to pee!"

Truck stops were similar along the nation's interstates. Some had reputations for being lizard pits plying the skin trade. Mostly, they were simply a place to park 53' trailers where drivers could eat and sleep. There would be a fuel island and an ever-present restaurant. The truck stop in Albuquerque could provide the two women with a shower and supper.

The experience was all new to Eve. She looked around apprehensively as the two women walked into the restaurant. Men were seated by twos, team drivers. Families sat together and most likely lived in their trucks. They had no brick and mortar to call home. Jill and Eve had passed a toddler no more than walking age wearing a T-shirt for a diaper. The young curly-haired boy came off the truck with simian dexterity. He hopped to the diesel-soaked concrete bare-footed and strode away with a sibling. 'Gypsies,' Eve thought to herself, 'American gypsies.'

Following the lite meal, Jill arranged bills of lading over the table and caught up with her logbook. Their waitress ran Jill's credit card, leaving it beside her plate. Eve glanced toward the door. She froze like a twelve-year-old caught shoplifting. Jill noticed the change of temperament. She followed Eve's gaze to a fifty-something couple. A waitress led them to a table as Eve grabbed a menu and held it to her nose, covering her eyes. The twosome strode by and was seated two booths away. Eve grabbed a napkin and a pen. She jotted, "Ex boyfriend's parents!" Eve's back was to the couple as Jill leaned out in the aisle, catching a full view of the man and woman. They were dressed to the nines, obviously not truck drivers. She glanced at Eve, "OK, this is how we're going to do this. When the woman gets up to use the john, and she will, we'll leave." Having said this, Jill scribbled her signature on the meal ticket and gathered her paperwork.

Perusing a menu and talking, the woman who had entered with her husband smiled and mumbled a few words. She slid out of the booth and strode away toward the restrooms. The man's back was to the young women. Jill signaled to Eve that it was time to vamoose. They slid out of their booth and made a bee-line toward the door. Jill brought up the rear as the two walked past the man and through the outer doors. The man focused on his menu as the young women hurried onto the parking lot.

"Don't look back, don't look back, "Jill gasped once outside. Finally seated in the truck, she asked, "What was that all about?"

"OK," Eve began. "Here's what it is." Jill got the big picture when Eve explained her last few weeks in Fort Collins. Gerald Ingalls was a slug that you wouldn't want your daughter bringing home to supper.

"That couple in the diner was Gerald's parents, Charles and Lynn Ingalls," Eve told Jill. "He's the reason I left Fort Collins and was hitchhiking on the road when I met you. I had to get away! Gerald is a verbose know-it-all with his friend Flynn, his matching sidekick low-life. Their goal was to consume beef jerky and argue the finer points of video games."

"Wow, you're on a roll," said Jill, "Is there more?" Eve thought Gerald may have gotten much too close because he soiled his dockers and may have grazed her virtue. He phoned his mom, the brave lad, and said he might have gotten a girl pregnant. His mother went berserk and insisted that the 'said girl' get a pregnancy test kit. All the while, Eve was in the bathroom at the rental house sobbing and putting on a pretty good show. She bailed that night, still owing her share of the month's house rent.

*   *   *

The Real estate market was booming in northern Colorado. Gerald's parents, Charles and Lynn, had a firm hold of the reins, knocking down a few listings every month. The percentages bore it out. Five percent of the real estate brokers sell ninety-five percent of real estate properties. They found themselves in that caliber of wheeler-dealers. They were looking forward to early retirement in their fifties, but one thing held them back. Their son Gerald was not a shaker and mover like themselves. Specifically, he had failed to launch from his parent's home after three years of freedom from high school. Gerald knew where his allowances were coming from and failed at getting serious about his future.

In a bold move, Gerald's mother suggested that he share expenses in a rental property among his close friends. He did just that, except one of his two friends was also a nonstarter. They had two gal pals, Trish and Eve, who decided to jump into the fray. Five young adults had set up housekeeping near downtown Fort Collins. The commune arrangement was off and running. It was a demonstration in perpetuity that only three of the team members had jobs. Gerald and Flynn sucked up the groceries living off the welfare of their housemates. The workers paid all utilities and kept the lawn spiffy. Gerald and Flynn hung out downtown and discussed social philosophy during the day, then retired to their video games for the evening. Such an arrangement couldn't possibly last. The only worker guy got fed up and split. Trish and Eve were bringing in all the income, but the wheels would soon fall off. Then the beer party happened. From there, a natural series of events took place.

The Ingalls copped a wait-and-see attitude following the initial shock that their son Gerald may have impregnated Eve. Since Eve left the group rental arrangement, Gerald's parents were concerned that she might be carrying their one and only grandchild. For the immediate future, they blew it off. After talking to Gerald, they decided to check out a retirement property in Sedona, Arizona. It was a coincidence that Eve and Jill were on the road heading in the same direction. Then Eve spotted them at the Albuquerque truck stop.

*   *   *

Following a restless night in the truck, Eve was awakened by Jill's very shrill alarm clock. Jill dressed quickly, then dropped her bills of lading and signatures of consignees into a packet and then dropped the whole package into a FedEx deposit box. From there, the paperwork would go to the terminal office in Phoenix for processing. The FedEx box was how Jill got paid for her efforts. With the job done, she returned to Eve and the truck.

"We'll start loading up, then get something to eat." Jill knew that her pick-up warehouse was a mere three miles away, pulling into traffic.

On entering the large warehouse complex, a gate attendant found Jill's paperwork and directed her to dock door seventeen. The warehouse was busy with aligned semi-tractor trailers loading or unloading. Backing into her designated door, Jill threw the truck out of gear and set the air brakes. She climbed out of the cab, opened, and latched the rear doors, climbed back into the cab, released the air brakes, and carefully nudged into the dock bumpers. Setting her air brakes again, she got out and chocked the rear tandem tires.

"Don't go away," she said to Eve through the driver's side window. After several minutes, she returned.

"It will be an hour or two before we're loaded. Come on, let's find a café." After a short walk to Candelaria Road, they found a day-diner.

Ordering cinnamon rolls and coffee, Jill asked Eve, "If you're on the run, why haven't you ditched your cell phone?" Dumbfounded, Eve couldn't formulate an answer.

"You do know, don't you? Your movements could be tracked by your cellphone. And I know you have a credit card, you used it last night to get a pregnancy test kit, or didn't you think I noticed?" Eve stammered, "Well, I'm not running from the FBI!" The two stared at one another for a few seconds.

"So, why haven't you used the test kit?"

"I don't have an answer to that question; maybe it's too early to check."

"When we fuel at Milan, get in the ladies' room and put that test kit to use," Jill said with affirmation, adding, "It wouldn't be my first rodeo, just do it!"

Walking back to the warehouse, the two women figured out a strategy about Eve's future.

"Why the interest in me," Eve asked as the two were searching for common ground.

"I see myself in you about two years ago playing house, no prospects, no future. I saw an ad on a bus stop bench. I had enough money saved to attend truck driver training."

"Where," asked Eve.

"I applied for training in Phoenix, completed the groundwork, and began driving in early October, about two Thanksgivings ago." Jill turned toward Eve as they walked and put a hand on her shoulder.

"The best move I ever made. I have no rent to pay. I travel to the lower 48 states and Canada. Let's see what else; oh yeah, bank accounts on both coasts with enough saved to put down roots. I'll keep driving until I decide what to do with the rest of my life." They trekked on in silence, but Eve's mind was racing. Was this an opportunity Eve might consider? She wondered.

* * *

Traveling miles ahead of Jill and Eve, the Ingalls had turned south from Flagstaff. They drove from I-40 onto Arizona state highway 89A. Morning sun sparkled through ash-leaf maples and willows as they went through Oak Creek Canyon. Sedona, less than an hour away, was their final destination. Charles had commonly exchanged favors with other brokers throughout the western states. This time, it would be a personal favor. The Arizona market was booming, and there were always people resettling, statistically about every seven years. Charles and Lynn had entered a fast-paced real estate office. Looking over his reading glasses, a former classmate of Charles dropped a stack of papers at his desk and walked toward the couple.

"How are you two doing? Great to see you!" Extending a hand to Charles and bear-hugging, the two greeted.

The old friend had been a marketing major at Colorado State one year ahead of Charles. They shared a few classes and formed a strong bond. That was 20 years ago, but the two stayed in touch.

"Let me take you to lunch, we'll hash over old times, and I can weasel my way of seeing why you're in this neck of the woods." The atmosphere was hectic around the large brokerage, but Charles' friend was happy to take the time and give the couple his full attention.

* * *

The truckers, Jill and Eve, on the same path were about to leave Albuquerque. It was a bit past high noon by the time Jill was loaded. She gathered her paperwork from the load manager slipped out the door only steps from dock door 17. Jill placed her paperwork on the driver's seat and prepared to leave. She paused for a mental assessment figuring out how to get back to westbound I-40. By the time Jill and Eve would reach Milan, New Mexico, they would have burned off 620 pounds of diesel fuel. There was a KAT Scale at Milan where she would fuel and find the gross weight of her rig. It would be thirteen hundred miles to her next fuel stop in California. A window frame load wouldn't be that heavy, she figured. By the time she and Eve crossed the scale at Blythe, California, the truck would burn fuel and be well under weight limitations. Six and a half miles per gallon for her rig was normal, mountainous terrain or not. Taking on fuel at Milan would put her well past L.A. and onto her next destination, wherever that might be. Jill loved this part of the job. Numbers were her jam.

Eve, riding along with Jill, took an interest in Jill's driving ability and responsibilities. She shadowed Jill for much of the time, learning how to help, not just sit. The next appointment was to unload the window frames in Compton, California. They would sleep somewhere along the route, and the Phoenix terminal was a secure bet. Jill reasoned that she might hide Eve in the sleeper, as passengers were not allowed unless they held a CDL license and registered with the company. Jill felt a bond with this runaway girl, and she had promised to get Eve to L.A.

Along the eighty-mile run to Milan, the two perfected a strategy that might pan out for Eve's future.

"Suppose you find a place to live and attend driver school in Longmont, Colorado?" As Jill posed the question, Eve jumped on it! She had seen enough to give professional driving some consideration. Maybe she could stay with her great aunt and uncle, Katie and Alfred, during her weeks of driver training. After floating the idea, Jill added that the two could team drive, get in more miles, and make a decent living for both of them.

"You don't have to drive semis for the rest of your life," Jill said.

"In a couple of years, you could put a down payment on a house in a great neighborhood, whatever city you choose. You could put in for somewhere that pays the big bucks if you like. How do you like Alaska?"

Both laughed at the prospect. Drivers could buy a tractor and lease it back to the company. That was how to make it in professional driving.

*   *   *

Miles to the southwest, Gerald's parents looked for a second home in Sedona. Charles and Lynn were not on a sightseeing trip. They were interested in an investment property, preferably renting one during the summer. Winters were different, and they might spend several months in

Sedona. The Real-estate broker seized the opportunity bringing along a top producer. His assistant had many years of experience in high-end Sedona real estate. The foursome soon found a quiet café frequented by locals. After some chit-chat, several ideas about properties were on the table. Wasting no time, the real-estate assistant opened her Ipad and took a seat between Charles and Lynn. She had a pleasant look on her face, both charming and disarming. Suave and coiffured, she took her time setting the atmosphere. The fragrance she wore said, 'money.'

"OK, what price range are we looking at." She tossed her question into the mix like she knew the answer?

The broker wanted the women to face off in discussion. 'Win the woman, get the sale.' It was a strategy he had perfected over the years. He sat forward in his chair, leaned back, loosened his jacket, and looked toward Charles.

"Played any golf lately?" Charles knew this sales game too.

Nose to nose, eyeball to eyeball with the broker assistant, Lynn said, "I think we could qualify for $2.5 million." Lynn and the assistant had a similar temperament, alpha dogs getting down to the nitty-gritty. Scrolling through her Ipad, the assistant brought her goods to the table.

"I have several that may interest you." One property on Bristlecone Pines Road was gorgeous but far above their price range. Two others on Moki Drive and Posse Ground Road would possibly be more to their liking. The Moki Drive home was in foreclosure.

"I can check on it for you," she murmured with a wink, "I'll find money figures on the foreclosure." Her dimples were bright and deep as she smiled broadly. After some haggling and speculation, they concluded the deal. All smiles, the Ingalls drove to their hotel on Horizon Drive. The realtors would lay the groundwork for an offer on the Moki Drive foreclosure. The Posse Ground Road home would be a 'fallback,' one to consider if the first didn't pan out. For Lynn, it was time to shop. Tomorrow, they would pay a visit to the Sedona properties.

* * *

In Fort Collins, Gerald was making plans. Finding himself at loose ends since Eve's departure, he was looking for something constructive to do. His parents had left Gerald in charge of their house as they departed for the southwest. They didn't think things could go wrong because Gerald remained in the house-sharing agreement. He seldom set foot in his folks 6,000 square foot home, that is, until they left. He and his buddy Flynn decided to check the place out, flush the six toilets, and look for anything interesting. There was a wall safe in the library. His parents had told him countless times, "If anything should happen to us, get into the safe, then call our lawyer." He got into the safe but skipped the lawyer part. His parents were fine and dandy too, as they had just called to tell him so, and they were out of town. That opened the door for Gerald and Flynn to pry into domestic affairs.

"Interesting," Flynn said as Gerald took possession of a safe deposit box key from where it sat in the safe. Gerald had no idea what the key was for, so Flynn filled him in. Gerald told Flynn where his parents banked.

"The thing is, I never heard they say anything about a safety deposit box," he told Flynn. He hefted the key in his hand, feeling the weight and odd shape of the thing.

"We'd better check this out," Gerald reasoned. "First, let's get a case of brew and head to the house."

Forty-five minutes later, they were guzzling beer and eating pizza along with their other fellow renter. Trish Saunders, on her day off, was cutting pizza slices. Slender and athletic, she wore blue shorts and a frilly top, somewhat mismatched. Her blonde, nearly shoulder-length hair was in ringlets due to the morning heat. She sweated from the unairconditioned house, which set her bitter mood. Male roomies Gerald and Flynn were engaged in a free for all water fight in the backyard.

Sopped and shivering from the garden hose, Gerald threw off his shirt as he entered the kitchen and headed for his room. There was a tiny metallic thunk sound as he departed the kitchen where Trish stood cutting the cold pizza. Flynn wasn't far behind, except he stopped to hurl in the kitchen sink. Trish, disgusted and giving up on the pizza, kicked at Flynn.

"Clean up after yourself." Her earrings jumped, and her face turned crimson as she shouted, "I've had enough of you two!"

Then she saw it, a wet safe deposit box key near the bread toaster. She slipped it in her jean shorts with the finesse of a carnival barker. Flynn, his head in the sink and retching, took little notice. Ignoring him, Trish marched out the back door, hopped in her beat-up Fiat, and drove to the First National Bank where she worked.

*   *   *

Eve, far away in New Mexico, was on no ones' s radar at the time. The truck rolled along I-17, through the saguaro-covered hills, and into Phoenix traffic. Jill spotted a Holiday Inn at Cactus Road. It was a quarter-mile ahead, plenty of time to maneuver the 53' trailer into the exit lane.

"This is it," she said, "Easy off and easy on." She made her turns slowly and carefully as four-wheelers buzzed around her rig.

"Don't want to smack anybody," she related to Eve. "If I do, it's driver error, meaning me." She maneuvered onto the Holiday Inn lot near the curb, parallel to the rushing traffic.

Eve hopped down, meeting the 107-degree heat of Phoenix. Then, she realized how well the cab air conditioning had been working. Jill threw the truck out of gear, set the air brakes, and put the engine at high idle. Climbing down to the baked concrete, she locked the doors and accompanied Eve toward the motel lobby. At that hour, there were several rooms available. The pool was empty, and there were no takers for the hot afternoon and a café adjacent to the lobby.

"Do you want to come up and shower?" Eve offered.

"No, there are women showers and lockers at the terminal, and I have to chat with my fleet manager before he goes off shift." Jill was road weary and made her exit saying, "I'll be back here, the same spot, around 9:30 tomorrow morning. I'll bring a driver application so you can get a preview of driver training." Jill wasn't sure if Eve would remain interested in the radical lifestyle change. It could be daunting, a challenge for the faint of heart, but the transportation industry also had its rewards.

*   *   *

Up north in Fort Collins, Trish parked the Fiat and entered the bank where she worked.

At the noon hour, several officers had gone to be with friends and coworkers two blocks away. Henri's Diner was a favorite. A skeleton crew was left at the bank to care for the few customers who might venture into the lobby. Two tellers attempted to look busy, balancing their drawers.

"Hey Steph," Trish said to a girl half awake at the lobby desk, "Toss me the box master. I need to check my contents; I haven't done it in a while." The girl sat back in her chair, opened the desk drawer, and fished out the safe deposit box master key. She tossed it to Trish.

Entering an off chute of the main vault, Trish grasped the master and her key to box C-333. It was a perk of the bank, having rent-free deposit boxes for employees. She opened her drawer near the floor. In a mad scramble of ill intent, she made a decision that would dog her for the rest of her days. It was simply too tempting. Her safety deposit box held little more than a pair of pearl earrings from her mother and her high school diploma.

On the key she had taken from the kitchen counter back home, a small piece of tape labeled the number L-3307. 'Stupid,' she thought. Numbskulls should never tape the box number to their keys. With the master, she opened that drawer. She discovered that the contents held far more than her drawer. Inside L-3307, among other paperwork, was an envelope with the handwritten words, 'Loving son Gerald.' Trish peeked inside and fished out nine money packets of $100 bills. She left one in the envelope. Muttering to herself, she mouthed the words, 'More than you deserve, you damn snake!' She placed $90K into her deposit box, locked both drawers, and walked out of the vault.

Thanks, Steph," she said, tossing the master key to her coworker. Trish had spent a lifetime wearing clothes from Goodwill and chasing a dream of financial independence. Thanks to the blow-hard Gerald back at the house, she had now taken a shortcut to prosperity. Now, the thought of covering her tracks loomed large in her immediate future.

She turned and dropped her small purse near Stephanie's desk as an afterthought. It contained a few items, some of which bounced out. There was nothing significant in the bag, and she wanted Steph to witness that.

"Sorry," she said, "I get tired of carrying that damn thing around." Collecting her near-empty clutch bag, Trish departed, saying, "Gotta go, catch ya later." The ruse had begun, but how to continue would become worrisome.

She returned to the house, set the Ingalls key L-3307 back on the kitchen counter, and took a slice of pizza and a cold brew from the refrigerator. Trish retired to a big screen T.V. in the living room. Her daytime soaps had come on. Soon, Gerald thumped his way down the stairs, clutching a towel about his waist. His hair wet and looking nervous, Gerald went straight to the kitchen. Breathing a sigh of relief, 'God, you idiot,' he told himself, after clutching the key to L-3307.

* * *

In Arizona, the fast pace of the Ingalls couple was picking up as they toured Sedona properties. The Ingalls' purchased the large home on Moki Drive. Following their bid with the bank, they got the place at the bargain price of $2.25 million. In Fort Collins, their son Gerald was thrilled to find ten thousand dollars in the safe deposit box L-3307 at his folks' bank. Ten thousand dollars, he scoffed, 'Oh my gosh!' The envelope had his name on it! 'Let sleeping dogs lie,' he muttered to himself. He would ride it out and not mention his snooping, and his folks already gave him a generous monthly allowance. He put the deposit box key back in his folk's wall safe at their house. He banged the door shut and spun the dial. His folks were due to return home from Sedona in a couple of days.

Over the ensuing days, Trish had severe misgivings about taking money out of the Ingalls deposit box. She couldn't put it back; Gerald had the key! Trish wondered, 'If I offered to give the money back to Gerald, would I still be a thief?' Then she remembered something her father had told her.

"Make your luck." Undecided about what she might do with $90,000, she had foolishly placed it in her deposit box C-333. Now what? She had known the Ingalls for some time and even waited on them occasionally at the bank. 'Just breath,' she told herself, 'No hurry, no worries.'

In the act of benevolence, Trish had Eve's cell phone number and called her. Eve had contacted Katie and Alfred, asking to stay with them. She was to start driver training in Longmont. Trish offered Eve $1,100 to cover the application costs and begin driver training. All was right with the world. Trish spread her good fortune around, and Eve was a life-long friend.

*　　*　　*

Three weeks after the heist, Katie and Alfred had finished breakfast and started their morning routines. As Katie cleared the table, she saw a beat-up Fiat roll into the yard. Eve had come back to Colorado from riding with Jill Clayborne. She was ready to start driver training in Longmont. Eve, with Trish, got out of the passenger side of the Fiat. Connecting the dots, she called to Alfred.

"She's here!" The two went to the entryway to welcome Eve and her friend into the kitchen. Trish was all aglow, wearing a brightly colored jacket, and went overboard about the friendship she shared with the long-lost Eve.

"Aunt Katie, this is my friend Trish," Eve said. They hugged one another, and Katie marveled at Eve's maturity. After a few passing remarks about Eve's mother in Florida, Katie invited her guests to sit and have coffee. Both Katie and Alfred were happy to see how Eve carried herself. All grown up, they decided, she seemed happy and well adjusted. The friend, Trish, bobbed along behind as Alfred brought coffee cups and crumpets to the table.

"So, what brings you out our way?" He glanced at his wife as they held their collective breath.

"Well, I need a place to stay while I'm attending truck driver school. I wouldn't be around much, and training starts early." Eve explained how she would be away before the sun came up and not return until late afternoon or evening. After three weeks, she would go out with a trainer for six weeks.

"If it's alright with you, I would be willing to rent the bunkhouse for a couple of months, three at the most. When I get my CDL and a truck of my own from the company, I will live on it permanently."

Alfred's head bobbed in approval. "So, how are you going to get to the Longmont school?" he asked.

Eve smiled, saying, "Trish is giving me her Fiat, the car in the driveway. She and I will go car shopping; Trish needs a newer set of wheels." It all came off logically and prudent as she relayed her immediate plans.

"Well then, I guess it's settled," Alfred said. "Plan your work and work your plan! You're welcome to stay for as long as you like!" Following some reassurance, the girls set off in the Fiat to go car shopping.

"I guess I'd better straighten up the bunkhouse," Katie said as the two young women drove away.

Chapter 2

NEW HORIZONS

March 2015

With financial help from Trish, Eve soon began driver training. One week after settling in at Katie and Alfred's, she drove to the training center in Longmont. The training area consisted of a large tract of land with several small buildings bordering the property. One served as a classroom. The instructor, a tall 60'ish man with impish red hair, started by saying, "I welcome you all. We have a nice mix of candidates. Why don't we go around the room and introduce ourselves?" The students found themselves with five men and one woman. They were a tribe looking out for one another. A man in his early fifties said he had retired from flying commercial aircraft.

"I've seen the country from 36,000 feet for 22 years, and I want to see it from ground level." Another said he had no choice in coming to the school.

"There is major construction around my parts store, and my customer base has disintegrated. I closed the shop temporarily. I don't fly fish, and I don't like to sit around, so here I am." When it came to Eve, she said she was there because she experienced truck driving from the passenger seat and wanted to drive a rig independently. Another, a tall pleasant looking guy, said, "My wife and I separated; I need something constructive to do while I figure out my future." A short guy in western togs and a cowboy hat said, "I've been servicing trucks at Johnson's Corner on I-25. It's time I join a new cast of characters." The final guy said, "I'll pass." Everyone looked at one other, nodding to say, we all have our stories; some are better left unsaid.

The instructor passed out a syllabus on the elements to be covered and the time frame.

"The basic structure of the class will be learning to handle tractor-trailer combinations safely and efficiently. If you pass our requirements and the test for your commercial driver's license successfully, you will have a job with us. The paperwork involved is your lifeblood. If you mess up the paperwork, it's as bad as jackknifing the truck or pulling one of many boo-boos that can get you fired. We will have your backs, but most of the mishaps are driver errors. The toughest one is this. We have a three-strike policy. We'll give you your walking papers if you have three fender benders. No, ifs and or buts! Are we clear on that?" A hushed silence swept over the driver candidates.

The instructor's tone was both strict and emphatic. Books on bills of lading and the structure of consignee obligations were essential parts of the paperwork. Rules and laws of the road are crucial to learning. The handling of hazardous materials loads or wide loads is covered. Each state has its own set of criteria for semi-trucks passing through. Bridge laws in Idaho are different from the rest of the country. The laws of Oregon are also dissimilar to other states. It's the only state in the union where ramp traffic coming onto a freeway has the right-of-way. The instructor droned on about the rudiments of the road and the load. The first two hours of class time went fast, then came a half-hour break.

"We teach the double-clutch method," the instructor said. "I'd suggest that you spend your idle time doing a few squats to build up your leg muscles." Most took to the outer doors on a classroom break, where they lit smokes and sat wide-eyed.

"This isn't going to be a cakewalk," one man said. They all nodded in agreement. The quiet guy asked, "What's a consignee?"

*　　*　　*

Lester Hays had worked at the same bank as Trish for several years. He was not an officer, but Les knew he was on the fast track to promotion at the bank, and he held a good deal of responsibility considering his position and pay grade. Les had admired Trish from the first time he saw her, and at the lunch hour he would make sure to seat himself across the table from her. The two or three other coworkers who had joined Les at Henri's dinner noticed his efforts, and so did Trish. He loved her from afar; it was apparent.

"Did you see that woman with the shopping bag this morning? She looked kind of suspicious leaving her grown son at the door," Les began.

"I had my eye on them," someone else said. The scenario of their lunch hour talks would have the group enthralled in stories of 'what if!' It would soon be time to trek back to their cubicles and continue the grind without concluding the outcome of their fantasies.

"March of the bean counters," the bank president would say as they entered the bank and returned to their appointed tasks. It was a friendly group with home life often the subject of their discourse.

Following Trish's escapade, taking $90 thousand from the Ingalls deposit box, she was getting frantic. She must move the contents to her deposit box out of the bank. How could she maneuver nine 10K money packets without arousing suspicion? Then came a revelation. Les mentioned that the bank regulator had discussed with the bank president that changes were coming. The regulator had recommended the bank reconfigure the safe-deposit boxes and rid the vault of those who hadn't paid their annual rental fees.

"Some of the owners," Les said, "haven't paid their fees for years! We have 42 deposit boxes that are sitting on the bubble awaiting eviction." It was customary to drill the boxes and the contents sent to their holding company for storage.

"Trish, I want you to take charge of the paperwork," said Les. "When the fun starts, things will move fast!"

"I'm in," she responded. Trish was ready to send letters asking people to bring their agreements up to date. There was one major hurdle. The Ingalls' box L-3307 was not on the list of delinquents. The wheels were turning in her mind as she knocked over her water goblet. Trish wondered how she could cover for herself and dodged Les's question.

"Are you OK," he asked, "you seem a bit preoccupied," Trish pondered how she ever got into such a mess.

"I'll be OK; just give me a moment," she said as she mopped up water with her napkin.

* * *

After buying the Sedona property, the Ingalls set out on their drive back to Colorado. They would retrace their route with one exception. An alternate route would take them north through Navajo country. The 12-hour drive gave them time to discuss the Sedona property and its environs. It was a great rental prospect, but Lynn hatched another idea.

"Suppose we get Gerald out of that awful rental property and have him occupy the Sedona house during the fall and winter months? If we should be lucky enough to rent it, he could have eyes on the property and live in the guest house." Charles gave her a side glance and asked, "Are you sure that's a good idea? Gerald hasn't shown many initiatives since graduating from high school."

"We could send him with a nest egg, maybe let him find his wings." Lynn proposed. They drove on in silence for a few miles along I-40, heading toward Chambers, Arizona, and route 191. The more Charles thought about Lynn's plan, the more he bought into the concept. They planned to spend a night at the Holiday Inn in Chinle and take a morning jeep tour of Canyon De Chelly.

Stopping for fuel at the Ganada convenience store, it was buzzing with humanity. Fort Defiance, to the east, was a place that Charles always wanted to see. He remembered a movie by the same name, 'Fort Defiance.' 'Well, maybe next time, he thought to himself.' Continuing north, the afternoon gave way to darkness as Lynn was dozing in the passenger seat. They arrived at the Chinle Holiday Inn.

* * *

Many miles to the south, the truck driver, Jill Clayborne, and Eve, her passenger, were on a different quest. Jill had not been honest with Eve as she dropped her off at the Holiday Inn on Cactus road. Leaving the lobby, she walked three doors west to a CVC Pharmacy. Jill purchased two bottles of Mountain Dew, a bag of Dorito Chips, and a Pack of Trojan, 'her pleasure' rubbers. The cashier smiled as she rang it up. "Have a good night," she said, with a smile and a wink. Jill, pursing her lips, smiled brightly in return. In the cab of her truck, she slung her purchases into a duffle, released the brakes, checked the mirrors, and wheeled out onto southbound I-17. She maneuvered the rig through late afternoon traffic toward southwest Phoenix and her home terminal on Buckeye road.

She shut the truck down at the company lot and departed with her duffle bag. The driver reception area was not teaming with drivers at that hour. A few were lounging around talking as Jill walked toward the partitioned glass offices of fleet managers. There, she took her truck key and tapped on the glass three times, SOS. It reverberated loudly. The seated drivers took notice. Momentarily, Chris Summers scooted his chair out of a cubical, glancing her way. He broke into a wide toothy grin. Standing there looking doleful, Jill unfastened the top button of her blouse and ran her tongue over her upper lip a couple of times. Her body language communique was effective and worked its magic. Chris punched the timeclock and escorted Jill out the door. They strolled arm in arm, kissing now and again toward his Chevy Impala in the east lot. She wouldn't be back in her truck until the next morning-tired, happy, and a bit frazzled.

*   *   *

Eve made the most of her solitude at the Holiday Inn on Cactus road by taking a leisurely bath in the oversized tub. She dressed quickly and coiffured her hair. The café was still open, and – surprisingly – the menu was delectable. Who knew? It was a hidden gem of a restaurant tucked away at a Holiday Inn. Her only thought was that she should be sharing her time with someone. Even Gerald would have been preferable to the empty chair across the table. He wasn't a bad guy, but immature for his age, even goofy, some would say. These thoughts carried her through a few scenarios. All were warm and assuring. Gerald was one of the reasons she had taken on the rental agreement in Fort Collins. They had hit it off while sharing the same house. Getting high on 3.2 beer and getting stupid was a total put-off a few nights ago. So why did she take off as she did? God only knows! For now, she considered her future and reminded herself that anything was possible.

*   *   *

Eve's friend Trish faced her own set of issues back in Fort Collins. She had stolen $90K, and no one seemed the wiser. She wanted to keep it that way. She desperately needed to cover her tracks. Trish sat in her workspace, considering sequels for future action. Contents of their deposit box had not been monitored regularly by the Ingalls.

"What the hell was I thinking?' she muttered to herself. She couldn't see herself confessing to the crime. She might make amends later. At the behest of Les Hays, Trish found herself preparing form letters. Warnings were going out to deposit box renters, and she would be the messenger. In the text, she forewarned bank patrons that their deposit boxes were in jeopardy of being closed. Rental payments were overdue! The hammer had come down, and she was doing the paperwork all Wednesday and Thursday.

She clarified the bank's position. If payment weren't forthcoming for fees in arrears, the bank would have no choice but to drill open and confiscate any contents of the boxes. She wrote assurances that the bank's holding company is in charge, pending further action. Lester Hays signed off on the letters as his signature block was at the bottom of the forms. He smiled at Trish, telling her, "Good job!" Initials under his signature were not 'ps' (Patricia Saunders) as the form preparer. Instead, she typed 'mr' (initials of the bank president) in an attempt to distance herself from the action. Trish anticipated that Les would overlook the sleight of hand. It was a typo with purpose and one that Les missed. She breathed a sigh of relief as the four boxes of letters were returned to her for sealing and mailing. All 143 were in the mail by Friday afternoon. Les had also overlooked the discrepancy that Trish had assigned the Ingalls' box number to a fictional owner. She promoted the idea that the Ingalls' had never rented a safety deposit box. Fortunately for Trish, no one was cross-checking her work.

Trish changed and saved the rental agreement and dates on her computer to reflect a bogus deal. The warning letter would not go to the Ingalls in Fort Collins. The last address of the box holder, she dreamed up, was a retirement home in Boca Raton, Florida. It was all fiction on her part. On the bank information, the rental agreement was 20 years old. In any event, she followed the ruse, making it air-tight. Trish had done microfiche research for the name out of newspaper birth notices in 1920. The Florida address didn't exist. Adding to the fraud, if the fictional character were alive, she would be 100 years old. "Fat chance," she told herself. She was safe with the fake name and bogus information.

The contents of L-3307 would be in a death spiral. Gone would be the envelope containing $10K for beloved son Gerald along with other scraps of paperwork. "Crying shame," she muttered. Trish felt like a race car driver walking away from a five-car pileup. Another perk for all bank employees, she carried insurance for errors and omissions. If any gross errors came to light, she could feign ignorance. 'Don't ask permission,' she told herself, 'Just beg forgiveness.' She considered the matter closed, well, almost. As for the nine $10K money packs in her deposit box C-333, she felt secure for the moment. She had a large tote bag, the marvel of most women at the bank. It came in handy as she removed the 90K from C-333 shortly after the letters went out. Trish did feel gratified about one thing. She benevolently loaned her friend Eve $1,100 to attend Truck Driver School in Longmont. What would she do with the rest of the money, all cash? It was a problem. She was petrified and perplexed at the same time.

*   *   *

Eve was renting from Katie and Alfred not far away at Carter Lake. A slight westerly breeze moved branches outside the bunkhouse windows. Two inches of snow had fallen as Eve awoke at 4:30 a.m. She hit the floor and dressed quickly. Eve dressed like going on a winter campout. Firing up her Fiat, she headed straight to Longmont. Eve approached the training center in a half hour. It was Monday as she gathered with trainee classmates at the Longmont site. Eve had drawn one of the eight diesel tractors she hoped to get. It was an older model Freightliner with a split windshield.

Along with her fellow drivers, they must maneuver their tractors out of a narrow chain-link gate and onto the practice lanes. All trainees fired up their diesel engines and built air pressure to release the brakes.

While sitting on the cold driver's seat, Eve contemplated her future. 'So, it's going to be like this, cold winter days before sun up, freezing my butt off waiting for air pressure to build.' When the heater came on, it was a blessed event. The windshield wipers (air pressure driven) trembled across the windshield. She was feeling similar tremors at the moment. The air pressure soon afforded her the comfort of raising her seat to a suitable height. Finally, the pressure buzzer stopped its infernal noise. She released the brakes. Eve, glancing at the dash gauge, saw that the needle had climbed above the red zone, and she was ready to head for the gate. She pushed the red pressure release knob with the heel of her right hand. The cab immediately crept slowly forward toward the chain-link fence. Instinctively, she hit the brake, and a gush of air locked all ten tractor wheels. It was so sudden. Eve thought she had hit something. 'Gosh, that was quick,' she said to herself. The fence was no longer two feet in front of her but a mere few inches away. Grinding the transmission into reverse and hitting the accelerator, the cab twisted and contorted, nearly killing the engine. She had forgotten to feather off the foot brake so the tractor could move. The resistance of the brake was a split second slower than the drive train. 'Feather the brakes, feather the brakes,' she told herself. Then one thing happened that would follow throughout her driving career; she must wait her turn. There were other tractors ahead of her, trying not to hit the gate posts. 'OK,' she reckoned, 'I have time to plan my next move.' She held her foot rigidly on the brake.

Her Freightliner was buried deep in the compound, alongside five others, their rear dualies nearly touching the tractor behind. Three instructors in orange glow vests were outside the gate in the darkness. They held red coned flashlights directing each vehicle into position. It was a luxury she would never see again. Someone was signaling where to go before she made a move. Finally, her turn, she threw her tractor in reverse, took her foot off the air brake, and crawled toward the gate glancing in her rearview mirrors. Clearance for the cab was far tighter than she had anticipated. 'I have to fit through that! Oh my God!' Slowly and deliberately, she made the big tractor fit through the narrow gate posts and back far enough to have a forward turning clearance. The vehicle didn't move into a small radius like her tiny Fiat. After a couple of backups and grinding the gears to move, she finally rolled into position. 'So now what,' she thought? The blessed sun was breaching over the horizon and blazed into all six of her rearview mirrors. An instructor climbed onto the driver's side running board and tapped his flashlight on the window glass. "You're doing great!" He smiled at her, "Now the fun starts."

*   *   *

Lynn and Charles spent a comfortable night at the Holiday Inn in Chinle, Arizona. The lodgings were spacious, and the restaurant was accommodating. There were several Navajos seated in the dining room drinking coffee at breakfast. Seeking a jeep tour excursion, Lynn approached one of the tables. Possibilities were endless, and tours were custom fit for individual parties. She chatted with a well-informed resident who lived on the canyon's north rim. His first effort was to explain that the name 'De Chelly' was a misspelling for the Navajo word, 'Tseyi.' It simply meant, 'People of the Rock.' When Spanish Conquistadors invaded the area in 1540, there were sixty ruins within the Canyon walls, and the Ingalls would only see a few of them. In the white culture history books, historians misspelled the names of the ruins. Other locations were left unrecorded. At present, most areas are off-limits to outsiders. Jeep tours were the only way tourists could see the Navajo cultural homeland.

It was an education that both Lynn and Charles could grasp. Their wish was that Gerald would be interested in anything other than adolescent pursuits. The jeep tour ended by late afternoon. Thanking the driver, they tipped him generously and traveled into southern Utah. The Navajo traditions expressed by their tour guide covered the binding of family ties. If only they could be so lucky with Gerald. They spent the night at Moab, Utah. They agreed to throw out some ideas for their son and see where it went. It might be a life-changing proposition. They also reasoned that time was short, and they needed to act. Gerald was turning into a dolt, and it was driving them crazy. They refused to believe that their son had a mind of his own.

*   *   *

Far away in Phoenix, at the Cactus Road Holiday Inn, Eve was trying to unravel her future as well. She would not be forced into a life with Gerald. Her relief was profound, and she could move on with personal plans. The self-administered pregnancy test gave her permission.

Returning to her truck then picking up Eve the following day, Jill was in a sullen mood. Her all-night foray with Chris Summers left her with several unanswered questions. As she and Chris had entered his Glendale apartment, it was time to throw off their clothes and get physical. The mountain dew and Dorito chips were an excellent precursor to their smoldering affair. Jill's philosophy was simple, feed and water Chris, then make whoopie.

As dawn approached, she went into the bathroom, showered, toweled off, and brushed her hair. Gathering herself while humming a sprightly tune, she glanced under a damp face towel. There in all its majesty was the baby blue pack of unopened Trojan rubbers she had handed Chris ten hours earlier.

"Oh shit," she told the face in the mirror. "Chris, a word, please!" She said it clearly, not raising her voice. Chris strode into the bathroom naked, looking pleased with himself. He leaned against the door jam and adjusted his stance.

"You didn't wear a raincoat, did you?" Mustering all the fortitude he could, Chris said, "I've told you time and again how I want us to settle down."

"And this is how you do it," Jill snapped, "Sending your little soldiers behind enemy lines to invade the citadel?" She picked up a hairbrush and tossed it backhanded at his lower appendage. Before she could mount further harassment, Chris swept in, cradling her arms in his. Held there for a few long seconds, Jill threw her head back, saying, "Oh, what the hell." It was time for a morning quickie. She loved everything about Chris; why fight the future.

Chris Summers had loved Jill from the first time he laid eyes on her. As her high school softball team was whaling on a cross-town rival, he was in the stands. It was their first encounter three years earlier. As Jill rounded first base and headed toward second on an infield fly, he loved how she filled out her softball uniform. Sleek and well-proportioned with slightly rounded hips, there she was, stealing his heart as she ran the bases. Jill's ponytail swung wildly as she rounded second base. The rival team had shown they could neither hit nor catch. The ball had come off her bat and popped very high. It dropped with a thud in front of the shortstop. Before she could field the ball, Jill was heading toward third. The third-base coach motioned for Jill to hold up. Ignoring the coach, Jill figured that the shortstop couldn't hit a bull in the rear with a banjo. As she sprinted toward home plate, the ball sailed over the catcher's head. "Home run on an infield fly," Chris said aloud, "I like this girl!" As fate would have it, the two soon met, mingled, and became infatuated with one another. Both their families were well connected. There were Bar-B-Ques and country club events to share. He liked her family, and she adored his family. Still, they were restless and wanted to explore their futures separately. The mothers compared notes but didn't push them along farther than the natural course of events would allow.

After graduating from NAU in Flagstaff, Chris worked in the transportation industry. Jill, on the other hand, took an alternate route. She didn't want to dispatch trucks. She intended to drive them. So, it went. Chris was Jill's Fleet manager with the same company. Jill hauled the goods, primarily dry freight. They made good money, but Jill had refused to settle with a home mortgage and the hassles of married life. They loved their jobs and stayed put. Still, there were the love nesting episodes that fueled their passions.

Chris's mother loved Jill like a daughter and convinced her son that good things come along rarely and great things even less seldom. Her discussions rang solid with her son. Chris and his girlfriend flew close to the flame, but she voiced little concern. Chris had no intention of forcing an ultimatum with Jill, but fate was fickle, and he was ready to accept the consequences. He was confident that Jill would face them with him. Nights of lovemaking ensued. This time around, he had forgone the protection that Jill thought he had taken. It was an unwritten rule that he willfully ignored. Whether or not she was pregnant didn't matter to Chris. He considered that Jill would love having his child. It would be a start for the future with the woman he loved, come what may. Though it might come sooner than expected, Jill was determined to make their prospects mélange.

"I guess we'll see what happens," she told him as he drove her to the company terminal. They kissed and separated with a knowing smile. She picked up Eve at the Holiday Inn, where she left her the night before.

*   *   *

Back at Carter Lake, Katie was apprehensive about Eve driving the big rigs. Retiring for the night, she asked Alfred if he thought it was customary, a woman attending truck driver training.

"I don't see why not," Alfred replied. "Many drivers out on the roads are women. Statistically, they hold better safety records than men." A driver himself in bygone years convinced Alfred of that! "I've known guys who have gotten into trouble more frequently than women. For what it's worth," he added, "Women are less aggressive, and they don't take chances. Husband/wife driver teams are the best." Still, Katie thought it prudent to call Eve's mother in Florida and get her opinion on the situation.

"It all rolls downhill," Katie said to Alfred. "If Kim doesn't know what Eve's up to, maybe she should!" Alfred was non-committal in his assessment but added, "I think you should give Eve the benefit of the doubt. Her mother flew Army chinooks during the gulf war as a warrant officer, and she wouldn't give a second thought about Eve driving over the road."

"Well, it isn't only the driving part," Katie continued, "What about all the other things that could happen, a woman alone at truck stops with a bunch of dirty old men?" It was late, and the two shuffled off to bed.

"I'll just say this, Katie, there are probably more dirty old men in the District of Columbia than there are in the entire transportation industry." Adjusting their CPAPS, they got into bed and held hands under the covers.

*   *   *

After work in Fort Collins, Les Hays and Trish Saunders were with coworkers at a local watering hole. When the subject of safe deposit boxes came up, Les offered a few figures. He mentioned that Trish had found 128 box holders whose owners brought their fees up to date. The bank changed hands seven years earlier. Trish was awaiting the chance to breach another subject when a coworker beat her to the punch. It was out of the blue and similar interest to her.

"What's your take on offshore banking?" Everyone leaned in for the discussion that followed.

"Well, I've followed the subject on a couple of blogs; it's not hard to do," answered Les. It was one of the tellers who had learned that you should open an offshore account in person. It was unnecessary to open with a balance but wire funds to your account number. You should arrive at a scheduled appointment and present your passport in person. Having an offshore account would give people global citizenship where investments were concerned. Music to her ears, Trish was taking mental notes at this point. Les observed Trish's interest and leaned closer to her.

"You want to take a cruise with me?" Dumbfounded but flattered, Trish locked her gaze on his and said, "I thought you'd never ask!"

*   *   *

Lynn and Charles Ingalls pulled into their driveway at Tarryall reservoir in north Fort Collins. They had traveled five hundred miles from Moab. An olive-drab pick-up truck with white government plates blocked access to their garage. Looking at each other in bewilderment, Charles murmured, "What the heck is this?" On approaching the front door of their home, they were surprised by an Army sergeant exiting the front door. He was dressed in desert fatigues and carried a briefcase. He shook hands with their son Gerald while Flynn stood off to one side. The sergeant hardly broke stride as he passed by Gerald's parents.

"Hello, Mr. and Mr. Ingalls," he said as he smiled and touched the brim of his hat. Turning to Gerald, his mom and dad stood in their tracks. Gerald said, "Flynn and I enlisted in the Army on the buddy system!" His parents looked at one another. "Are you kidding me?" Charles was baffled, and Lynn stood captivated by what she had heard.

"Well, come on in, I'll tell you all about it," said Gerald.

"I'm all ears!" Charles said to his son as he gave Flynn a wry smile.

*   *   *

Trish was driving weekly to the gambling houses in Central City and Blackhawk, Colorado. Once there, she would buy $5K in chips and play at the roulette wheel for a few turns. Trish liked blackjack too. If she won, Trish would keep on playing with house money. If she dipped into her nest egg, she would cash in her chips.

"I don't like to carry cash around," she would say to the lady in the cage.

"Please make out a cashier's check for the full amount."

Trish had seen the movie 'Hell or High Water. The storyline was about bank robbers who would take their booty across the state line to Oklahoma and launder the stolen cash. She followed their methodology.

Casino cashiers figured Trish was a rich kid playing with her sugar daddy's money. Most casino patrons were repeaters just like her. All were attempting to get rich quickly, with Trish in that same category of people. Such was her modus operandi, going through thousands of dollars in cash. She made one trip down to Payson, Arizona, and dribbled $2,500 through her system. If she went to the casinos with Les and other friends, she would only take a couple of hundred dollars to avoid suspicion. She had bank accounts set up with two institutions in northern Colorado and a couple in Denver. Trish also took out certificates of deposit or simply put cash into savings accounts.

"I won big in Black Hawk," she would say to her friends. So far, she had laundered a considerable chunk of the stolen deposit box cash. Push came to shove, and Trish decided it was time to take Les up on his offer and cruise down to Nassau and open an offshore account. He was hot on her trail, and the feeling was mutual.

Their amicable relationship blossomed into a full-blown romance. Les would be prudent to take a few thousand dollars in travelers' checks and open the Nassau account with a fair balance. Vacations rolled around at the bank, and several employees won Bahama trips, a fringe benefit for being good employees.

So why not me, Trish figured. She would bat her baby blues at Les and make the trip with him. Making bank officer, Les was living the dream and had fallen for his lovely girl 'Friday.' Trish had laundered roughly $65K in supposed casino winnings. It was time to move on to the next phase of her plan. The airport shuttle rolled up, taking them to Denver International Airport. The flight to Orlando went well, and it was time to party.

*　　*　　*

Eve's curriculum was simple. For the first week in Longmont, the driver candidates would simply reverse with their tractors, backing for twenty-five yards then going forward again. Each vehicle had its lane in which to execute the maneuver. Seldom did they shift into third or fourth gear of nine or 13-speed transmissions. Daily, the trainees would switch tractors to get a feel for the different gear trains and the climb of RPMs. They were never permitted to go above 1800 RPM. Unnecessary wear on the gear train was company policy. If mechanics found an abundance of steel filings in the bottom of an oil pan, there could be consequences. Eve and her classmates were able to master double clutching. Candidates would do the same with 53' flatbeds and cargo vans. The practice is on a 100-yard driving lane. When Eve had trouble backing up, her key instructor had her try an alternate maneuver. Through the entire circumference of a three-acre practice area, she would back her trailers around the whole circumference, then repeat the exercise. By the end of the second week, she was very proficient. Meanwhile, morning class time holds instruction on bills of lading and logbook procedures that every driver must learn for the business end of their training.

The instructor would be on the passenger side, saying to the drivers, "OK, first gear, no acceleration, double-clutch and go to second, climb to 1500 RPM on the accelerator and double-clutch into third gear." Performing a ninety-degree turn at a stoplight, the instructor would say, "Get five feet from the right-hand curb, then go fifteen feet into the intersection before you turn the steering wheel. Keep the tractor in the left lane until the rear tandem clears the right curb. Watch your mirrors!" With a tractor pulling a fifty-three-foot trailer, there are fifteen feet of off-tracking. Eve became acuity aware of the mirrors in making her turns. She would instinctively swerve into the right-hand lane and go through the gear train to fifth. Double clutching as she progressed, she soon found a smooth acceleration pattern. Third or fourth gear was fast enough for the city driving on secondary roads to observe a 35mph speed limit.

Both city and mountain driving are practiced. The term 'lost in the gearbox' was a common theme. Mountain roads on I-70 west of Denver were a proving ground. The jake brakes to retard two or four of the eight engine cylinders would save wear and tear on the brakes. Some of the candidates couldn't master the maneuvers right away. While downshifting on a downhill grade, it would be necessary to find a lower gear.

"Bring your RPMs up to 1500 before you downshift. Do it one gear at a time," the instructors would often repeat. Eve was a fast learner. She became one with the truck, the air brakes, transmission, Jake brakes, double-clutching, and she seldom ground the gears. Eve had been fascinated to learn that, unlike passenger vehicles, a truck's turn signals do not go off on their own; the driver must manually turn them off. Eve rarely failed to manage this small task.

"I'm dang good at this," she crowed when her instructor pointed that out. Eve loved being in total control of the vehicle. The whole experience gave her a feeling of command, power, and exhilaration.

After the third week, all drivers were proficient in the morning classes that covered paperwork and logbook efficiency. Now they must pass their CDL road test. The license would allow drivers the ability to make a good living. The company already guaranteed jobs. On passing her CDL, it was time for Eve to go with an instructor for six weeks. Her first load would be from a box company in Denver to an outlet warehouse in California. "Settle the nerves," she advised herself, "I've got this!"

Eve became excited to meet her driver-instructor. Jill Clayborne would be Eve's trainer for the next six weeks. Eve had Alfred take her out of the Johnson's Corner truck stop on I-25. From there, she and Jill would be working the eleven western states hauling freight to complete her training cycle. 'On the Road Again,' by Willie Nelson, played on the speakers as Eve settled behind the wheel. California, here we come!

Chapter 3

ROADBLOCKS AHEAD

April 2015

Katie wasn't about to let Eve, her only grand-niece, go out into the world as a truck driver unless her mother in Florida knew and approved of the venture. Dialing up the Florida area code with her niece's phone number, the call went directly to voice-mail. Frustrated, she left a message for Kim to call Katie and Alfred in Colorado.

"I'm telling you, Katie, that ship has sailed!" said Alfred. "Eve will do what she's been training to do these past few weeks. She's twenty years old! You have no say in the matter!" Still, it was a sore point with Katie, and she was left feeling uneasy.

"Well, there's more to the story, something you may find interesting," she said. "Come with me!" Katie took Alfred down to the bunkhouse where Eve had stayed for several weeks.

"I was dusting and straightening up the place. Look what I found." Katie took a large lamp with a ceramic base off the side table near the bed. Turning it over, she pointed out two bundles inside the hollow portion of the lamp base. She had discovered two money packs of $100 bills.

"There are about eighteen thousand dollars in there!" she said to Alfred, "I counted it! What has she been up to?" A moment of silence slipped by before Alfred concluded that there must be some reasonable explanation.

"Just put it back the way you found it . . . leave it be!"

Locking the bunkhouse door, they moseyed back up to the house as the kitchen phone was ringing. Catching the phone in time, Katie answered. The call was from the Naples, Florida, area code.

"Oh, Hi Kim, let me sit down. I'm a bit winded." Changing the phone to her other ear, Katie took a seat and exchanged a few pleasantries with her niece Kim Chambers. "Well," she went on, "You know your daughter Evelyn has been staying with us a few weeks. I thought you should know. I don't know how to say this. I was straightening up her room and discovered a large amount of cash by the bed." Following a short silence, she said, "Oh . . . well, I didn't realize that." Alfred leaning into the conversation said, "Put it on speaker!" Katie did, so she and Alfred listened to Kim for several minutes.

"It's all good," Kim was saying, "It was Casino winnings from her friend Trish, and she loaned that money to Eve."

"Well, that's a relief, I ugh, didn't realize, but it's good to know," said Katie. The conversation lasted for twenty minutes as Katie caught up with Kim on other family matters.

"OK, we'll keep it under our hats about the money." She hung up the phone. Looking at Alfred, still wearing his ball-hat, Katie took on a coy and evasive posture.

"Can we just forget that I was snooping where I shouldn't have been snooping?" Later that evening, she was startled while watching 'Wheel of Fortune' and said to Alfred, "I remember what it was that I forgot to ask Kim. Why didn't Eve put her casino winnings in the bank?"

"Good question," said Alfred, "I'm sure she has her reasons."

*   *   *

Lynn and Charles treated Gerald and Flynn to brunch at the Fort Collins Country Club. The foursome had cleared the air concerning the young men's dual enlistment in the Army. It was determined to be a good choice for further development and speculation. The next three years would give both young men a measure of domestication and a sense of direction. They made their way by bus to Army MEPS. The military entrance processing station was a stop-gap for physicals and paperwork before basic training would begin. Both Gerald and Flynn scored above 80 on the ASVAB test. They would receive further technical training following Army basic at Fort Bliss, Texas.

During the physical, Flynn was getting cold feet. Wearing his boxers, he was bleeding from the blood drawn moments before. Flynn adjusted the specimen container, so a couple of drops fell into his urine specimen. Continuing along a marked corridor, he dropped his specimen at a designated laboratory window then sat among other recruits. Then, a very intrusive physical examination began. After the physicals, both young men returned to the Remington street house for a few days.

The Army recruiter called Flynn and said he might have a urinary tract infection. His laboratory test results indicated as much. He was to clear the matter up with his physician before pursuing a future with the U.S. Army. Much to the chagrin of Gerald, he advised Flynn to see a doctor for further evaluation. The two parted company and would not see one another until months later. Gerald and ninety-two other recruits took the oath and entered the U.S. Army on April 6, 2015. Gerald was left on his own to face basic training with a bunch of strangers, or so he thought. He was about to have a few surprises and introspection during the ensuing weeks. His true character was about to be revealed.

*   *   *

Trish and Les were preparing to dress for 'Pirate night' on the 'Disney Dream.' They laid, naked and glistening, smiling into each other's eyes.

"You first," said Les. The only other sound was a tingling of metal closet hangers as their ship sailed toward Nassau harbor in the dark of night. Beyond their state-room veranda, two other vessels were heading for the same destination. They were tiny pin-pricks of light against a black velvet canvas of sea and sky. Trish rose from the bed, but not before kissing Less's firm six-pack. After a few minutes of getting acquainted with the shower features, they were fully awake. The couple dressed, with lingering looks that put a solicitous stamp of approval on previous hours of love-making.

Strolling arm in arm along a through-way next to the jewelry store, they stopped to look at an exquisite jewelry collection. In the glass case was a set of emerald necklaces and earrings. The price tag was $7,000.

"Would you like to try them on?" asked the clerk.

"Sure, why not," said Trish.

"If you want, you can wear them for the evening and return them before we close at ten."

"I would love to," said Trish. She signed a form to wear the jewelry. It was like checking a book out from the Fort Collins library. Against her tan skin, the jewelry pieces looked right at home. Her pert blonde hair and symmetrical features added to the intrigue. Breathing her fragrance, Les was weak-kneed at the sight of her. They continued arm in arm toward the dining room.

"I have a confession to make," said Trish as they were walking. "I could make a habit of this, the cruise, and you along as my companion."

"Are you proposing to me?" asked Les.

"Let's just say I'm impressed." she answered, "You are a delight." She squeezed his tall frame next to hers.

"Let's eat." he said, "You've given me an appetite."

The Disney Dream docked in Nassau harbor an hour after sunrise. Most passengers were anxious to get off the boat to walk on solid ground. At the deboarding gate, they were subject to an electronic badge check. It was built in security, allowing them to reboard later in the day. Trish and Les kept their boarding passes, and passports close at hand. Most passengers went to Paradise Island. It was a place where local citizens were not allowed to visit and ply their trade. Most passengers wouldn't see the dark side of Nassau, the yellow underbelly of the beast. The ship would depart in the late afternoon for Castaway Cay. Missing the departure would be stressful, and most people attentively watched the clock. For Trish and Les, it was business first, then sightseeing later.

The Commonwealth Bank of the Bahamas was the first stop on their schedule. Les had done his homework, and Trish was an apt pupil for discoveries they may share in the future. They awaited a taxi van that would take them to the bank. The wait was tense. They felt uneasy as menacing men loitered nearby and spoke on cellphones with a thick Bahamian dialect. Some took pictures of them. Among foreign ports,

Nassau held a reputation where tourists must exercise caution. Robberies were a risk, along with other forms of ill-treatment. The contents of Trish's fanny pack didn't allow her any measure of security. Time drug on, but finally, their designated driver arrived. He was twenty minutes late, and all apologies. Other passengers dressed in business attire made their way through Nassau's congested streets. The narrower the roads, the faster the van sped along. Their boarding passes swung to and fro from the neck lanyards their wore. Most passengers, it was assumed, were opening offshore accounts just like Les and Trish. The discussion was spirited and lively but guarded. Discretion was palpable among the riders, but they also shared similar values. All wanted to accumulate wealth and hold on to it.

A primary interest of Les was to establish credibility for real estate investments in the Bahamas. Trish had a different plan. She wanted to park a great deal of cash away from the prying eyes of the U.S. government and the IRS. The matter of passing the required KYC (Know-Your-Customer) background check was of concern to her. When she brought it up with Les, he asked her, "Have you ever been subjected to a banking or financial enforcement action?"

"Well . . . no," she responded.

"Then you have no worries. Enjoy the moment; it will be fun and educational." Less's reassurance was adequate, and Trish put her cares aside.

Their dual appointment for the banking interview went smoothly. Les seemed well in control of particulars. He was a U.S. bank officer and talked the lingo. What could go wrong? The atmosphere was friendly and business-like. When it came time to hand over a cash amount for deposit, Trish reached into her fanny-pack and pulled out the hefty sum of $5,000 in U.S. currency. Les had cashier's checks in a similar amount. They both received account numbers pending further transactions. From that moment on, they could make deposits from anywhere in the world. It could be from U.S. soil for any amount of wire transfers. Established as global financial citizens, they could do as they wished in securing monetary rewards. When Trish got home, she would secure a hard copy of her offshore account number and put it in her safety deposit box. Life was good.

Before their ship would sail from Nassau harbor, Les and Trish took a sightseeing tour of the old city. Les had some idea of changes made for the commonwealth when the city transitioned from British rule. His parents had visited in the years before Les was born. Thousands of boat passengers now skipped the town. Instead, they took boat transport to Paradise Island. Changes were profound. The iconic white-uniformed police officers in pith hats were gone. Long walks through residential areas to see and smell the flowering hibiscus seemed risky. Groups of British boys playing rugby on open fields were a thing of the past. Looking in the eyes of vendors at the Straw Market, they seemed unhappy, desperately trying to hawk their wares. Their customer base had gone to Paradise Island, where the vendors were not allowed. Paradise Island, formerly called Pig island, had been an over-grown mango-covered jungle in prior times. Following radical development, it was now a tourist attraction. The boat people largely forgot the old city of Nassau. As Les, with Trish on his arm, toured the Pirate museum, they were mostly on their own. Only a handful of boat people were on tour.

An iconic display of a pirate in a bygone era hung in the museum. The man, head down, arms covering his face, was on a small strand of a deserted island. The caption read, 'Marooned.' According to the Pirates Code of Conduct – Articles 2 and 3 . . . for infraction of desertion, lying and stealing . . . with one bottle of powder, one bottle of water, one small arm and shot. (Pirate museum, Nassau, New Providence, Bahamas). The image epitomized the fate of Nassau itself in its present state. Except for offshore banks and Paradise Island, the people of Nassau seemed primarily forgotten. The Queen's Staircase, another attraction, witnessed only a few tourists. "How sad," said Trish, "Let's go back to our corner of the world onboard the ship." They passed through the port gate in a down-pour. It was an apt signature that ended their tour of the old city.

* * *

Following their return trip from Sedona, Lynn and Charles proceeded with their well-laid plans for the new home in Sedona. The Army enlistment of their only son was a shot out of the left-field! They didn't see it coming. What would become of the arrangements with Gerald, living in the Sedona house as care-taker and rent collector? Gerald was committed for the next three years. As they mulled over the future, the Ingalls' decided they should remove the $100K they had laid aside for their son years earlier. They might die suddenly, was their thought, a plane wreck, or a car crash while showing houses in their real-estate business.

"It was an over-reaction," said Charles.

"Yes . . . you're right," said Lynn, "We should put his nest egg into certificates of deposit in his name." A hundred thousand dollars should be making interest instead of lying idle in a bank vault.

"I'll get on it Monday when the bank opens," assured Charles. He sipped his Martini while Lynn nursed a Manhattan out on their deck by the pool. The blue-lit pool water shimmered in the moonlight. A warm breeze blew in from the south. A moment of silence went by when Lynn blurted out, "A few classes at CSU, I could see, but the Army?"

"First thing Monday, hon, first thing Monday," Charles reassured Lynn as he touched her hand.

*   *   *

The president of the First National Bank saw him coming from across the street. It was 11:30 Monday morning. He thought Charles Ingalls might be dropping by to arrange a golf date at the Country Club. One of the loan officers greeted him by name as he entered the building. Not breaking stride, Charles walked directly to the president's glassed office and rapped on the door frame. He leaned into the doorway. "Not a social call; I'm here on business. We have funds in a safety deposit box, and I want them for C.D.s." The president set a few papers aside, folded his hands on his desk, and said, "OK, I'll have my assistant take care of it for you." Buzzing the intercom, he summoned his assistant. "Could you come in here for a moment?" The woman slipped quietly into the office, "What is it?" "Escort Mr. Ingalls to the deposit box vault, would you please?" She shuffled off to her desk for a few seconds and returned with the deposit box master key. They walked briskly to the bank's outer vault with Charles tagging along. Finding the bar-screen open, they entered the small room, and she asked, "Which one, Mr. Ingalls?"

"Let's see, let's see," said Charles as he fumbled for his key, turned it over, right side up, and squinted at a number taped to it. He adjusted his glasses. "Looks like L-3307. Should be right down there near the floor, one of the oversized ones." The two looked over the bloc of boxes near the floor. It seemed to be missing.

*   *   *

Gerald Ingalls departed his parent's home in an Army shuttle-van. The point of departure to Texas was Denver's Union Train station. On arrival after the 55-mile drive, other young men were milling about the train platform. Five young men stepped out of the van and blended into the larger group. Soon a U.S. Army sedan pulled to the curb. A Sergeant first class in combat fatigues stepped forward and brought the group together.

"OK, now listen up," he began. His orders were explicit and to the point. "All of you will be going by train to Del Hart, Texas. On arrival, you will change trains for the last leg of your transportation to El Paso, Texas. When you arrive there, an Army drill instructor will meet you. Then you will be taken by bus to Fort Bliss. Any questions?" No one had any questions and stood around in clusters. All wondered what the next two or three months were going to bring. To a man, they realized they were not going to summer camp. Following a moment of silence, the sergeant said in a loud voice, "Gerald Ingalls, step forward!" Surprised, Gerald stepped to the front of the group.

"I am giving this man your travel and food vouchers for the train," said the sergeant. Before Gerald could ask any questions, the sergeant handed over a sizeable manila envelope.

"Do as this man says, be prompt, be punctual, and don't give him any trouble." His lingering gaze swiveled around the entire group of ninety-two young men. He purposely made eye contact with almost all of them. Gerald didn't know why he was the designated leader, but he followed the sergeant's orders. 'So, it begins,' he thought to himself, 'so it begins.'

*   *   *

Eve Chambers spent most of her morning detailing truck 3186. It was not under a load and sat bobtail (no trailer attached) in the Phoenix terminal of the west lot near the wash rack. Jill Clayborne had been replaced with the new instructor due to Jill's pregnancy. Eve met the new instructor for the first time as she descended from the truck.

She said to Eve, "I need to turn in my paperwork, and then I need sleep." Tall and gaunt, the woman wore a beat-up western straw hat, jeans, and a denim jacket cut off at the shoulders. Before walking toward the terminal office, she turned and asked Eve, "Are you a smoker?"

"No, I'm not," Eve answered.

"Good! No smoking anywhere around my truck!" With that, she strode off to dispatch, paperwork in hand. Returning ten minutes later, she said to Eve, "I'm Riley Baxter." With that, she walked past Eve, climbed into the truck, entered the sleeper berth, and closed the curtains.

'Well, OK then,' Eve said to herself. She continued cleaning bugs off the grill of the truck. Some were so huge; they looked like they wore jerseys. She opened the hood then sidled around to the engine compartment. There, she climbed onto the mainframe and Windexed the windshield and all the mirrors. Completing that, she went to the dispatch office lounge and selected several items from the vending machine.

Plopping down in a comfortable chair, she nodded at a burly man sitting next to her. He was in his forties, reading Games People Play by Eric Berne.

"Required reading in my Psych 101 class two years ago," Eve said. The man nodded and stuck out his hand. They shook hands and carried on a two-hour conversation about people and how they affect everyone around them. Eve was captivated by his articulate view on many subjects near and dear to her.

"What's your story?" he finally asked with a twinkle in his expressive blue eyes.

"Do you want the short or the long version?" Eve asked.

"Start with the short one. If I ever see you out in the driving world, you can bring me up to speed." With that, Eve said she had started driving with her first trainer about a month before. The trainer learned that she was pregnant and had to leave her driving job. "Now I'm with this new woman who seems kind of quiet but blurts out exactly what's on her mind. When she gets her rest, we have a load waiting near Sky Harbor Airport."

"Yeah, but what about you?" the man insisted.

Eve was not keen on spilling her guts but said, "I have this boyfriend back home. Or at least I thought he was. I got to know him fairly well, and then he 'came on' to me. It was a bit much! I ran away and got picked up hitchhiking in New Mexico by the woman who became my first trainer, the one who's pregnant. So, here I am."

"Did he rape you?" asked the man. Eve looked at the ceiling, "No, not really; he just got too close when we were in a compromising position, and I thought I might have become pregnant." The man laughed, "Oh my God!" Eve told him that she and a few friends were sharing houserent in Fort Collins.

"I've lost touch with him; Gerald is his name. If he hadn't been such a juvenile basket case, our relationship might have gone somewhere."

"Sounds like you may have something going on with this guy," the man said.

"Maybe so, we'll see," Eve looked away, losing interest in the conversation. Drivers were crowding into the dispatch area. Shortly after that, here came her newly assigned trainer, Riley Baxter.

"Gotta go!" Riley said to Eve.

"Bye . . . nice meeting you," Eve said to the man.

"Keep the dirty side down," he replied. Eve's new trainer seemed to be in a big hurry. She felt rushed as they walked briskly out to truck 3186.

*   *   *

Katie, quilting in her sewing room, listened to a radio broadcast of 'Focus on the Family.' It was interesting to hear the perspective of someone half her age dispensing advice. The subject matter was on questions of human nature refocused through Bible-based resolutions. There were many Prodigal son stories, and it had happened in her own family with nephews and nieces. She and Alfred's relationship with Eve were unique; they loved her like their own. Still, Katie worried. A female out on the nation's roadways seemed risky. Alfred convinced Katie that Eve's problems revolved around a boyfriend. Was Eve running from the boy? Time would dictate an outcome.

"Eve can support herself, and she's engaged in her passions," Alfred said. "It is no different than a young woman hitchhiking around the world. She is in the U.S. and a safer environment." The tumultuous years came to most people, and then they were gone, hopefully. You could wallow in self-regret or learn from life's experience and move on. As Alfred saw it, that was Eve's ambition, go away for a while, and grow up!

Alfred had come in from watering the stock. The stock consisted of deer, elk, squirrels, rabbits, wild turkeys, a few coyotes, wildlife that wandered onto the place. Both bears or cougars could be in the trees surrounding their home. The bruins had a habit of destroying anything that stood in their path while searching for food. They were not neat, but they were beautiful animals, muscles rippling beneath thick wavey coats of fur as they strolled on all fours. They were flukes in a sense, never learning table manners. Still, all bears and most people were adorable creatures. Wildlife came to water at Alfred and Katie's place as welcome guests. All animals and people were worthy of love and kindness. It was the Lord's way.

*   *   *

"What do you mean, there's no L3307?" demanded Charles. He was more than a little flustered, reaching the point of apoplexy. The bank officer assisting him thought there must be some error. Examining the deposit box key, she asked Charles, "Are you sure you have the right number taped here?" As the morning played out, the bank president brought up the information on his computer. Sure enough, there was a mistake. Box L3307 belonged to a different patron of the bank. An older woman hadn't used the box nor paid rent in five years. "How could that be?" demanded Charles, "We've rented this box for years!"

"We'll conduct a full investigation as soon as we can!" said the bank president. "Make it quick," he said to his assistant, "Give me the full registration on Box L3307." Charles Ingalls had charged out of the bank by this time. What would he tell his wife Lynn when he arrived home?

Once Ingalls had departed, a bank officer summoned the bank's attorney. "Let him know there may be a breach in the chain of custody for box L3307," said the president. The holding company was then called and asked to present all their paperwork. Within thirty minutes, a representative was on the phone giving particulars on their end about the apparent mix-up.

"What are the contents of the box?" asked the bank president. The holding company representative said an envelope containing $10K with the inscription, 'To our beloved son Gerald.' Other than that, there were a few documents on the discharge of deeds on houses. They were homes owned by Lynn and Charles Ingalls in joint tenancy.

"Well, that proves that the box did belong to the Ingalls," said the president.

"It appears so," came the reply on the other end of the phone.

"We'll get to the bottom of this." All parties were embarrassed about the mix-up.

"Do you have our lawyer on the phone?" His bank officer patched the call through to her boss.

"You know, we have a problem here," he said to the attorney," "What's the game plan?"

*   *   *

Eve was about to make her first trip with a new trainer in Arizona. Riley Baxter handed over paperwork to Eve as they drove around the truck lot, looking for trailer No. 53746. "It's a 53-footer," said Riley, "Empty and scrubbed out." Finding the trailer, Riley snapped the tractor around and jacked in for the hook-up.

"Check the kingpin," she ordered, "Raise the dolly, connect the electrical and the airlines. See that the trailer is empty, close and latch the doors!" Riley was quick to give orders to Eve. She snapped them off like a drill sergeant. So far, Riley hadn't told Eve anything she didn't know. Eve had some experience simply riding with Jill Clayborne and attending driver training. 'This is going to be ruff,' thought Eve. 'Just my luck, drawing the Dragon lady for a trainer.'

They were looking for the warehouse on the east side of the Phoenix Sky Harbor airport. Once they found it, they learned there was no loading dock. A forklift would bring loaded and shrink-wrapped pallets of freight down the warehouse ramp. Once placed on the trailer's tail, it was up to Riley or Eve to maneuver an electric pallet-jack, putting the load in place.

"I've got this," said Eve. She handled the jack with skill and know-how. Securing all thirty-two pallets on the truck in perfect position, Riley exclaimed, "Well, look at you; you might come in handy after all." It was an ice-breaker. From that moment on, Riley chilled her attitude and smiled at Eve. Riley routed the truck along Arizona Highway 93 toward Wiki-up, Arizona. Their first delivery would be Henderson, Nevada, 285 miles to the northwest.

"If I were you, I'd crawl into the top bunk of the sleeper and get some shut-eye. You can relieve me at Kingman," said Riley. Eve hadn't rested for the run. She said a brief farewell, taking her time to get comfortable in the sleeper-berth. Riley had the truck on Highway 93 high-balling toward a pee-stop at Wiki-Up.

After three hours of fit-full rest, Eve awoke as maneuvers of the truck jarred her awake. Riley scratched her fingernails on the plastic curtain of the sleeper.

"Let's take a little break, hit the john, and maybe grab some treats." She had pulled off onto the shoulder near a few gas pumps of a convenience store. A handful of Navajo kids were pitching pennies against the store's wall. Riley and Eve left the truck.

"I'm sorry to interrupt your rest," Riley said to Eve, "I'm a bitch when I don't sleep." Riley was apologetic, saying it was the last stop before fueling at Kingman and heading north into Nevada. After their brief respite, the two returned to 3186. With Riley at the wheel and after releasing the brakes, she said to Eve, "See those kids pitching pennies? Don't take your eyes off the truck." With that, she put the truck in reverse and nudged the fifth wheel into the kingpin. "Just making sure," she said. "The oldest trick in the book is to have someone pull your fifth wheel. You take off without your trailer. While they stand there laughing, you wind up with broken airlines, and you must find two forklifts to raise your trailer for re-hooking." That said, she put the transmission in second gear and waved to the kids pitching pennies.

"Sorry boys, maybe next time."

* * *

At Denver's Union train station, young Army recruits were boarding a passenger train. Gerald Ingalls climbed onto a Pullman car along with 92 other young men. They left Denver's Union Station in the late afternoon. A few girlfriends and mothers especially were near tears as their young men said farewell. Gerald ambled his way toward the observation car with travel vouchers for all the group. He eventually got seated among fellow inductees. Not knowing most, he was somewhat familiar with a few faces. They had gone through induction at MEPS together. They recognized Gerald as the guy in charge with the yellow voucher envelope in hand. He handed over travel vouchers to the train conductor.

The train rumbled out of Denver. It stopped at a couple of switching side-tracks before dark. They occasionally waited on a side rail as freight trains rushed past, heading north. Conversation among the men was hesitant. Some stared out the windows and ogled the rushing landscape. Others engaged in discussions about their home life or why they enlisted. Some were reluctant participants, while others seemed more patriotic. The inductees filled the hours' in anticipation of reaching Del Hart, Texas, and switching trains. Many civilian passengers were on board going on about their lives, oblivious to the Army inductees. They seemed carefree, not knowing how lucky they were. They were in charge of their futures, and the inductees were not. They were about to lose all manner of privacy and personal aims. Night fell as the train progressed along its southern route. Gerald took up residence in his sleeper berth with a familiar face from Laramie, Wyoming. He climbed to the upper berth.

The men awoke in the darkness at a Pueblo, Colorado, switching yard. The night wore on as Gerald starred into the ceiling of the car one foot above his head. With a sudden jerk, the train continued along its route. It seemed to move at a snail's pace. As morning approached, some men were not stirring as Gerald went along the corridor knocking on doors. It was time for breakfast. A porter walked by, saying, "I'll bet they get up tomorrow!" Gerald handed over meal vouchers in the dining car as men formed small bonds. Appetites were skimpy.

Near mid-morning, the train slowed and ground to a halt. Del Hart, Texas, were the words on a sign needing paint. The place looked like an old west movie set. A porter announced that all passengers bound for El Paso, Texas, must depart the train. Ninety-three Army inductees stepped down to red earth and sand. Other train passengers gazed out the windows. Some were dumbfounded as the numerous young men scrambled away in the middle of nowhere. There wasn't a soul in sight save for a young man in an old pick-up truck. The next passenger train the inductees were to find was across a switching yard, seventy-five yards away. The young driver of the pick-up said, "You want a ride?" It was the only transportation provided for the next leg of the journey. The pick-up springs bottomed out as twelve men boarded. The rest, Gerald among them, walked toward the adjacent train platform. After unloading riders, the pick-up truck departed. The young driver said, "Good luck, guys!" The young men stood around waiting for the next train going west. They were left to wonder if any form of transportation might arrive. Finally, a speck from the east grew much more prominent. Two engines rushed by with a gust of wind as the train eventually halted. The young men climbed aboard. With a whoosh of spraying sand, the train moved away at high noon. It carried a fraction of the total men trained to defend our country from foreign and domestic enemies.

Chapter 4

KINDRED SPIRITS

May 2015

Eve, the future maid of honor for her friends' wedding, traveled north on Nevada US highway 93 with her trainer Riley. As evening fell, they crossed the Hoover dam bridge bound for Henderson. Nine hundred feet above the Colorado River, the bridge wasn't a fear factor. Eve was doing great in the driver's seat and woke Riley from her scheduled rest. The lights of Henderson came into view. Riley slid to the passenger seat and asked about their fuel level. Following their delivery in Henderson, there would be a pickup in Vegas.

"I see between half and a quarter on the gauge," said Eve.

"Tell you what," said Riley, "Let's take a room at Caesars Palace after we unload tomorrow morning."

Eve, used to living on the truck, looked at Riley askance, "Excuse me, Caesars Palace?" Riley answered that it was her custom to spend a night in a spacious hotel along delivery routes every few days. It took the monotony away from being on a permanent camping trip. Dispatch had a pick up waiting just east of I-15 two days hence. There was time to burn, and burning time in Vegas was a treat.

Unloading in Henderson was scheduled for 9:00 a.m. The gate guard directed them to a spot where they could sleep. Lined up in the yard, a mom-and-pop driver team was on their right. Riley rolled down her window and pounded lightly on the outer door. The man rolled down his window, and she asked, "Have you delivered here before?"

"Ah yeah," said the man, "We've been here a time or two. Once the load crew starts, you should be out of here in a couple of hours."

"Where you from?" asked the woman in the passenger seat.

"Oh, here and there, same for my trainee," Riley said, "and you?" The man answered, "We call Des Moines home, but we're rarely there." It was Riley's practice not to give information to strangers. Her short response sparked Eve's annoyance. She leaned forward, looking past Riley, "I'm from Colorado and Arizona mostly." Riley looked at her disgust and rolled up the window. She sat for a while, then said, "Don't share anything with strangers! If they ask what you're hauling, you say, sailboat fuel. If they ask you where you're going next, you say, I don't know. There's evil out on the interstates." Unfazed by Riley's diatribe, Eve's thoughts soon turned to Gerald. It wasn't in her nature to smolder over trivialities. She thought to herself, 'Why did I run from Gerald?'

*   *   *

In Arizona, Eve's friend Jill was making plans of a different sort. Wedding plans for Jill Clayborne and Chris Summers were progressing smoothly. Jill's mother, Connie, had the venue in place and flower arrangements on order. The wedding was to be held, alfresco Sedona. Invitations had gone out one week after Jill revealed to her mother that she and Chris were bringing a new life into the family.

A bluff near the vortex in the Sedona valley was the setting for countless weddings. The vortex is where, according to legend, swirling masses of energy rose from the earth. Pending a sandstorm or freak monsoon sprinkle, it would be the perfect wedding location. Jill, the bride-to-be, loved the idea as she and her family spent all their years in the area. They were deeply rooted through family and civically. The rental home on Moki Drive could accommodate several hundred people for an outdoor reception. It had a spacious commercial kitchen for the caterer. Connie's friend and real estate broker made the arrangements.

"I know the perfect setting for the reception," she had told Connie. A couple living in Fort Collins, Colorado, had purchased the ranch-style manor. They would not be occupying the place regularly.

"Who do you want for bride's maids?" her mother wanted to know. Jill didn't hesitate. Eve would be her maid of honor. The two had spent countless hours together in the truck and found they held similar values. They also had mutual respect.

"You don't know someone until you've traveled through the western states together," Jill said. "I would also like to have two teammates from my old high school softball team." Jill's sisters could be bridesmaids too. The Clayborne girls were well known for their reputations and well respected. Meanwhile, Jill worked in her mother's boutique. As the two women spent hours side by side, wedding arrangements fell into place. Connie made a solid suggestion for her daughter. "I've made appointments for you to see my OB/GYN."

*   *   *

West of Loveland, Colorado, Katie and Alfred was busy with chores. Katie vacuumed and dusted the bunkhouse as Alfred popped in the door, "Once Eve gets her certification, I guess we won't see much of her." Eve was out on the road but still rented the bunkhouse. A week earlier, she had stopped by to collect a few belongings. The road ahead would be busy, working dry freight throughout the US and Canada with her new trainer, Riley Baxter.

"Not much to keep Eve in northern Colorado," said Katie. Before moving out, Eve had dropped an envelope into Katie's hand, saying with a smile, "Rent money." Katie had set the envelope aside. It lay on her dining room table for a couple of days until curiosity got the best of her. Peeking into the envelope, Katie gasped, "Greenbacks and a lot of them!" There were 125 crisp twenty-dollar bills. Alfred dropped the sports section of his newspaper and stared at the packet of bills in his wife's hand.

"Well, I guess we can put a down payment on a new hot tub."

"Or take a road trip," suggested Katie, "You know, we could go down to Sedona by way of Ojo Caliente and soak in the hot springs. Eve did say she would be a maid of honor at her friend's wedding. I don't see why we couldn't visit her."

"If we get a wedding invitation, that would be even better," Alfred said. "If we're going to make a trip, now is the time before the tourist season, and kids are out of school."

*   *   *

Trish and Les, away in Florida, were not concerned about anything except each other. They were about to deboard the Disney Dream as it arrived at Port Canaveral. They had come to terms with the relationship they shared. They had also set a few precedents about financial matters. They held a mutual agreement to send money to their respective offshore accounts as profits might accumulate. Trish had a knack for enterprise, or so she said. She ruminated about telling Les of her ill-gotten gains. No matter how Trish sugar-coated it for herself, 'Conniving thief' flashed repeatedly in her imagination like a neon sign. Telling a boyfriend about her past was one thing; If their relationship became more serious, how much would she reveal to a husband. The clock was ticking.

Les was honing his skills for the sake of investments and considered dabbling in futures trading. Their cruise adventures had come to a standstill when he popped the question about getting married. Their ship had docked at Castaway Cay thirteen hours north of Nassau. He asked Trish to hike out to a small bay for the morning of the land excursion. Disney cruisers had several options when it came to memorable moments. A morning of snorkeling gave the couple some great photo opts as they swam among stingrays. Then, they went with a group to see and hear about the local foliage.

"Don't eat that," their tour guide would say, "It will kill you!" Still, other species of plant life were 'eater friendly.' At the end of their hike, the group could return to a central staging area where their ship awaited. Each couple would use two-person kayaks. Les boasted to Trish about his travels down Colorado's Arkansas River.

"Don't worry about a thing," he said, "We've got this."

The kayak boarding area came into view. More seasoned boaters boarded and paddled smartly in the proper direction. When it came

Les and Trish's turn to leave the small estuary, the surf suddenly came up. Wind racing above miles of open water brought two-foot waves. Trish made it into the front cockpit. Les kept asking Trish to put an oar in the water to stabilize the small craft. Finally, he established proper seating behind Trish, preparing to cast off. Trish was still sitting with both hands on the gunwales with no oar in the water. Before Les could get ready to paddle, a menacing wave heaved the kayak skyward. Trish sailed high into the air like being thrown from a saddle bronc. Her tan body was inverted and unceremoniously spread-eagled. She seemed to stop in midair as time stood still. Les found himself in four feet of water. He attempted to find the bottom with his feet, but the waves' oncoming rhythm kept him flailing. As Les found his footing, he reached out, grabbed Trish, and shouted, "Put your feet down!" He forgot that she was only five feet tall. Clinging to one another in their Senior Frog tee shirts, Les said the first thing that entered his mind.

"Trish Saunders, will you marry me?" His question sobered the small contingent of onlookers as they laughed and burst into applause. Trish wrapped her legs around his waist, brushed blonde tresses from her face, and exclaimed, "You betcha sailor!"

* * *

Away in Texas, Gerald was apprehensive. The passenger train carrying himself and other recruits had arrived in El Paso. After crossing miles of arid wasteland, the train station was a welcome sight. There were palm plants and greenery—people scurrying off the train, searching out loved ones. An Army sergeant wearing his drill instructor hat looked from car to car. 'He must be here for us.' mused Gerald. As recruits scrambled to the platform, Gerald approached the sergeant and offered the empty travel voucher envelope. The sergeant asked, "Did you use all the vouchers?" Gerald said that he had. Not wasting time and being more polite than Gerald expected, the sergeant directed the men onto two waiting buses. The buses made their way through El Paso traffic. 'So far, so good,' Gerald thought, 'no yelling, at least not yet.'

Old Fort Bliss was a surprise to the men, with large structures reminiscent of college dorms of bygone years. The buses didn't stop there. They went to a quadrangle of single-story Army barracks and a mess hall.

"Get off my bus!" yelled a rather direct Army sergeant at the front. The one who had met them at the train station was nowhere in sight. 'So much for calm,' Gerald thought. Men scrambled off as though the buses had caught fire. They were formed into two squads of men by four yelling sergeants. The instructor to pupil ratio was changing. Like a school of fish, men jockeyed for position.

"Eyes straight ahead," shouted one of the sergeants.

"Don't look at the ground, them rocks is Uncle Sam's rocks!" Instead of being marched away, the two squads stood, immobile. A drill instructor walked by yelling, "Just let me see somebody move!" There they waited. An old axiom of Army life was, 'Hurry up and wait.' Wait, they did, for more than an hour.

"Stand still," shouted another sergeant eyeing the men, "No one told ya'll to move!"

The sun was crossing the sky. As Gerald stood at attention with his squad, he could see ground shadows morphing to longer and longer angles. Finally, as some guys started twitching, they were marched to the mess hall.

"MOVE, BOY! Yo mama ain't here to per-tek you!" If someone bobbed along out of step, a sergeant was on him like a maggot, "Drop and give me fifty!" There was little room for error! Once in the mess hall, "Move dat chow line! Dis ain't no dam Hilton hoe-tel." The sergeants in command were fair but firm, with no room for individuality among the recruits! They also seemed to be talking another language. 'Southern boys,' Gerald thought.

'OK,' thought Gerald. 'I'll play your silly little game.' And it would be a game for eight weeks of basic training, which wouldn't start for another week. The entire cycle of men hadn't yet arrived at the training center. Being singled out for any infraction was taboo. He would get through this. When someone said jump, he simply jumped, didn't ask how high or how far. He also learned a few things. Don't think about talking back. Just melt into the squad.

Gerald and those in his company learned how to survive as a unit. They learned to work as one, with no room for creativity. Before the infiltration practice with M-60 machine guns firing three feet off the ground, one of the sergeants yelled, "Listen to that bad mudda-fucker! I wanna see one of Y'all stand up and ax a question!" 'I think he's being facetious.' Gerald thought with a snicker.

The recruits were not there to think; they were there to react. They performed as one on the firing range, as a troop while marching, eating, sleeping, using the lavatory, or painting rocks. Yes, some rocks needed painting! They came to Army basic training as individuals of different sizes and dispositions. By the time graduation rolled around, they were similar in size, lean and hard-muscled, and didn't ask questions. They had acquired a can-do attitude. 'It's not all about me,' thought Gerald, 'It's about the mission.' Mission was a non sequitur in civilian life. Now it meant following orders, pure and simple, and having a new attitude regarding mind over matter.

It was finally time to go home on leave. Gerald had made it through Army basic training with a sharpshooter badge and mosquito wings on his shoulders.

*   *   *

Eve also learned to follow orders and act as a unit with her new driving instructor. Riley directed Eve to the Las Vegas Wild West truck stop on their first visits to the city. As they came north on I-15, Exit 37, came into view.

"In the old days, this used to be called Boomtown," said Riley. "We can get a taxi to Caesars Palace." The truck park was handy as it had a shuttle service to the fuel desk. The plan was to fuel before noon the next day. Their load would be off Tropicana boulevard, a mile east of I-15. The truck park was buzzing with other drivers who had similar ideas of killing time in Vegas. Riley saw familiar faces at the fuel desk and introduced Eve to a husband/wife driving team. Riley had crossed paths with them in Texas.

"Didn't I have breakfast with you in Midland, Texas?" Riley asked the woman and her husband. The three collaborated for a while. Riley was reminiscing with the lady about a run she would never forget.

"I had run out of fuel between Odessa and Midland. Dispatch said, according to the computer, I had plenty of fuel. The truck didn't know that." In due course, the couple had rescued Riley. She had cruised to the side of Texas Highway 191, set her triangles, and waited.

"I got on the CB and asked if anyone could get me to town, 2:00 a.m., of course." She turned to Eve and said, "That's why I carry that 3-foot wooden dipstick. Don't trust your fuel gauge in a hilly country. When the gauge reads less than a quarter tank, the fuel intake is sucking air as you go uphill." Eve made mental notes.

"We're going over to the Palace. Can we share a cab?" asked Riley. Caesars Palace catered to an older crowd.

"Well, sure," said her friend. Backpacks in hand, off they went to a waiting line of taxi cabs. On the ride across I-15, they would have supper at the Bacchanal Buffet, then see what might shake out for the rest of the evening. Rooms were available from $99. They were giddy as adolescents going on their first bungee jump. As they separated at check-in, the foursome would meet again later.

"I don't have much to wear," said Eve, "Just jeans and a halter top. Do I have time to shop for something?"

"You can wear about anything you want, but we can shop," said Riley. "The Forum Shops have some glitzy outfits." Eve settled on a midnight blue cocktail dress, form-fitting, sassy, and she loved it! She had never owned anything like it. There was a large walk-in shower in their room and two king-size beds.

"This certainly beats sleeping in the truck," said Eve. Like a couple of college girls on a Friday night, they showered, prepared themselves, and headed for the elevator.

During supper, Eve won $87 playing Keno. It paid for the dress she was wearing. The food was great, and it was 7:30 in the evening.

"I feel like dancing," said Riley. While their friends went to the casino and played the slots, Riley and Eve took a cab to Club Rio. At the Masquerade garage, their cab driver pointed toward the elevators. From there, they went to the 51st floor, home of the Voodoo Rooftop nightclub. The music was just getting started. Riley summoned a cocktail waitress and ordered a couple of glasses of chardonnay.

"We don't want to get smashed," she advised, "Just establish some good vibes." The women enjoyed themselves with plenty of dance partners. Most of the crowd had connections, but many young and not-so-young revelers loved to dance. Everyone enjoyed themselves, some more than others.

"Tell you what," said Riley above the beat of the music, "If things get a little too cozy, I'll rescue you if you will do the same for me." "How will I know?" Eve asked.

"Oh, you'll know." said Riley, "Trust me!"

As the evening wore on, the dress Eve wore and how she filled it created a bit of voodoo magic of its own. A couple of guys, in particular, were hovering around her and having a good time. When she wasn't dancing with one, she was dancing with the other. Riley had her own set of admirers. As her cell phone alarm chimed promptly at ten p.m., Riley, phone in hand, excused herself from a trio of new friends. She walked hastily through the crowd of gyrating dancers to Eve's side. A young man had cozied in tight with Eve. He was in the process of asking her where she was staying. As Riley approached them holding her cell phone, she said rather loudly, "Your husband is on the phone. Little Jasper is hungry and needs his mommy." The young stud with Eve lost interest and bowed out to roam for other prospects.

"Let's go home," said Riley, "Busy day tomorrow!"

*   *   *

The wedding for Jill and Chris was two days away. Guests were arriving in town, and the hills west of Sedona had received a light rainfall with mid-seventy-degree temperatures. Fragrance from the wet Creosote bushes presented an earthy ambiance. The vortex, the site for the wedding, would take people on a narrow dirt road. Around the alter, majestic red stone cliffs ascended. There would be a catered lunch and dancing at the house on Moki Drive. One unexpected occurrence needed immediate attention.

The Ingalls, owners of the manor, would be there. They had left Fort Collins for a one-week respite in Sedona. The short flight from Denver put them into Flagstaff shortly before 7:00 p.m. on Thursday. From there, they rented a Porsche Cayenne for the short drive south. The home was under contract for a wedding party over Saturday and Sunday. Their broker had told them of the conflict and asked if they could stay in the guest house for a couple of days.

"Oh, that will be wonderful," said Lynn Ingalls. "We can see how the place operates for a large gathering." Having completed Army basic training, their son Gerald would be with them. They wanted to spend time with him before his next duty assignment. They could mingle with everyone at the wedding and pretend they are friends of the bride.

The bride streamed forward on her Father's arm at the wedding venue. The young couple, Jill and Chris, were married in a double-ring ceremony. The Father of the bride said his line beautifully and took a seat next to his wife, Connie. She gave him a warm knowing glance as he kissed her lightly on the cheek. There was a tense moment at the lighting of candles. Those in attendance hoped Jill wouldn't set her veil on fire. It would be in character with Jill. She had always been the animated one of the Clayborne girls. Fortunately, things went well. After exchanging a theatrical, back arching kiss, a caravan proceeded to the Moki house. Throwing the bouquet and removing Jill's blue garter would be at Moki Drive manor.

Gerald was happy to visit his parents and considered the wedding reception a bonus. When they arrived in Sedona, it was time to dine. Gerald answered his parents' many questions with outdoor seating at the View 180 Restaurant. They dined on an extravagant menu and shared a bottle of Brut champagne. His parents wanted to know what he would be doing for the next three years of enlistment. He explained about his secondary MOS-71Q20.

"That's military lingo for reporter/photographer," he explained. They wanted to know what his primary MOS would be.

"If you have that for secondary, what's the primary?" asked his father. Gerald explained, "My primary military occupational specialty is rifleman; I'm a soldier after all." His parents didn't like the sound of that. Nevertheless, they hung in for the rest of his briefing. He explained that he would be attending the Department of Defense Information School at Fort Mead, Maryland. The school trains men and women from all branches of the military service. They are an internal corps of professional journalists and broadcasters. Following that, he would be assigned to an Army post somewhere in the US. He would work on the unit newspaper. He might go to journalism school on the GI bill following the Army.

"If I'm lucky," Gerald added, "I might work in print media or take a job in radio and television."

The Ingalls drove to Moki drive and settled in at the guest house as late evening approached. In their spare bedroom, Charles and Lynn were preparing to retire. They were pleased to see that Gerald had found a sense of direction in this life.

"He seems like a confident young man, our son," said Charles.

"He certainly does," responded Lynn, "and it comes none too soon!" The Ingalls slept soundly with the knowledge that Gerald was doing well.

*   *   *

Away in Florida, Les and Trish were back from a Bahama cruise and began to make some wedding plans. When their ship docked near Orlando, departing passengers were scurrying about, weaving along thruways. Passengers were deboarding in mass. Going through customs, the port authority agent asked Trish and Les if they had anything to declare.

"Well," Trish hesitated for effect, "I found this man beside me. What do you think he's worth?" Amused, the customs agent smiled and waved them along. The couple found ground transportation to Orlando International Airport. Trish talked Les into making a short flight to Naples as they rode on the shuttle bus. She wanted to visit Kim Chambers, Eve's mother. She suggested they follow up on their marriage plans in the Gulf coastal town.

"We could make it legal and hold a reception later," she proposed.

"We'll have family and friends to help us celebrate at the Fort Collins Country Club, maybe in a month or two." Les had no objections.

"Why quibble over trivialities when you've found the love of your life?" he told her.

*   *   *

Eve's mother, Kim, took a phone call while at the Fort Myers Airport. She was about to take a tourist couple on a helicopter flight along the Gulf coast.

"You're sure about that?" Kim said into her cellphone, "You want to get married here in Naples. When?"

"Would tomorrow be too soon?" answered Trish.

"Les Hays and I are eloping! We'll get a marriage license and blood tests as soon as we arrive."

"Well," said Kim, "I certainly won't try to stop you!" She thought about the relationship that Trish held with Eve. Three years earlier, Eve and Trish Saunders had shared a Naples apartment right out of high school. They made the trip to Colorado and CSU to pursue higher education. Both took elective classes in general studies and hadn't declared a major. Following their first year, the two moved off campus to a house on Remington Street. They made it through their sophomore year then dropped out for lack of funds. The plan was to work and save money for tuition and fees. Trish found a job at the First National Bank, and Eve worked as a hostess at the Silver Grill Café in old town Fort Collins.

'Fate was a fickle friend,' Kim thought. Trish was getting married to a co-worker at the bank, and her daughter was a truck driver. "Well, isn't life grand," she said to Trish.

Before ending their conversation, Kim asked, "When could we find a suitable husband for Eve?" There was a moment of silence on the other end of the conversation. Trish asserted, "Maybe we have found him, but it will take some work."

*   *   *

Eve and her trainer Riley were loading out of a warehouse east of the Las Vegas strip. They had a 48-foot trailer allowing them to enter Canada. Dispatch knew what trailer length they had; computers took notice of such things. A 53-footer or a set of cubes (double trailers) couldn't travel north of the Canadian border because of bridge laws. Distance between the steering axle and the rear tandem hubs would be too long. Eve wasn't crazy about getting so far from the Phoenix terminal. Riley sensed Eve's apprehension.

"So, what's the problem?" asked Riley. Eve explained that her previous trainer, who had become a close friend, was getting married in ten days. She was to be maid of honor at her wedding in Sedona. Riley assured Eve that the company was sensitive about such matters. The company would fly her to Arizona from anywhere in the US or Canada.

"Didn't you mention that the groom worked as one of our fleet managers?" asked Riley. When Eve said he did, Riley assured her that all would go well. In any event, the six weeks training would have concluded by then. Eve would be assigned her tractor once Riley signed off on Eve's certification. Both drivers needed rest before striking out on the thirteen hundred-mile drive to Vancouver, British Columbia.

Riley estimated the drive time would be around 22 hours. Her calculations included eating, showering, and fueling.

"If we can pull away from this dock by midnight, we should be there after dark two days from now," she told Eve. Dispatch had their appointment time set for the morning following their arrival in Vancouver. It would all work out.

"There was a late snow moving into the northwest; we may have to chain up on Grant's Pass north of Medford, Oregon," said Riley. Soon, Eve had them backed into the dock and chocked the rear tandem. Not sure when the warehouse crew would get to them, Riley had Eve let down the dolly and pull the fifth wheel. Riley instructed Eve to leave the airlines attached, drop the cab airbags and pull the truck forward an inch or two. The load team would be running in and out of the trailer for a couple of hours with forklifts. Set up the way Riley recommended, the two could get some shuteye without being jolted awake.

"The load crew will wake us," she said. Before they slept, Eve put in a request and got time off to participate in Jill's wedding.

*　　*　　*

After the Ingalls had set a homey atmosphere in their Sedona guest house, they became observers for the weekend wedding about to take place. Charles and Gerald got in a round of golf at the seven Canyons Club. Father and son returned home to shower. Lynn looked out the window and observed some professional vendors working on the grounds below. She summoned Charles to her side. He was out of the shower, dressed in his bathrobe.

"Charles, do you see that young woman with those other two ladies by the pool?" she asked.

"Wow, she looks vaguely familiar!" he answered.

"Isn't that Eve Chambers, the girl who lived in the rental house with Gerald and those others?" They both stepped in for a closer look and realized that it certainly was Eve!

"I wonder what she's doing here," Charles said.

"More importantly, wasn't she the girl that Gerald may have drawn a bit too close? We'd best keep this to ourselves." Minutes later, Gerald entered the room. He tied his shoes as Lynn stepped to the window and closed the curtain.

"The sun's a little hot," she said.

Following the wedding early Saturday, people began streaming in for the reception. A band arrived and set up in an alcove near a portable dance floor. Gerald entered the fray in his Army dress uniform, and his parents were close behind. A couple of hundred people wandered about the spacious backyard. The wedding party soon arrived. With her back to a group of young women, the new bride, Jill Summers, was about to toss her bouquet. Five girls of all ages were cloistered and waiting for her toss. Among the waiting women stood Eve, in position to catch the flower arrangement.

The gorgeous woman had vanished from his life in Fort Collins. Her hair was much shorter than Gerald remembered. As the bouquet arched high in the air, Eve caught it and looked about the revelers with a gracious smile. At that moment, their eyes met. Gerald marshaled his way to her side, "Eve? Eve Chambers?" Startled, Eve smiled and said, "Gerald?"

Chapter 5

FOLLOW THE LEADER

June 2015

A bit hesitant initially, Eve laid out the timeline since seeing Gerald at the Remington street house four months earlier. "I'm not sure what I was thinking," she said. "I left the house after you, and I got a little too entwined. Maybe it was for the fact I was between semesters at CSU, or perhaps because I liked you and I felt pressured. My mother told me long ago that I was a mistake, and I didn't want to continue the pattern. Jill Clayborne picked me up in the mountains east of Santa Fe. She was driving for the same company where I now work. We became very close. After driver training and on my own, I became the maid of honor for her wedding today. I'll spare you all the details, so what about you?" she asked Gerald.

"Without you, I had nothing holding me in Fort Collins," he said. "I thought about you a lot and made some inquiries. Except for Trish, no one knew where you were, and she wasn't talking. I figured you were safe and on your own." Gerald turned and looked out at the crowded reception.

"My parents bought this place as an investment and retirement property. I was to become a caretaker and rent collector. That didn't sound too exciting, so I took the oath. In two weeks, I report to The Defense Information School at Fort Meade, Maryland."

Eve didn't say much, pulled him close by his necktie, and kissed him softly on the lips.

"Let's stay in touch," she whispered. With tears welling up in Gerald's eyes, he said, "OK, by me." The fragrance of the two mingled on the air, unwarily stimulating their senses.

Gerald's mother, seated near the cash bar, saw her son with Eve. As a spy might do, she kept nudging Charles with tidbits of information.

Eve and Gerald were entwined in a slow dance, hardly moving, oblivious to the rhythm or anyone around them. They didn't pry, just danced, eyes closed, finding one on one serenity. Leaning back and giving Gerald elevator eyes, Eve asked, "So, you joined the Army?" Acknowledging that he had, Gerald twirled Eve around slowly.

"Yes, I guess the uniform gave me away. What are you doing these days," Gerald asked. They were at arm's length, eyeing each other. Gerald nearly lost his footing when Eve said she was a long-haul truck driver. Letting the moment pass, he smiled and looked her in the eyes.

"Why does that not surprise me?" The two justified themselves concerning the months since Eve's departure.

"Let's have a glass of wine, and we'll talk some more," Eve suggested.

"I no longer drink." said Gerald, "I'll just watch you and listen."

"Oh my gosh, she pulled him in and kissed him!" Lynn said breathlessly to Charles.

"We should go over there and listen in on the conversation." Charles and Lynn made their way through the dance floor with drinks in hand and sidled up to their son.

"Hello there," said Lynn, "Aren't you Eve Chambers who lived at the Remington house with Gerald and the gang, my, my, how did you end up here?" She said this as charming and disarming as she could muster. Gerald made an effort at re-introductions.

"Yeah," he said, "You remember Eve Chambers? She lived at the house but went AWOL!"

"Shall we move to a table?" suggested Charles.

With no vacant tables available, they moved to the veranda, away from the blaring music. They spread out on cushioned wicker settees. Gerald mentioned that he didn't recognize Eve at first because of her shorter hair. Eve revealed that she hadn't seen Gerald with his shorter hair. They smiled. The musicians disassembled as a Mariachi band made its way onto the veranda. They got into full swing with 'Que de Raro Tiene.' A lively atmosphere permeated the premises with lots of brass instruments. Personal conversations were futile. As the veranda became saturated with more and more revelers, the Ingalls looked around to see that Gerald and Eve had gone. Lynn caught the arm of a bystander.

"Do you know that girl, Eve Chambers?"

"I do," said the girl, "Eve is a friend of the bride and her maid of honor. She was a driver trainee with Jill."

"Driver trainee?" inquired Charles looking over his bifocals. He poured the remainder of his scotch and soda in a nearby planter, took Lynn's hand, and said, "Let's go to our room, honey. We have a few things to discuss." Lynn noted that the keys to the Porsche Cayenne were missing. In their place was a note.

"Don't wait up; tomorrow's breakfast is on me, Gerald."

Gerald and Eve, in the Porsche, on the driveway slowed to a halt. He asked, "Did you drive your truck to the wedding? Eve said she had, and it was behind the downtown Walmart. She would be idle for two more days before dispatch had a pickup for her in Flagstaff. Eve hesitated briefly, then fished out her Freightliner key and handed it to Gerald.

"Let's go to my place!" He glanced at Eve, who was expressing a warm smile.

"This could be complicated," said Gerald with a twinkle in his eye. He turned onto 89A and headed toward Eve's truck at the Walmart store.

The following morning Eve lay in Gerald's arms. She had left the truck on high idle, so the two would have overnight air conditioning. The rumble of the diesel engine was an accompaniment to their love-making. As morning sun glowed through the windshield, Eve's hazel eyes looked intently into Gerald's.

"You don't think I'm too short, do you?" she asked. She nuzzled in close for Gerald's answer.

"You're tall enough, and your nipple fits right into my belly button. All the other places fit nicely too." She swatted him playfully on the hip, "Stop that!" she said. He asked, "Where did you get that little heart tattoo on your pelvis. The one with initials, 'G I,' in in the middle?"

"Riley and I got tattoos at a parlor outside Terminal Island in LA. It stands for soldier boy." She winked and touched the tip of his nose with her tongue.

"I need to shower," she said, "It smells like something wild has been going on in here." Dressing and getting into the Porsche, Eve suggested going to the Clayborne house and shower. "They're troupers. They won't mind," she said.

*   *   *

Trish and Les hopped on Southwest Airlines to the Fort Myers/ Naples Airport. By contacting Kim Chambers, they could lay the groundwork for their elopement. It would require a three-day waiting period for the marriage license to activate. Their plane landed not far from the chopper pad and hanger facilities where Kim worked as a pilot.

Kim was about to depart with a couple who wanted to view Naples' territory.

"I won't be gone long," she assured Trish. Kim would be on a half-hour to forty-five-minute flight at most. "When I get back, I'd like to take you up if you want." Without hesitation, Trish said that would be great! The couple found a comfortable outdoor food court, parked their bags, ordered brunch, and settled in to wait for Kim.

"One thing about Kim," Trish said," Whatever she says, just nod your head and agree. She didn't get through Army chopper school being a namby-pamby." Trish told Les that they competed on the gymnastics team when she and Eve were high schoolers. Many times, the two girls needed encouragement and the support of Eve's mother.

Les held Trish's hand while she told of her history with Eve. He listened intently, discovering that the two had a special bond. Trish and Eve were inseparable; sisters joined at the hip.

"So, why did you and Eve make the long trip from Florida to Colorado?" he asked. Trish explained their acceptance to several colleges, and Colorado State University was their final choice. As it turned out, tuition and fees became an issue in their sophomore year. They ran out of money. The two girls dropped out of college to work for a semester, and then life got in the way. Eve got a hostess job at a restaurant, and Trish worked at a bank.

They finished their French fries as Kim walked to their table. With her was the couple from their morning flight. They discussed the abundance of inland water seen from three hundred feet about the coastline.

"Yeah, that's Florida for you, a water wonderland," Kim was saying. Parting ways, she handed a business card to the woman with a word of encouragement. She mentioned water access construction problems and elaborated on peculiar building codes they may encounter. As the couple walked away, Kim turned to address Trish.

"My mechanic is refueling the chopper. I'll grab lunch, and then we can take off for a run if you like." Noon was fast approaching, and the food court was humming with day-trippers. People had water swim masks, snorkel gear, and Nimrod air guns. Les excused himself to hit the men's room, leaving the two women to talk.

"So?" asked Kim, "Is he a good one?" Her eyes darted toward Les as he walked away. "Yeah," said Trish, "He can handle the workload, no problemo!" The two winked at each other.

When Les returned, he wore a tank top, shorts, and sandals. He had gone native. Kim, much the same, wore a tank top over a swimsuit. Settled in her Rubicon jeep, they were ten minutes from the chopper pad.

"We flew this Loach-type model for reconnaissance. I went to CH-47 Chinooks once I certified on the advanced airframe," Kim told them. "This one has a lot of maneuverability; the CH-47 was like flying a gravel truck. Who wants upfront with me?" Trish sat up front to the right of Kim with Les in the rear passenger section. They communicated through headsets. Kim took notice of the tower chatter, overseeing their lift-off. Once airborne, Kim took them up to the 300-foot low ceiling limit and flew along the gulf coastline north from Naples.

"We're not supposed to fly too low," she said, "Sun worshippers might be buck naked and raise a stink." To the far horizon, multi-storied resorts rose above the shoreline. Boats were leaving wakes along the coastline with little direction or forethought. The light green surfside of the beach gave way to the blue of deeper water. Open doors of the craft and the seating arrangement were like sitting on the edge of a 300-foot cliff.

"Glad I'm buckled in," said Trish.

"Have you ever done an autorotation," asked Kim? Her riders motioned that they had not. Climbing to 3,200 feet, she calmly shut down the ignition system. The craft went into a free fall. The rotors spun to slow their descent as they remained level. Les watched the altimeter go round and round backward as the surf became larger. The loose tank top he wore billowed out in from of him. Trish's water bottle floated eerily in front of her face. Only safety harnesses keep them from leaving their seats.

"Gravity's a bitch, isn't it?" Kim said through the headphones. At 1,500 feet, she re-engaged the ignition system, and their bodies settled back into the seats.

"Don't say anything to my partner about this; he would have a fit." Les noted the vacant lots along the coast, always looking at the possibilities. 'Anything and everything has its price,' he thought to himself.

The two nights that Trish and Les spent at Kim's bungalow in Naples brought much conversation and reminiscing about life in Florida. A Justice of the Peach at the Collier County Courthouse joined the Colorado couple in matrimony. Les was curious why his new wife hadn't bothered to look up her parents.

"You don't want your Mom and Dad as witnesses?" he asked Trish. Trish forced a short laugh answering that she wouldn't know how to look for them. The conversation ended there. Kim had no comment and looked away from the couple. Les didn't want to be intrusive and shelved his thoughts. The following morning, they all had breakfast at Bill's Café, then headed for Miami.

To spend a few more hours together, Kim drove the couple to the Miami International Airport. She could have flown the couple by helicopter, but they chose Kim's Jeep, allowing more time to talk. The two-hour drive across Florida's Alligator alley went through the Big Cypress National Preserve. It was nonstop, where Kim could further bond with Trish. Les wasn't part of the discussion. He watched Trish's body language as his new wife was talking. He loved what he saw and learned about her former years. It was a no holds barred discussion about Kim accepting Trish as a daughter when she was in high school. Trish and Eve shared the same home, and they were family. Trish's neglectful parents were coming off drug issues in an attempt to maintain sobriety. Kim went in place of Trish's parents to High School gymnastic events and back-to-school nights. The two girls were often taken for sisters by other classmates. Trish's father was nabbed in a Ponzi scheme and arrested as things deteriorated. Then Eve's name came up.

Trish said she was apprehensive about Eve attending driver training.

"I can't see it as any life for a young woman alone." Kim hesitated momentarily before giving her take on the matter.

"Yeah, that seems like a stretch," she said, "But I can only use myself as an example; she is her mother's child." Eve had been born near the end of her mother's military career.

"I was in the S-1 office at Fort Rucker. I was also flying the group commander around for training inspections and briefings. The major and I were walking up to one of the units when this tall, handsome captain met us. This guy, Pete, wasn't anything like the men I had run into before. He was knowledgeable and had an easy-going manner that made my defenses drop. He wasn't wearing a ring. My group commander encouraged me when Pete asked me out following the inspection. I knew it was a setup." As she said this, Kim laughed and continued her story. The two did have that date, and further contact quickly turned physical. Pete came down on orders as a flight instructor soon after the couple set a marriage date. Before taking on a cadre of trainees, Kim did get his engagement ring. The marriage date was set for early 1995 during their mutual thirty-day leaves. There was a long pause for a quarter mile as the Jeep sped toward Miami.

"It was on a Sunday when the major called me to say that Pete's UH-60 Blackhawk chopper had crashed during flight training. Hours later, I was no longer engaged to the love of my life, and I was pregnant. Along with Pete, two other pilot trainees died that day. When the bodies were recovered, I was at the flight line when his silver-gray casket was loaded onto a C-130 bound for Cheyenne. Only the end tag gave his name, rank, and service number. I stood on the flight line in the rain. I took my engagement ring, kissed it, and stuffed it under the flag on Pete's casket. I don't remember much after that." Kim smiled faintly, then turned to Trish, "Here's our exit, next stop, Miami International departures."

*   *   *

Over four hours of flight time between Fort Myers and Denver allowed Trish and Les to discuss their careers. Les, it was decided, could stay at the bank and continue in his role as a bank officer. Trish chose to resign from her position.

"I would like to spend more time working the commodities market," she said. "With a bit of coaching from you, I could make better money than punching a time-clock." They would live in Les's apartment for the immediate future then find suitable housing later.

Deboarding the plane, they collected their baggage and caught the Fort Collins shuttle to the Fairfield Hotel.

"I'm spending the night with you, no more sleeping single in a double bed," said Trish.

"Do ya think?" responded Les.

"I have to call Eve and tell her the news; she will be green with envy! As far as I know, she's still in Sedona following her friends wedding."

*   *   *

Thursday morning, with Trish at his side, she and Les circled the bank interior. Employees stopped what they were doing and gawked at the couple. Trish held up her left hand, displaying her ring finger. The boss came to their side.

"So, what happened in the Bahamas?" He looked around the lobby as people gathered in close. Les stated the obvious.

"I would like to introduce my lovely wife, Trish Hays. We got married in Naples, Florida!" Employees and bank customers alike burst into applause. Some girls stepped forward to see the rock on Trish's left hand.

"I'll be back at work tomorrow," said Les, and Trish will be a stay-at-home wife.

"Well, well," said the bank president, you do have a few things to catch up on! We expected you Monday, and here it is Thursday."

"Better to beg forgiveness, then ask permission," Les said. With smiles all around, the lunch hour approached. Women friends walked to Henri's diner along with Trish admiring her rings. Two men congratulated Les saying, "You got your dream girl. The entire crew wanted to hear details about the elopement. At the bank, the president didn't want to spoil the festivity. Friday would be soon enough to mention that the bank was under investigation.

Les entered the bank promptly at 8:30 a.m. Friday. Following a few moments of small talk, the boss broached a sore subject. The bank may have been party to fraud. The president elaborated about the missing $90K from one of the deposit boxes.

"We had four boxes drilled because we couldn't contact the owners. Customers rented the boxes before the First National took over in 2008." He explained how the contractors who handled the drilling had muffed the job. They successfully drilled three boxes but ruined the lock housing on the fourth, the one in question. It was just rotten luck that the box belonged to the Ingalls'. By the time they got wind of the matter, Charles Ingalls had insisted that it contained $100K.

People taking out a safety deposit box do so at their own risk. The bank couldn't be held liable. The name on the rental contract was an older woman living in a Florida nursing home who had passed away five years ago. Somehow the paperwork hadn't been updated, which cited the Ingalls as owners.

"That's not all, and It turns out that the owners of the box are friends of my wife and me," said the president. "We know they are the true owners because of other paperwork found in the box. I invested $5K in their son's name to help make it up to them. I put the whole matter in the hands of a financial group. They will manage the portfolio."

Les asked, "So, who was the proven owner of the box?" The president hesitated for dramatic effect then told him it was Charles and Lynn Ingalls and not some deceased woman in Florida. Les stood walked to the window.

"You know, Trish and I may have a stake in this too." The president leaned back in his chair and stared at his loan officer.

"What do you mean by that?" he asked.

"Trish and I are friends of Eve, and she is on a fast-track relationship with Gerald Ingalls. We could easily donate $5K to strengthen the bank's position. It wouldn't be a burden."

*   *   *

"So, you've taken up with Gerald Ingalls again," Trish teased. She had called her friend to hear the latest.

"You could say that," Eve replied, "We've been spending some quality time together." She was nonapologetic as she held Gerald's hands while talking to Trish. Eve changed the subject following a lengthy pause and asked Trish if she was house hunting. They ended the call by promising to speak again soon.

While Les was catching up on activities at the bank, Trish had found a rather sizeable rambling brick home in the Indian Hills neighborhood of Fort Collins. Constructed in the fifties, it connected the rooms with an intercom system.

"How quaint; I can summon my husband to the bedroom with the push of a button." The real estate agent smiled and suggested they look over the kitchen and utility area. Trish wanted Les to see the place because it was a house with great potential. As she walked toward the front door, she turned and took one last look at the living room. "This might be the one," she said.

Les had several meetings concerning bank security with the lawyers. The lawyers' heads swiveled between the bank president and his chief loan officer. Les mentioned that the $5K portfolio set up for Gerald Ingalls was a good start. It could take some stings out of the whole affair.

"Trish and I would like to enhance the base sum of the investment to $10K. My wife and Eve grew up in Florida together. They were practically sisters living in the same home with Eve's mother. The two were quite close, and they still are. With a financial group handling the portfolio, I could see the investment grow to a tidy sum in a few years. If the portfolio could acquire fifteen percent per annum, that would be a substantial sum of money to take some sting out of the loss for Charles and Lynn. As they thought about the plan, the bank president said, "That doesn't address the problem why the money came up missing in the first place."

"True," said Les, "But who cares, it happened, and now it's over, we may never know, pending further investigation." Les insisted that the effort they were willing to make was generous. The bank could do nothing and let the chips fall where they may. The contract that the Ingalls signed protected the bank.

"The way I'm suggesting," Les said, "You and I are out $5K each. The Ingalls would have some of the lost money back for their son in a few years. That would make a nice wedding gift when Gerald completes his Army enlistment."

"OK, said his boss, we'll let that sink in for a few days." The meeting broke up, and the lawyers were left to wonder why they were there.

* * *

Jill and Chris Summers considered going on an abbreviated honeymoon. Once the wedding ended and the guests departed, they lived in Chris' Phoenix condominium. A honeymoon would have to wait as Chris had to work. Jill was anxious to move to a new assignment, something other than driving. The home they occupied off Bell Road in Phoenix needed a woman's touch. She threw herself into bringing a warmer mood to the place. At the start, accommodations were much too confining. It looked like a bachelor pad when Chris carried her over the threshold. There was immediate access to the main thoroughfares, and a high wall circled the condo. It was reminiscent of a fortress. She had been there for many televised Cardinal football games. There were beer and pizza blasts with friends when they were both single. Things were different now. Jill didn't want to force changes on her new husband because he had lived solo for years.

Jill looked in the hall mirror and said aloud, "I need to be strong but tactful!" She fell into her job search as a distraction. They would be having their first child in December. "Oh my Gosh, I need to arrange a nursery." There were a few instructions that Jill's OB/GYN had for her.

"See a dentist," she was advised, "The sooner, the better. Delivering a baby is one thing, but doing it with a toothache would be excessive."

Chris was working his fleet manager position for a platoon of drivers. During a staff meeting, he brought up his concern.

"Could we find something for Jill to do, something not too nerve-racking?" The company fuel manager suggested that she work in fuel allocations. Keeping seventeen hundred trucks from running short on diesel was crucial.

"OK," Chris said, "I'll run it by her." The fuel manager caught Chris at the door when the meeting broke up.

"I don't want it to seem hard nose, but fuel is the number one commodity that keeps the wheels turning. It's an important slot and has its ups and downs." Chris took mental notes and got on his cellphone. He gave Jill the news.

"Do you want me to set up an interview for you in fuel allocation?" Eager for the challenge, Jill would be doing her share, adding to their income.

"Oh yeah," she said, "If we're going to have a baby in this boar's nest, I need to make some alterations." Chris didn't answer. Not long after the conversation, Jill went online shopping for the nursery room accessories. Chris thought, 'What does she mean, Boar's nest?'

*   *   *

Gerald would be floating around Sedona with Eve for a couple of days. Time was short, and Eve was obligated to load out of Flagstaff the next day. She would be taking thirty-two pallets of dry dog food to Ohio. Following a reception at the guest house, Lynn broke the ice by asking her son and Eve to shed light on; she stumbled for the word, "Your union."

"Union, yes, well, I'm glad you brought that up, mom." Gerald let his reply flutter indifferently for all to hear.

"Eve and I have had a thing for each other for some time." He looked at Eve, winked, and continued. "We never got around to consummating our relationship." Lynn sat straightening her skirt and adjusted her concho belt.

"Well, I see." With that out in the open, they proceeded to discuss their plans. Gerald mentioned again that he was on orders and traveling to Fort Meade within the week. Eve would continue her driving career.

Tired of seeing the heads swivel back and forth between the older couple and their son, Eve piped up and became proactive.

"Mr. and Mrs. Ingalls, I am working to pay my way through CSU. I will be a junior when I go back, 'if I go back. I'm majoring in Organizational leadership." The senior Ingalls sat up straight and listened as Eve continued talking.

"I grew up with a single mother. She lives in Naples, Florida. A friend and I, Trish Hays, came out to Colorado three years ago. I don't know Trish's plans, but I may eventually go back to CSU and finish my degree program." Lynn stood looking directly at Eve.

"That's marvelous!" She felt closer to Eve after the discussion. She placed both her hands on the girl's shoulders and said, "I know we will be great friends. How could we help with your plans?" Eve looked at Gerald.

"Thank you so much. Let Gerald and I think about that."

*   *   *

Kim Chambers was ending another workday in Naples. Her cellphone chimed; it was Lynn Ingalls.

"Hello, ah, hello, is this Kim?" Lynn asked.

"Yeah, who is this?"

Lynn proceeded to tell Kim that they had a couple of things in common, their kids. Kim's daughter Eve was essentially engaged to Lynn's son Gerald.

"Well, well, that's news," Kim said. Following a brief pause, Lynn said bizarre things about an apparent romance between Gerald and Eve.

"I wasn't aware of this," Kim said. If Eve was considering an engagement, her daughter would have said something. Lynn had called a bit late, considering the change in time zones. The two women finally got on the same page following an awkward moment.

Eve had told her mother, nothing about her romance with Gerald. It was alarming from what Trish Hays had told Kim about sharing the same house with Gerald. She didn't think her daughter liked the guy!

"Well, this is news," Kim repeated. "She isn't pregnant, is she?" On the other end of the conversation, Lynn was tongue-tied.

"Well, I haven't given that much thought. I certainly hope not!" Kim was walking toward her Jeep for the drive home after work.

"Tell you what," Kim said," Let me call my daughter, so I'll get her opinion on the matter. I'll get back to you." They ended the conversation with some assurance they would compare notes. Kim got to her Jeep, sat behind the wheel, and concluded that her daughter might be involved, once again, with this guy, Gerald Ingalls.

Chapter 6

MEETING OF THE MINDS

July 2015

Eve would be going back to work four days after Jill's wedding. The Ingalls had taken up residence in the main house and hired a cook. Lynn's mood was hard to read for the younger couple after brunch. Eve loved Gerald, but the stress of putting up with Lynn was demeaning. Eve sat in the blue dress she had purchased at Caesars Palace. It was a bit formal, but all her other clothes were driver fare. Lynn was attempting to bring Eve online with their family values. Eve needed to get back on the road, but part of her wanted to spend a few moments alone with Gerald. She got up from the table, saying, "I have to run, duty calls, and I must answer." Before leaving the house, Lynn gave her a big hug as Charles remained ogling the two women from the table. He hadn't bothered to put down his newspaper.

Gerald drove Eve to her semi on the Walmart lot. She unlocked the door, stepped up on the top runner, and toggled the start switch. Diesel exhaust was pungent on the crystal clear air. The tractor rumbled to a start as dark plumes shot skyward from dual exhausts. She glanced down to see Gerald gazing up at her with a wry smile.

"You should wear shorts when you drive," he said.

"Voyeur," Eve said with a mischievous smile. She set the engine at high idle, gathered the dress to her thighs, and hopped to the ground. Eve took Gerald by the hand and did a walk-around truck inspection with him. Releasing and popping the hood, she checked for fluid leaks. The hub cups were pliable, and all the tires were sound. She was ready to roll.

"Well, I guess this is goodbye for now." She gave Gerald a prolonged kiss and told him, "Let me know how it goes with your Information school." Gerald responded in kind, telling her to be cautious on the roadways. He stepped away as Eve gathered her dress and settled into the driver's seat. She released the air brakes. Before pulling away, she rolled down the window, saying, "At least we had Sedona." Gerald laughed and motioned her away, "Get out of here," he said, "You're burning daylight." Eve laughed and waved him away.

She delivered dry freight for several months in the eleven western states. Getting around southern California, the bay area of San Francisco, Seattle, Phoenix, and Denver, without maps, came with experience. The only thing that gave her pause was chaining up on the snowy mountain passes in winter. With chain laws in effect, she and other truck drivers must apply 70-pound chains to the driver axles on the front tandem and a drag chain on the outside rear of the trailer. Considering that a single set of chains were more than half her body weight, it could be a nightmare.

Eve had to be careful with the touchy air brakes, not under the weight of a load. There was little weight on the drive axle. A hard stop could put the tractor into a spin. Getting onto I-17 northbound, she soon had Flagstaff in sight. The Purina warehouse bordered I-40 and was visible from the interstate.

"You're just in time," said the guy at the gate. Once she entered the drop yard, Eve took her paperwork to the loading office. Her trailer, No: 52386, was just short of 53 thousand pounds and well within weight limitations. Returning to her truck, Eve coupled to the trailer, giving it a slight tug. The kingpin locked. She cranked up the dolly and connected her lines when she got out of the cab. The yard dog driver wished her, "Bon voyage." Eve climbed into the sleeper and put on her driving togs. She had been in this warehouse once before and recognized the yard dog guy. Personnel at docks were mostly nonchalant about drivers. The men working drop yards with Eve and other women were more pleasant. Most guys had wives and girlfriends; they knew the rules.

*　　*　　*

Chris Summers had allowed Eve's truck to sit for more than the limit. Rolling stock wasn't supposed to sit idle for more than three days. In response, Eve would take the Flagstaff Purina load to Ohio as a thank you. She would not repower in Colorado as previously planned. Until now, Eve preferred to stay out west. Following the Ohio run, she could contact East coast dispatch and deliver goods along the eastern seaboard and perhaps Fort Meade. She may drop in on Gerald with a bit of luck, and the two could break some tension. It was a matter of knowing how much free time Gerald would have in his training schedule. It would be tricky, how the loads would go and how much free time she might have.

The Phoenix transportation company had contracted with Miller brewing in Milwaukee. Company drivers could drag beer loads throughout the eastern states for weeks. If they chose, they could take on trans-continental loads returning to more familiar turf. It all seemed feasible. There would likely be a beer warehouse where Eve could get under a load and continue to the Atlantic states. The only problem she foresaw was how to get along with a new dispatch protocol. A beer contract with a brewery could be demanding. 'Life is a gamble,' she muttered to herself, 'Just do it!"

*　　*　　*

Delmer Cullen, yard-dog at the Purina warehouse that Eve had seen in Flagstaff, was there for a summer job. He thought a lot about her from the first time she loaded out. This time, she wore a skimpy dress when she arrived. As he moved con-gears around, Eve had climbed down from her truck. She had to hike up her skirt revealing black panties with turquoise tiger stripes. Mr. Happy noticed her too! He wanted desperately to engage her in conversation. She seemed to be in such a damned big hurry. As she departed, all he could muster was, "Bon Voyage." You idiot, he told himself, 'Bon Voyage' was all you could say? Eve climbed back into her truck with the same exhibition as before. 'I gotta see about her,' Delmer told himself. He loved confident women. She took off out of the yard like a bat out of hell.

Walking into dispatch, Delmer asked if he could see the manifest on the last load going out. The clerk handed him a stack of papers, and he proceeded to rifle through the load sheets.

"That last driver that was in here is this the trailer number, 52386?" The clerk, a middle-aged woman, pushed herself from the file desk and rolled her office chair over to Delmer.

"Yeah, that's the one," she said, "Why, are you stalking that sassy little driver? She was a pretty little thing! And that dress, my-my." Delmer dropped the paperwork to his waist and said, "No, I'm not stalking her! What do you think I am, some pervert?"

"You just have a look," the woman said, "I've known guys like you all my life, and you have one thing on your mind!"

"Come on now," Delmer said, "I just wanted to see if she got the right trailer." With this, he handed the paperwork back to the dispatch clerk and walked out of the office. 'Hah,' Delmer said under his breath. The load sheet had the driver's name and cellphone number. Eve was a phone call away. 'You're a damn genius,' he told himself. Delmer went back to moving trailers around the drop yard.

*   *   *

Charles Ingalls drove his son to Phoenix Sky Harbor Airport. Gerald could travel at half fare if space were available, and he wore his Army dress uniform. As he left his father at departures, Gerald snatched his duffle bag from the Porsche.

"Thanks, Dad. I'll give you the thumbs up when I get there." The two shook hands, and Charles sped away. Gerald checked in at the departure kiosks and later removed his shoes, placed the contents of his pockets, and duffle bag on the security conveyor. The departure gate on terminal number four was a good walk from the security checkpoint.

Settling into a chair, he doffed his hat and called Eve's cellphone number. The call went to voice-mail. He looked around and saw several other Army personnel within vocal distance.

"Where you headed?" he asked one of the nearest soldiers.

"Florida," came the response. He sat adjacent to Gerald, and they proceeded to talk about the horrors of basic training and how happy they were that it was over. The man bound for Florida would be serving in a missile unit. The Air defense command (ARADCOM) had defensive positions around all major cities. They exchanged a few details about basic and talked about their relief of not being on orders for advanced infantry training (AIT). Each looked away from the other in silence.

"Looks like my gate is boarding," said the other soldier. He stood, straightened his dress uniform, and took up a position at the end of the queue. About that time, Gerald's phone rang. It was Eve.

"How's it going, stud?"

Gerald sulked, "Don't torture me like that!" Eve wasn't sure how long any cellphone tower would be able to carry their conversation.

"I'm on the move about 10 miles west of Winslow, Arizona. I'll be in Columbus, Ohio, two days from now." She proceeded to tell him about her plan to get on east coast dispatch. Maybe she could see him on weekends. Gerald's mood lifted.

"Oh man, that would be awesome!" The two were reliving their passions in Sedona when the call reception became spotty.

"Gotta let you go," Eve said, "Winslow is coming up, and I need to put the Eagles 'Take it Easy' on the sound system. I do it every time I'm cruising by on I-40." They signed off. "Love, love that girl," he said to an older woman sitting nearby. She smiled at Gerald, saying, "Give it time, sonny, just give it time."

*   *   *

With nothing pressing in Fort Collins, Charles and Lynn had a few more days in Sedona. It might be interesting to call on the bride's parents from the wedding. They had met them briefly along with the bride and groom. All they knew for sure, their real estate contact had set up the wedding venue. It was over, and the Ingalls rattled around the big house. They drove over to the Tlaquepaque shopping area after

Gerald left for Maryland. Parking was scarce during the tourist season. The weather was quite warm, with temperatures hovering near 90.

They strolled through the shopping area before coming to The Blossom. The boutique was quite chic. Lynn was surprised to see so many notable brand-name items. One of the clerks greeted the Ingalls.

"Where are you from?"

"Is the owner in?" asked Lynn, ignoring the woman's question.

"She's in her office." The clerk walked to Connie's office. Lynn glanced at a Stitch Fix blouse. She showed the price tag to Charles.

"Only $175, very nice," she said.

"Should be, for that amount," Charles said. The clerk popped her head into the back office.

"There's a couple out here asking for you." Connie looked over her eyeglasses, "Who might that be?"

"I think it's the owners of the Moki Drive house."

"Oh crap," said Connie, "I hope we didn't break something during the wedding reception!"

Connie went to the Ingalls in her showroom and placed her hand on Lynn's shoulder.

"Welcome; I'm happy to see that you finally made it in to see our little set-up." Lynn came to the point following a few remarks about the parking and the hot weather.

"Our son Gerald is quite taken with your daughter's maid of honor." She went on to fill Connie in about what she knew concerning Eve.

"Tell you what," said Connie, "Allow me to send off an order. We can go next door; they have a cardamom chai that's to die for." Connie retraced her steps and finished placing her order. She asked the clerk, "Could you watch the store for a while?" The Ingalls followed Connie to the nearby cafe and took seats on the veranda.

"So, what do you need to know about Eve?" Connie asked. The Ingalls caught it right away that she said 'need' and not 'want' to know about Eve.

"I believe there's more going on than just hand-holding between Eve and our son," Lynn said. Connie squirmed a bit in her chair, saying that she hadn't noticed. To lighten the mood, Connie suggested that they were young adults with raging hormones.

"Eve did leave for her driving job yesterday; you may not see her again. You won't see Gerald for a while either; he's on the east coast. Is there a problem?" Connie gazed back and forth between Lynn and her husband.

"Well, she's so young, and she's a truck driver, for God's sake!" Lynn was on the verge of hyperventilating.

"We were all young once," Connie said, "And more promiscuous than we are now. As for her driving career, you should know that my daughter Jill was also a truck driver! A good percentage of the people moving things around this country are women!" Lynn began to tear up and pushed her chair from the table, following Connie's expressed opinion. Connie and Lynn locked eyes on one another.

"Let's go," Lynn said to her husband and, "the sooner, the better!" Three Chai tea orders came to the table as Lynn and Charles walked hastily out the door. Connie asked the waitress, "Could you make that to go?" Walking into the Blossom, she said to her staff, "Chai tea, anyone?"

Lynn Ingalls had plenty of practice as an elitist. With a degree in marketing research, she saw it as her duty to cut the competition and eliminate barriers. Unfortunately, her character flaws cut across several lines in her private life. The only person with the knowledge and ability to reign her in was Charles. If he did so, he would receive the silent treatment. Lynn would sulk. Charles learned early in their marriage to allow Lynn the chain of her frustrations. He would dive out of the storm clouds so his wife could soothe her angst when she came back to reality.

* * *

Newlyweds Jill and Chris Summers were engrossed in their work at the Phoenix transportation company. They were also absorbed in each other. As they made time for themselves, they also anticipated their new arrival. Jill and Chris considered baby names.

"No, if it's a boy, we're not naming him Zeke," she would tell Chris. Jill was still putting a woman's touch on their condo. Chris was busy as a fleet manager, and Jill worked long hours at fuel allocation. Both were valued employees and understood their responsibilities.

Jill was taking calls from drivers needing COM-check fuel money. One driver was about to be stranded between Pocatello and Boise, Idaho.

"I'm showing less than a quarter on the gage," he said over his cell phone. Jill asked if he could make it to Jerome, Idaho.

"I doubt it," he answered, "I'll be pushing my luck to make Twin Falls." It was a cardinal rule not to let fuel tank capacity go less than one quarter. Jill scrolled through her computer screen for Twin Falls fuel.

"OK," she said," There is fuel at Twin Falls, but I'll have to open an account. It is not one of our designated stops." The company had prearranged fuel stops. They were on contract to get bargain fuel prices at specific locations. Drivers did not use personal funds for fuel. At her orientation, it was a hot topic because fuel costs set the company back $850 thousand per day. The fuel capacity on each saddle tank of a truck was 150 gallons. At current diesel fuel prices, it would require the driver to pay $650.00 out of pocket. No transportation company would put that burden on their drivers. The drivers wouldn't stick around. It would also mess with the demographics of the rolling stock. Trucks got around 6.5 miles per gallon. If not, the tractor may need an engine overhaul. Jill and her fellow specialists were made aware of this information ad nauseum. Company trucks were rolling down the road with a thirteen hundred-mile fuel range. Jill had realized that her challenges were detail-oriented. She had to be diplomatic with fuel stops all over the western states.

She repeated to the driver, "There is a Flying-J in Twin Falls, but you will have to sit while I open a contract with their corporate office." These arrangements are made to the detriment of the driver. Trip masters and satellite location devices are on each truck. Speed is monitored at the touch of a keystroke. If drivers run their engines over eighteen hundred RPM too often, it's an infraction of company rules. Regulations placed on drivers seemed overwhelming. They were also given their walking papers after a third minor accident. A large percentage of such accidents would happen by backing up at less than five miles an hour. It made no difference, three strikes and you were out of a job!

When Jill drove with Eve, she didn't pay much attention to these matters. Perhaps she should have. She could have been fired for picking up Eve when she was hitchhiking. Fortunately, it went below the radar. All ride-along passengers had to be CDL licensed and work for the company. Spouses could ride along, but they must have a permit. Drivers were like cats with fewer than two lives. Driver error was the official reason for almost any mishap. What they did have to their advantage was dispatch. They never had to be responsible for arranging their loads and the logistics for running them. That was Chris Summer's job.

*   *   *

Delmer Cullen, a student at Northern Arizona University (NAU), was a part-time worker for the transportation industry. His life was manageable. He loaded trucks and put in his time moving trailers and congears around the two-acre drop yard. He had seen Eve only twice in three months. The first time Delmer noticed her, she was a dead ringer for actress Amy Adams. A few months later, there she was again! A skimpy outfit was not normal wear for women drivers. She wore one with grace and downright perfection. Watching any woman get in and out of a sports car wearing a tailored outfit was an attention-getter. Climbing down out of a semi-tractor was drop-dead captivating. It could leave any red-blooded American boy weak in the knees. That was yesterday. He went home after work with Eve's name and cell phone number, which was enough for the moment. The next time he talked to her, it would be something more than the despicable 'Bon Voyage' he had said to her yesterday. As he sat in his work clothes at home in the declining light of the day, he drank a Coors lite beer, then another. Now or never, he thought to himself.

Grasping his cell phone, he dropped it the first time. Then he doffed his ball cap, got up his nerve, and dialed her number. She picked up on the second bounce.

"Who is this dialing me from area code 928?" the soft female voice said on the other end. Delmer told her that it was the yard-dog at the Purina warehouse in Flagstaff. Delmer's courage was full-blown after the two Coors beers he had consumed.

"Yeah, ah, this is Del Cullen from the Purina warehouse; you just picked up from us yesterday in Flagstaff." He let the statement hang in midair like a fish on the end of a very long line.

"What's the matter, Del?" My God, she called him Del, he dropped the phone again. Scrambling to pick it up without disconnecting, he said, "I'm surprised that you answered so quick. Don't you have both hands on the wheel?" Eve paused for a moment.

"I'm wearing a headset," she finally said.

"A what?" Del asked.

"Say, did I mess up my paperwork yesterday or something. Why are you calling me?" Eve could tell that the guy was feeling frisky.

"Well, it's this way," Del said, "The first time I saw you come on the lot, I swore to God you were Amy Adams!"

"Amy Adams?" said Eve, "The movie actress, she's twice my age!"

"Well, ah, I meant that you looked like a much younger, ah, ah, Amy Adams."

"OK, so what's this about?" Eve was pressing the matter, knowing full well that the guy was in over his head.

"Well, Eve, I want to marry you; I want you to have my children!" Eve paused for dramatic effect, smiled to herself, then answered.

"Well, Mr. Del Purina, before things get that far, we'll have to become friends first." Delmer could do nothing but roll with the punches.

"I, I'm sorry," said Del, "When I saw you climb out of that Freightliner yesterday, I almost lost it."

"So that's it!" Eve let the words sink in.

"You were the guy straining his eyeballs before I could change into my driver outfit?"

"That was me," said Del, "and I won't apologize."

"Well, that's very charming, Mr. Del Purina, but I'm at my exit; I have to get off the interstate and fuel the truck. I'll call you back in an hour!"

"Say what?" said Del.

"You're not getting off that easy, Mr. Del Purina!" Eve was adamant! The phone went dead, and Delmer was left wondering if Eve would call. He doubted it, and he might get fired from his job. She would likely contact the warehouse and complain. He slumped down on his sofa, opened another Coors Lite, and waited for the phone to ring.

"Oh shit, what have I done," he said to his cat. Before he could finish his beer, Delmer was asleep. He awoke at 2:15 a.m. There was a text message on his cell phone. When Eve had called, Delmer wasn't available to answer. The text read, "Good night sweet prince, your secret is safe, we did have Flagstaff -- Eve." Delmer looked down at the cat standing on the floor, looking back up at him, "Meow!"

*   *   *

On east coast dispatch, Eve ran hard for Miller brewing. They didn't require refrigerated trailers, which was one less thing to worry her. She got her fill with narrow eastern sideroads and had a horrendous experience in New York City. She dialed up her old trainer, Riley Baxter, to vent.

"Four-wheelers don't pay much attention to trucks!" Eve said. "They run around like you're invisible, taking up your turn radius. If you hit one, it's your fault!" The streets were so narrow; I took the middle of two lanes on all my turns. One woman screamed that she had the truck number and would call my boss!

"It was hard keeping it together," she said. Eve paused to take a breath.

"And the tolls, ninety bucks just to cross that damn George Washington bridge! I kept asking myself, how bad can it get, then it got worse! Route planning had done little good! I often had to turn around in shopping mall parking lots trying to figure where the hell I was and how I was going to get where I needed to go!" she expressed to Riley.

"All the while, people were laying on their horns and giving me the finger."

"Eve, Evie, stop," Riley said. "I know you're upset. Stay away from New York, Philadelphia, and Chicago. It's not worth it!" After a silence, Eve said, "I'm never going east of the Mississippi River again!"

Eve then mentioned that she was on her way to LA. Riley gave her an ultimatum.

"Why don't you have Chris Summers give you some time off. Maybe you could go back to Sedona and work for the Clayborne's.

"I don't know if I want to go back to CSU," said Eve, "I'm considering Northern Arizona University in Flagstaff. Jill's mother said they would love having me around. I've come to love Connie's other daughters, and I need that right now."

"Well, it's settled then," said Riley, "Park that damn truck at the Phoenix terminal and walk away; you're my over-the-road sis, and I want what's best for you!"

*   *   *

In Naples, Florida, Kim Chambers was coming off downtime with friends. She had flown them to Key West for a long weekend. Arriving home, Kim was toweling her hair after stepping from the shower.

Taking her time to dress casually, she peeked through the curtains. Kim saw a relatively short, balding man with a loud shirt and sunglasses. Answering the door, the man asked, "Kim Chambers?" Standing there with the towel, she replied, "Yeah, who's asking?"

"Allow me to introduce myself," the man said.

"I'm John Sebastian, a licensed Private Investigator with the state of Florida." Kim remained silent, standing in her doorway peering at him.

"My client in Cheyenne, Wyoming, asked me to locate the person who left this engagement ring on her brother's coffin twenty years ago." He held out a blue velvet ring box at arm's length. Kim threw the towel on a deck chair stepped out the door.

"You better sit, Mr. Sebastian, and tell me what you're getting at." She took a seat across from the man.

"I know this is a shock, Ms. Chambers, but my client was very adamant and paid me a tidy sum to locate you."

"Well," said Kim, "How much do I have to pay you to tell your client you didn't find me?" Sebastian shook his head.

"Too late for that. I already gave my client your name, phone number, email address, and pertinent information about your company. I realize it's hard for you to digest, but there it is, plain and simple." Kim softened her stance, let out a sigh, and stared daggers at him.

"So, explain this to me," she said. "Why dredge up something that happened so long ago?"

"Well," said Sebastian. Kim cut him off and said, "Would you like a beer? I know I could use one. And stop calling me Ms. Chambers, call me Kim." Sebastian accepted Kim's offer and waited. She returned shortly with two cold bottles of Pop's Porter beer.

Sebastian explained that his client, Sylvia Mildenhall, was the sister of Peter Mildenhall. Sylvia hadn't known about the ring until her mother, in declining health, told her. The survival assistance officer found the ring. It was there when the C-130 landed at the Cheyenne airport.

"Pete Mildenhall's body was delivered to Cheyenne in 1995. Sylvia's parents had kept it quiet about the ring all these years," said Sebastian.

There was a long pause with no reaction from Kim. Sebastian continued, "Pete's mother passed away, and the father passed away five years ago. It was easy to get a file photo and television footage when the tragedy occurred. Kim, you were in a photo and the local television footage." She was near the casket, and her name tag was easily discernable.

"We know it was you, Pete had written to his sister telling her your name, but he hadn't mentioned any engagement with you. We have the letters, but Pete's sister had not known about the ring until two weeks ago," Sebastian said.

"There's one question I need to ask you. Please brace yourself." Kim sat with tears welling in her eyes, "I'm listening."

"Pete's sister wants to know if you may have been expecting Pete's child."

"What if I said no," Kim answered.

"Please, Kim, I've been doing this for thirty years. I could get into hospital records, DNA, and all means of investigative material. Just tell me the truth." At this point, Kim was crying. Sebastian waited until she composed herself.

"I realize this has hit you like a ton of bricks. If you like, I can come back later and fill you in on a few more details." He excused himself and handed Kim a business card.

"I'm at the Springhill Suites in Fort Myers, call, and we can talk some more."

Following a second meeting with Sebastian, Kim was forthcoming with her daughter about Pete Mildenhall. Sylvia Mildenhall wanted to meet Kim, especially Pete's progeny, Eve. The timing of events unfolded quickly. Eve would be arriving at Denver International Airport in little more than a week. Kim had explained to her daughter that she could very well be heir-apparent with the Mildenhall family. Having heard a great deal about her late father, Eve readily accepted her fate. She held a deep curiosity about the man and what he must have meant to her mother. She never knew a father's love; it was a driving force to meet her aunt and make a connection.

*   *   *

Gerald arrived at his new duty station bag and baggage. Fort Meade, Maryland, had all the accouterments of a small eastern town.

His orders were to report to the Staff duty NCO building. As a Private E-1, Gerald was in an assigned barracks. His in-processing took three days. After getting his quarters assignment, Gerald was free for the day.

Freedom for him meant going to the day room and contacting other people in his unit. Among them were men and women to be trained as Information Specialists. There was an orientation at 0800 the following day. Then there would be a physical examination and dental work if necessary. Gerald began his radio broadcast and print media journalism classes on day three in personnel operations. They were instructions in combat camera leadership, content management, intermediate public affairs, and intermediate photojournalism classes.

Gerald would receive further orders for an in-country assignment following his training. He could be anywhere in the continental United States, Alaska, or Hawaii. With the attainment of SP/5 E-5, he might receive orders for a foreign duty assignment in a few months. Gerald's training would be fine-tuned through OJT (on-the-job training). 'I can do this.' Gerald thought, 'bring it!'

Chapter 7

A CALL TO ARMS

September 2015

As Eve made her way from San Francisco, she took an alternate route on the run toward Phoenix. Her thought was to get off I-5 and find something more exciting. The monotony of running I-5 to Los Angeles had been so ingrained it became tedious. Most of her driving experience in California was along designated interstate routes. Today, she would find a new path, making her way toward Barstow. There, she would fuel the truck at the Flying J travel center and catch some shut-eye in the sleeper. From Barstow, it would be another six-hour drive along I-10 to the Phoenix terminal. Barstow would cut down on the driving distance and make an excellent place to stop. She would fly out of Sky Harbor in three days, bound for Denver.

By Eve's reckoning, distances were psychological. Cut the driving time here and there, and you could satisfy the logbook and have more peace of mind along the way. A rest stop came into view on the Mojave road. There was plenty of pull-through truck parking. Entering a slot among other trucks, Eve set her brakes. Local Indians had their wares set out for tourists. In these circumstances, Eve became a tourist herself. You wouldn't find anything like this along the I-5. She bought four sets of onyx earrings and necklaces for those who awaited her in Colorado. The gemstones came from the nearby Black mountains to the south.

Back in the cab of her truck, the series 60 Detroit engine kept the cab quite cool. Eve did a tire check for the sake of being vigilant. She was supposed to do one every 250 miles by company regulations. Her method of checking tires was as old as truck driving itself. She had a heavy hickory baton. There should be a resounding ring by putting her hand on the tread then hitting the tire edge. If you didn't hear that ring, you had a problem. On one of the rear dual sets, there came a dull thud. It was like a fly swatter hitting a bed pillow. One of her inside duals on the back tandem was flat. Without getting it fixed, she would be throwing rubber off that tire on the next leg of her drive to Barstow. She did sweat it a bit, and she had to get to Denver. The wine load she carried was running just shy of 80,000 pounds. Each duel tire has a rating of 36,000 pounds. She had a net safety margin of 28 thousand pounds between the seven remaining tires on the rear tandem. All was good unless another tire blew. She had a good chance of making Barstow before things might become dicey. She entered the cab and rolled down her windows to bring in the cool September air. Traveling at a slower sixty miles per hour, the rubber on that flat would stay intact. Truck drivers call rubber laying on the highways' alligators'. Company radials had steel mesh holding them together. Eve rolled down the windows and listened to nothing more than the wind flowing through the mirrors. It was soothing but mind-numbing. Chewing a stick of Dentine gum way past its due date rendered a similar experience. Finally, Eve felt like a mariner who found a safe harbor with Barstow, California, just ahead.

The tire crew got her into the service bay right away. After climbing from the cab, Eve took a seat in the waiting area and checked out the magazines. They were all about auto racing. When she looked up, a familiar face moved past the shop window. It was Riley Baxter, her second trainer. She jumped up, hurried to the door, and shouted, "Hey lady, get a life!"

*   *   *

Meanwhile, Delmer Cullen worked the night shift at the Flagstaff Purina warehouse. He was bored. There would be no more loadouts for the day. He shouted, "Mind if I take off for the evening?" His supervisor gave him the thumbs up, so he clocked out early. Since Del had set eyes on Eve two months earlier, she was constantly on his mind. Lovesick, he was stuck on her like the peel on an orange. Del decided he would call Eve from the Starbucks near his apartment. She would hear the background chatter and figure he was not sitting alone in his apartment with his cat.

Del dialed Eve's number once he got his coffee and lemon pound cake. Her phone chimed four times. He was about to sign off when she answered.

"Hi Evie," he said, trying to maintain command of his nervous energy.

"Well, hi there, Del Purina!" said Eve.

"Could you just call me Del or Delmer?" he insisted.

"I've got some advice for you, Del," Eve cooed.

"OK, I'm listening," he said.

"I want you to think of three girls living in Flagstaff that are on your radar. Do you have anyone in mind?"

"OK, let's see, there's Griffee in my speech class, a girl who works at the Campus café and, oh yeah, a girl whose father owns the Chevy franchise here in town."

"Wow, I'm impressed; you're a go-getter!" Eve said, "The next time you see any one of the three girls, I want you to walk right up, look down at her shoes, then raise your eyes to their level and say these words.

"Hi, I've been noticing you for some time, and I think we should get to know each other."

There was a short pause. "That's it?" asked Del.

"That's it. The next two words that you hear will tell you all you need to know," said Eve. "You will know how to take it from there."

"Suppose I ask you that question?" asked Del.

"Well, you just drive on over here to Barstow, and we'll give it a go! You did mention something that interests me," added Eve.

"What's that?"

"This Griffee gal in your speech class, what school?"

"I'm a sophomore at Northern Arizona, majoring in English Language Arts."

"Hmm," said Eve. "I'm going to be checking out NAU. You may see me there when you least expect it."

"You're thinking of attending Northern Arizona University?" he asked with considerable enthusiasm.

"Yes, I am. I may run into you when I drop by in a few days. That is unless you hit it off with one of those girls." Ending the call, Eve said, "Night, night, sweet prince, let me know how it goes."

Delmer would count the days before he might see Eve again. The two said their goodbyes. Eve asked Riley, "Where were we?" Riley answered, "Careful Eve, when you're not near the one you love, you might love the one you're near."

"Not this time," Eve said, "My main squeeze is on the east coast."

*   *   *

Sylvia Bijou Mildenhall was born in February 1967. She had a sibling, Peter, who inherited the title role in the Mildenhall Oil Industry because Sylvia had other interests. As a child, Syl, as her friends called her, was bright and always well dressed. Dresses with sashes, out of character for a girl growing up in the 1980s, were out of style, but she wore them proudly. Her mother, a product of Texas University, was a homemaker in Cheyenne, Wyoming, and had married well. Her husband was the son of Bartolomeu Mildenhall, who founded a Cheyenne Oil refinery that came online in the mid-1930s.

Syl excelled in her studies. She graduated from high school in 1985 with a perfect 4.0-grade point average. Accepted to The Colorado School of Mines, her parents were delighted that she might pursue an interest in the family oil business. Pete, her younger brother, was equally adept at his studies. Instead of chasing a college degree, he enlisted in the Army, trained as a helicopter pilot, and became an instructor. His life ended tragically in a training accident at Fort Rucker, Alabama. Syl would be left alone to take the reins of the family oil fortune.

During her years at The School of Mines, Syl was active on archeological digs during her summers. She was equally at home, collecting nonmarine mollusks of Late Cretaceous age near Cokeville,

Wyoming, or dusting artifacts at the Tombs of Saqqara south of Cairo, Egypt.

The Middle East's political climate became a threat in June of 1987. Thomas Sutherland, a dean of the faculty at the American University, was kidnapped by the Islamic Jihad near Beirut. The Mildenhall family was uneasy about their daughter's travels in the middle-east. After college graduation, Syl came home to serve within the family oil business.

When her parents had passed away, Syl had no extended family. On her death bed, her mother told Syl about an engagement ring found under the American flag on her brother's casket. Knowing this new information prompted a search for the possibility that her brother and his betrothed may have produced an heir. It was a long shot, but Syl readily undertook the search for her peace of mind. The head of her security team, John Sebastian, was asked to look into the matter.

To Sylvia's surprise and satisfaction, Sebastian found the woman that Pete Mildenhall was engaged to, living in Naples, Florida. Twenty years earlier, the survival assistance officer found the engagement ring and presented it to Pete's parents. He mentioned the incident to no one other than the head of the family. The officer's responsibility was to protect the integrity of the Mildenhall family. If they wished to pursue the matter, it would be their discretion. They put the ring inside a dresser drawer and never spoke of it. They were numb from Pete's death and would remain so for years. The older Mildenhalls didn't wish to have anyone lay claim to the family fortune other than Syl. Following the revelation to her daughter by a dying mother, Syl had a different perspective.

If her brother had produced an heir, she wanted to know who that person might be. Provided she had a niece or nephew, she would disclose family interests to that individual. That person turned out to be Evelyn Chambers. Eve could take her place alongside Syl in the Mildenhall family legacy if she desired.

*   *   *

Two days before the Cheyenne meeting, Eve was parking her semi-tractor trailer on the terminal lot in Phoenix. Fleet manager, Chris

Summers, granted her some downtime. She had decided to transfer two years of credits from CSU to Northern Arizona University. She would investigate her prospects of living in Flagstaff and study the NAU course catalog. Chris and Jill Summers loaned her one of their cars. Eve drove through Sedona on her way to Flagstaff and spent one night with Jill's family, the Clayborne's.

Kim called Eve and strongly suggested a change of immediate plans. She considered that Eve had not taken the Cheyenne meeting seriously enough.

"What's this about?" Eve asked. Kim filled her in about the investigation by Sebastian concerning her birth father. She must be in Cheyenne for a meeting with Sylvia Mildenhall.

"The family I'm speaking of," Kim said, "is your father's family. There are a few things that you need to know."

"Like what?" Eve asked.

"I'll just tell you this much, a blood relative wants to meet you, and it could be crucial."

"Well, OK then, I guess, I'll bust my rear and be there. First, I have to stop by NAU and check out their course catalog."

"Fine," said her mother Kim, "Just be at the Cheyenne meeting! Get to Katie and Alfred's as soon as you can, even if you have to fly into DIA. I will meet you there." Eve looked at her host Connie across the breakfast table, "Well, I guess I have to be in Cheyenne in two days."

*   *   *

The Ingalls remained in close contact with their son as he trained at Fort Meade. Gerald, along with troop mates, could go off post and mingle. His parents took advantage of the opportunity and brought a companion for their son. It was an effort to keep him connected with Fort Collins. It was typical that married service members chose women who lived far from home. The senior Ingalls didn't want that to happen, and Jean Suthers filled the bill. She was a Fort Collins High School graduate and daughter of an affluent family. Lynn and Jean's mother saw social engineering as necessary short of a pre-marriage arrangement. Anything to take Gerald's mind off Eve Chambers was crucial for Lynn and Charles.

Gerald and Jean had dated in High School. The girl's parents were connected with the Country club atmosphere and owned a 24-foot Chaparral cabin cruiser on Horsetooth reservoir. Both families shared a lot of time on the boat. The senior Ingalls would be good chaperones, and Jean's parents were OK with the idea. The Ingalls took a couple of rooms at the Candlewood Suites on the Fort Meade Army post. Lynn and Jean took one room while Charles would be their suitemate. Gerald was not aware that Jean Suthers had made the trip with his parents. Sure, he liked her, and she liked him, but it was a long shot as far as romance was concerned. Jean was a yellow Cadillac with tan leather upholstery if girls were cars. Eve was a cobalt blue Lamborghini with gull-wing doors and a disposition to match.

Jean would do whatever her parents asked of her. Lynn and Mrs. Suthers considered it far-sighted that the two get reacquainted. Gerald met his parents at a local restaurant as the Colorado contingent arrived. When he saw that Jean had made the trip, he was a bit put out. Match-making was in the works, and Gerald didn't like it.

The menu ranged from seafood to the best beef entrees. They ate, talked, and shared a bottle of Johannesburg Riesling. When Lynn would attempt to steer the conversation in one direction, Gerald would set boundaries. Charles would put in his two cents, keeping the discussion civil. Jean Suthers wouldn't be a party to either persuasion and stood neutral. It was like a tennis match as the foursome ate, talked, and drank the wine.

*   *   *

Back in Arizona, other concerns were brewing. Eve visited the Northern Arizona University campus before her trip to Cheyenne. She could be enrolled for the fall semester beginning in two weeks. A seasoned professional driver, Eve witnessed numerous irregularities that cost people time, money, and in a few cases, their lives. She wasn't sure how many credits might transfer to Flagstaff; her new ambition was to change her major and pursue a law degree.

In Eve's view, our national electric grid was the nervous system of our nation. The transportation industry was the lifeblood. She had seen how the system worked, indeed how the country worked. Products and services moved from point A to point B. The rules that made it all work together were in the law. Interstate commerce was a tricky business. The United States was a nation of laws, and she would find her place in that system. Would it be easy? No, but it would be feasible and doable. She asked herself where she would be in five years. She wanted to become a lawyer. She drove to Flagstaff early Monday morning.

The only friend she had known at the University was Delmer Cullen, the yard dog at the Purina warehouse. He was taking classes on Monday, Wednesday, and Friday. Del was a wounded soul, but he might understand Eve's situation. He was attempting to better his life the same as she. On-campus, Eve took a chance and dialed Delmer's phone. A young woman answered, "Hello, who's calling?" The voice was cheery but direct. Eve hesitated before answering, "I was looking for Del Cullen." Eve could hear the phone transfer from one person to another.

Del took the phone and stood straight when he heard Eve's voice on the other end.

"My gosh, Eve, what brings you to call me?" She explained her predicament and asked if he had time to go with her to the registrar's office on campus. She didn't have much time and must make her inquiries promptly. He assured her that he could help her navigate the campus. For the moment, he was having coffee with a friend in the student center. Eve had seen the building and would be there in a few minutes.

"Guess who I'm having coffee with," he asked Eve.

"No, no, really, one of the girls on your radar?" After winking at the girl sitting across the table, Del said, "Come on over and meet Laura Griffee."

*   *   *

In Maryland, the Ingalls and Jean Suthers made small talk and asked for refills on the wine. When table conversation had gone on long enough, Gerald asked Jean, "Would you like to go for a walk?"

"Sure, Ger, let's do it!" They excused themselves from the table. Before leaving, Gerald asked his parents to order decaf.

"We'll be back in a bit; sit tight." Lynn Ingalls looked around nervously for their waiter.

The younger couple went off toward an outside exit.

"You know Jean," Gerald said, "It looks like we've been thrown together in a matchmaking duet." Jean couldn't agree more. She explained that her mother forced her to come on the trip to dissuade a love interest back home. She had been going out with an acquaintance several years older, and her mother was coming unglued. Gerald told about his situation. His mother disapproved of his girlfriend in Arizona.

"How would you like to handle this?" Gerald asked. They agreed that both parents would be upset if nothing came of their meeting. They decided not to fake any feelings for one another. They could say no sparks were flying once everyone returned home.

"Is it a deal?" asked Gerald.

"Absolutely," said Jean.

When the couple returned to their table, there was decaff waiting. Lynn looked at the two and swayed slightly in her seat.

"So, what did you two talk about?" Gerald looked at his iPhone and suggested they get back to the Candlewood.

"I have an early morning formation, and we should leave." It was a lie.

*   *   *

Undergraduate courses at NAU would be a good fit for Eve. She could change her studies concentration to Political science, Philosophy, History, or English. She chose to declare English as her major. For the present, she was earning $48K annually, driving for the transportation company. With a law degree, she could triple that salary. The objective of passing the bar exam hadn't registered with her as she walked briskly across campus. Entering Starbucks, she made an initial pass through the seating area as she searched for the young man she had seen only twice at the Purina Warehouse. The place was abuzz. Gone was the preppie look of people wearing cardigan sweaters with open laptops on their tables. These were students on break from their computers. Delmer stood as Eve recognized him and walked toward the table he and Laura shared.

"Nice to see you, stranger," said Del. The two foxy chicks were seated with him. Eve gave him the look of not selling himself short. She performed the same routine that she taught Del. Looking at his shoes, she raised her eyes to meet his. Knowing her modus operandi, Del smiled and pulled out a chair for her.

"You clean up pretty good," Eve said. She was wearing a loose-fitting outfit, nothing to show off her attributes. Laura was a modest dresser too. Both women had the common sense not to attract attention. Each recognized right away one another's choice of attire. They didn't need to dazzle.

"I have to make this short," Eve said. "After I get a caramel macchiato, I'll have just a few hours. I have an appointment to transfer some credits, and I have to work fast."

"Hold on a minute," Del said, "Why are you leaving the transportation company? It seems sudden."

"A girl is entitled to change her mind," Eve said. "I intended to drive just a few months and no longer. Now I can return to the study grind." Laura asked, feeling left out of the conversation, "Will you be pledging a sorority?" Eve hadn't given it much thought, but she seemed open to the idea.

"We would love to have a girl like you in Tri Delts," Laura assured her.

*　　*　　*

In Wyoming, Sylvia Mildenhall would hold the meeting with Eve and her mother at her childhood family home on Cheyenne's 5th street. She and her brother Pete had grown up in the house. She secured the two-story brick structure in agreement with her parents. It was now a meeting place for the upper management of Mildenhall Oil Corporation. Their grandfather, Bartholomew Mildenhall, had founded the Cheyenne Petroleum Company in 1934. It was situated along I-80 and ran on for more than a mile. Sylvia owned 51% of the voting stock on the board of trustees. She had a Ph.D. in Petrochemical engineering. In the company family atmosphere, everyone referred to her simply as Syl. She had the countenance of her father with an ardor for simple truth, a Wyoming girl. A few years older than her brother Pete, Syl Mildenhall could spot a phony from five miles away.

Syl's apprehension vanished when her niece, Eve Chambers, entered the meeting room. Eve had arrived alongside her mother. They sat in the

English Tutor drawing-room. A few members of the company's board of trustees were also present. Along with them were Katie, Alfred, and John Sebastian, the private Investigator who had located Eve. Syl's cadre of officers had driven from the Cheyenne airport in an older Ford station wagon. It wasn't posh and kept a low profile for appearance's sake.

Connie Clayborne had outfitted Eve and Kim in Sedona. They wore southwestern attire, not too flashy but modern and fashionable. The first person to speak at the meeting was not Syl. It was her secretary, a man in his forties.

"We want to thank you all for coming here," he began. The purpose of our meeting is to break the news that the Mildenhall family has an addition to their estate. It became known only recently. He was a bit formal, but Syl allowed his dissertation to continue for several minutes. While he was elaborating, she had her eyes fixed on Eve. Lady Mary of Downton Abby came to mind. Eve Chambers and her mother sat with backs straight on the outer portion of the settee they shared. They sat straight with their hands folded in their laps. Their smiles said it all. They were charming but gave nothing away in their mutual deportment. Finally, Syl stood, crossed the room, and took the younger woman's hands in hers.

"You are my brother's child; I don't need a DNA test to tell me that! We can save such things for our Texas cattle operation." Syl was referring to the ranch she owned south of Abilene, Texas. Eve spoke for the first time.

"I'm happy to meet you, Aunt Sylvia." Syl stood silent for the moment, brushing away a tear.

"If you and your mother would like to step this way, I want to show you the rest of the house." Syl's posture turned from Eve to Kim. In doing so, she asked when lunch might be ready.

"We'll be ready about 11:30," came a response from the resident wait staff. Syl took her would-be sister-in-law, Kim, by the arm and said.

"Tell me about you and Pete."

The company secretary took Alfred aside and said the oil operation came online when WW II needed fuel for the war effort. The company has a cadre of engineers and maintenance people who look to find weak spots in operation and fix them. Piping is in constant need of repair and replacement. The population of Cheyenne has grown considerably since 2010. Mildenhall Oil has 250 maintenance people on staff to keep things running. The engineers are constantly struggling to work at the molecular level to refine crude oil in the making of gasoline, diesel, and propane. As the two talked, the other men chatted among themselves.

A company lawyer strongly suggested that Eve should produce a DNA sample.

"I heard what Syl said, but just the same, I want a swab of that girl's pretty little mouth." Looking to his legal assistant, he added, "I want you to get it for me." In the lawyer's view, they couldn't risk turning a nine billion dollar market cap operation over to a stranger.

"Anything can happen, and we can't run the risk," he added, "Our Texas Pearsall formation has 90 producing wells. It will be a shame if we let that fall into the wrong hands. What would we tell our stockholders? We don't need some shylock trying to move in on us. There have been plenty of those!" The legal assistant said he would get on the DNA sample; "I'll get that swab before the morning ends," he assured his boss.

Sylvia took Eve and Kim to the second floor by elevator. She told them about the house renovation and described her state-of-the-art business center.

"This," she said, "was your father's room when he attended grade school." At that early hour, two young office women were producing spreadsheets. A fragrance of warm paper permeated the air as two printers ran simultaneously.

Kim entered the room and walked about, trying to sense the atmosphere when the man she loved had lived here. At the southwest bank of windows, she had visions of a tousle-headed kid playing catch on the front lawn.

"I'm going to run my mascara," she said, "If we don't get out of here." Syl understood completely and loved Kim for saying what she did.

"That was all a long time ago," said Syl, "But look what we have for the relationship you shared with Pete." She turned and took Eve in her arms and held her for a moment. Looking at her niece, she said, "Look what God brought us, what love inspired." With a glance at Kim, Syl said, "Brunch is probably ready. We can use the stairs. I want to show you our family photos on the staircase."

The legal assistant got to the dining room ahead of the others. He took a precursory glance at the seating arrangement. He quickly took Eve's name tag and placed it on the left of his own. The tag of their company comptroller he set to the left of Eve.

"I saw you do that, you young rascal," It was a voice from behind him. He turned and stared at the kitchen helper staring back at him.

"Can you blame me," he said, "I want to sit next to Eve. I've got the hots for her." The kitchen helper gave him a frown, turned, and strode back to the kitchen.

As people entered the room, the secretary directed each person to their place. The young lawyer dove to assist before Eve could move her chair and take a seat.

"Thank you," she said, "Wow, such a gentleman!" The kitchen helper filled water goblets and came to the assistant's chair. He was fiddling with the forks between his own and Eve's place setting. Eve smiled at him, saying, "If you want a DNA sample, just ask for one." Sayings that, she snatched his goblet and dumped the contents into the nearby pitcher. She spat into the empty goblet and handed it to him.

"See, that wasn't so hard, was it?" She turned to her left and said to the company comptroller, "Wow, what a nice piece of blue Kingman turquoise you have in that bolo tie!" For most of the Brunch, she and the comptroller discussed the finer points of turquoise and where it originated. The senior lawyer glared at his legal assistant seated next to Eve from the table corner. The young man shrugged and gave him a feeble thumbs-up very meekly.

*   *   *

Gerald finished his training by Christmas. His parents sent him a $10K cashier's check to go out and buy a set of wheels. His Army pay would only allow him to fly commercial and rent cars when affordable. They sent the money as a graduation gift for completing the tasks that gave him an Army career. They were thankful that he wouldn't be going to Advanced Infantry Training with all the repercussions that it might bring. A Twix came down from the Department of the Army in a manifest. The Twix wasn't a chocolate bar. It was Army jargon for a message. The message listed the names of men and women and where they would be going for their state-side duty assignments. His assignment came for an Army post in Homestead, Florida. All Army posts had a unit newspaper, and he would be a reporter/photographer for 'The Defender.' He and his classmates had a week to prepare for departure. Some purchased plane tickets and traveled on orders. Gerald made the rounds with two of his buddies to find a decent used automobile.

In Laurel, Maryland, the third dealership they went to had a few higher mileage fleet cars in their inventory. Gerald was still short for two of the vehicles he liked with the money his parents sent. He called Eve. She had returned from the Cheyenne meeting and was on the Northern Arizona University Campus. She was perusing a bulletin board for off-campus housing in the student union building. As her phone chimed, she took the call lackadaisically from her backpack and answered.

"Eve, this is Gerald!" She switched ears on her cell phone and hurried toward the food court where she could sit and talk. Gerald explained his situation and hesitated before saying.

"My parents sent me ten grand to buy a used car. I wondered if I could borrow some money to help get the one I wanted. I don't want to ask my parents for more money; I called you."

Gerald didn't know what had transpired with Eve over the last week. He would ask for $1,200. Gerald had no way of knowing that Eve had come into a money situation with Sylvia Mildenhall. Eve asked him to describe what cars he had found. The first was a 2011 Honda Acura MDX for $11,200 with 141 thousand miles.

"Wow, that's a lot of miles, anything else?" Eve asked. Gerald explained that there was a 2014 Toyota Camry for $12,995. It had 65 thousand miles on it.

"Get the Toyota; I'll wire you $4K to make up the difference."

"That's too much!" Gerald said. Eve rationalized that he needed plates and insurance.

"I didn't think you would have that much cheddar laying around. How can you afford to wire me that much cash?"

"It's a long story," said Eve, "Just tell me where to wire the funds."

Chapter 8

NEW BEGINNINGS

December 2015

Though she couldn't be with her friend as she gave birth to fraternal twins, Eve would be their Godmother. On speakerphone, she called from the Mildenhall Ranch. "You snuck up on me, pretty lady," said Eve. "You had twins? Are you kidding me!" The young women had their conversation after Jill's family had left the hospital.

Jill Summers was in her ninth month of pregnancy. Two months, liberated from her cubical, she worked from home. On Thursday, December 3rd, at 10:45 a.m. Jill called her husband Chris to say her water had broken. Her mother, Connie, drove her to the Phoenix Thunderbird Medical Center. When the two women pulled into the hospital parking lot, Chris's car was already there.

The atmosphere was jubilant and efficient as Jill processed into the center. Specialists had been called to the ward to handle all the precautions for the birth of Owen and Chloe. The babies arrived right away after the resident doctor gave Jill an epidural. The brother and sister were healthy and whole. Owen weighed five pounds fourteen ounces, and Chloe weighed three ounces less than her brother. Jill did not see her twins until six hours after the delivery, a bummer after doing all the work. Jill's whole family was there – mother, father, sisters, the new aunts, all looking forward to doting on the new arrivals. A nonsmoker, Chris passed around Titleist golf balls at work.

When things had settled down and Jill could rest for several hours, she contacted Eve to update her situation.

"What are you doing in Texas?" Jill asked.

"My Aunt Sylvia suggested that I take riding lessons over the weekend. She had Bert and Ernie fly mom and me to her Abilene ranch."

"Take you to a ranch in Abilene, Texas. That's like a gazillion miles. How did you manage that?"

"Well, Aunt Syl owns an airplane, so here we are," said Eve.

"Uh-huh, tell me another one." Eve explained how her father's family was in the oil business.

"I've become a fairy princess of sorts, and I didn't even have to kiss a frog."

"OK, said Jill," You lost me completely. What's this about being a fairy prince? And who are Bert and Ernie?"

*   *   *

Eve and her mother had taken part in an orientation. They were in Cheyenne learning about the Mildenhall oil business. Sylvia had taken them aside and suggested that Eve and her mother needed to know their family history.

"I don't want to alter your lives, but I do want you to consider the future of Mildenhall Oil and your place in it," Syl advised the two women.

"I'm planning to start classes at NAU this semester," replied Eve. Kim had a thriving business in Naples, Florida, which she had developed for many years.

"I don't want to alter your plans," Syl said again, "But I do want to lighten your burden if I could. The future will take us where we need to go, and I'll be in favor of your wishes."

Syl offered to pay for Eve's tuition and fees while working on her degree program.

"I would also like to help you with your living accommodations," she added. Eve looked for off-campus housing the day before she made the Cheyenne trip.

"I have real estate connections in Abilene," Syl said, "I could have them pull some strings and find a condo or townhome in Flagstaff. If you like, we'll buy your home and turn it over when you finish your degree." Eve and her mother looked at one another with skepticism. Syl read their thoughts. She suggested that they take a break and spend a couple of days at her Abilene ranch.

Syl asked her secretary to link up with Bert and Ernie and have the Global ready for takeoff to Abilene, Texas.

"It's an inside joke," said Syl, "Our pilots are always together coordinating company flight schedules. It's a nickname. If they are not sitting on the runway or here at the house, they lease the Global out through our air charter service. Once we leave Cheyenne, we can be on the ranch airstrip in little more than a couple of hours." Eve and Kim settled into the Ford Suburban with Syl and several board members. Who were they to spoil the party atmosphere?

"What do you mean Global, Aunt Syl?"

"Oh, it's our nickname for the plane, a Bombardier Global 5000, our 13-passenger jet." "OK," said Eve. With the luggage compartment closed. The ground crew was assembled away from the jet blast and marveled at the plane.

"You don't see many like that coming into Cheyenne," said one of the ground crew.

"That's Mildenhall Oil money," said another, "They do a lot of running around with oil interest in Texas and a few southeastern states. I've seen their flight plans for Dubai, about a twenty-hour hop. It must be nice."

Seated next to Eve on the plane, Sylvia gestured toward the Mildenhall refinery.

"Goodbye Freddy," She said, "See you soon!"

"You must have nicknames for everything," said Eve, "It's kind of cute, but it is a little odd." Syl looked at Eve.

"It keeps me grounded, all the responsibility of having a majority of the voting stock, I must remind myself of who I am once in a while." As the plane gained altitude, the flight was smooth and the cabin very roomy.

"When we get to the Abilene ranch, you and your mother will have your second-floor suite. It has a veranda on three sides. As a kid, I would sunbathe up there in the buff. When I got into my teens, mother would insist that I wear something."

"You will have a new life, Eve," Syl said, changing the subject, "I won't be intrusive with your plans, but there are things you will need to know." She went on to explain some of the ins and outs of wealth. Having money was a lot like building sandcastles on the beach. They can be as large and intricate as time and money will allow. When the tide comes and washes it all away, it's sad. In a perfect world, sandcastles are on cement pylons. They would hold the main structure above an advancing tide.

"Did you see that family we picked up at the airport?" Syl asked, changing the subject. "They're my comptroller's boys, and that's his wife next to them. You had a conversation with him this morning. The loyalty we build with people runs very deep. I haven't accumulated all our wealth so that I can hide on the Abilene ranch. I have it to make our lives better, your life, and most everyone involved with the company. We also supply a good deal of domestic oil. Your mother isn't just anyone, Eve. She is my sister-in-law, and you are my niece, a blood relative. You are Pete's lovely daughter, and nothing can change that. Their love brought you into the world. This morning when you walked into the 5th street house, you had all the moves and features of my brother. All I ask of you is that you consider our relationship permanent. You can go to law school wherever you want if that's your desire. You can go to Harvard; you can go to Cambridge, England, if you like and meet all the requirements. I'm convinced that you will. You need to know that you will be under scrutiny, not by me, but by others that may have their motives. We have the good, the bad, and the ugly in this world: the good and the ugly we can tolerate. The bad actors we need to ferret out. I've had three men ask me to marry them. They were sincere to a point, but they didn't love me, and I didn't love them. I'm married to

Freddy -- Mildenhall Oil. Tomorrow morning, my secretary will fill you and your mother in on the details of our working relationship. For now, let's get into a bottle of Moet Chandon champagne."

Saturday morning, Eve and her mother descended a wide oak staircase to a large drawing-room. Off to their left, they smelled bacon and omelets. A few of the kitchen staff were present as they walked into a large dining area with place settings for a dozen people. The legal assistant and his boss were at the coffee urn, drawing a morning wake-up. Both appeared to be ready for a horse ride. The assistant turned to Eve and her mother, "Syl and the rest of them will be down in a few minutes. Help yourselves to some coffee."

"It looks like you two are going out for a spin on horseback," said Kim.

"You must not have gotten the memo; we're all going riding." Syl and the remainder of her entourage entered the room about that time.

"We'll all go riding later this morning; first, we have some business to discuss." On her left was Syl's secretary, who carried an extensive portfolio.

"We're all informal here," he said, "Just help yourselves to breakfast, and then we'll go out on the veranda later."

"Gosh, another meeting?" asked Kim.

"This one will have more substance," said the lawyer. He gave her a furrowed glance to emphasize the importance. The entire party filled their plates and found places at the table.

"I forgot to mention, there are closets full of riding clothes," said Syl.

"They're all laundered and ready to go. I'm sure we have sizes to fit you." She said this to Eve, Kim, and the comptroller's wife.

One of the kitchen staff asked Syl if there was anything else she could do for the group. Syl motioned her away, "Beautiful job, get off your feet and relax." The younger of the two boys at the table asked.

"Aunt Syl, can I go out on Chopper today?"

Syl nodded, saying," Chopper's a lot of horse. Are you sure you're ready? If it's alright with your mom and dad, then it's OK with me." The legal assistant asked Eve, "Do you ride?" Eve and Kim looked at one another. Kim answered.

"Eve and Trish, one of her close friends, have been riding bareback since grade school. They would muck out stalls at Showboat Stables in Naples for riding lessons. I flew the owners to a lot of meetings."

"Yes, I ride," Eve said. The assistant looked at Eve over his coffee cup with a suggestive smile, "And bareback too, I'm impressed!"

After a moment's silence, Syl said, "I'm sorry, you haven't met our ground crewman for the Global. She pointed out a man in mechanic's clothes across the table. He lifted his orange juice glass in salute.

"He keeps the Global from crashing while it's on the ground."

Eve asked, "I would like to do a walk around the plane if it's not too much trouble. I've been driving a semi-tractor trailer over the eleven western states and Canada for the last few months. I did some of my truck maintenance; I'd love to see how flight maintenance works."

"Not a problem, you can wash windows." Said the mechanic.

"Oh, don't you wish," said Syl. She smiled and wadded up her napkin, tossing it at her maintenance man. "Eve has better things to do."

The cook stepped back into the room.

"Syl, the veranda is set up whenever you're ready." Within thirty minutes, the group stood, and the legal assistant pulled Eve's chair out for her as he had done in Cheyenne.

"Still the gentleman," Eve said, "You don't give up easily, do you?" He leaned in and whispered, "I deserved what you did in Cheyenne. I'll be a good boy from now on." Eve gave him a look to express that she had her doubts.

The veranda faced south, and the morning sun was visible above the mesquite. Eve and her mother had gone upstairs to their room. In the hall were two portable closets of riding clothes. They found what they liked and changed. A bit baggy for their taste, the two looked into a floor-length mirror and giggled. In times past, they had ridden bareback for miles along the Naples beeches in swimsuits and little else.

"When in Rome, do as the Romans do," Kim said. They even found Dover riding helmets that fit.

Another get-together was soon in progress on the lower veranda. The comptroller's wife and her boys were already off to the riding stables. The Global maintenance man had also departed. The airplane was visible in front of its hangar to the east, less than a half-mile away.

"Let's get started before it gets too warm," said the secretary. Eve and her mother were facing Syl and her secretary across the table. Others settled in with their laptops and iphones.

"The first order of business this morning," said the secretary, "Is to establish a genetic tie between the Mildenhall family and Evelyn Chambers. The legal assistant sat straight with flushed cheeks. Eve grinned and gave him a protracted wink.

"Other than DNA analysis, there is the matter of legal ties. Kim Chambers and Pete Mildenhall were not married. Sylvia Mildenhall will proceed with a 'Kinship adoption' of Eve. Syl must sign documentation that she will assume responsibility for Eve. It's only a formality, considering Eve will soon be twenty-one years old. In the legal proceedings, Eve will assume the Mildenhall name. We will file for a new birth certificate in the name of Evelyn Chambers Mildenhall. Custody law is all-encompassing, so we will have the lawyers draw up documents, and an officer of the court will review and sign them. The only thing we must have before drawing up the documentation is Eve's written permission to proceed. Since she is no longer a minor, her mother has no legal say in rendering an opinion."

All eyes were on Eve and Kim as the legal procedures were explained. Kim was first to speak.

"Pete and I would have been married if it were not for his untimely death. I have no objection with my daughter becoming a Mildenhall." As Eve watched her mother's reaction to the arrangement, she agreed to the terms. Eve looked over the paperwork. She signed it, following a short study of the wording. Sylvia came around the table to take Kim and Eve in a huddle hug.

"You won't regret this," she said. Kim and Syl wiped away tears as Syl addressed the rest of the people at the table.

"Well, that's it for now, let's go riding. Later this afternoon or tomorrow, we will discuss financial strategies." Not sure of what was meant by Syl's remark, Eve asked," Financial strategies?" The lawyer answered, "You will enjoy some compensation for the immediate future." With that, the group boarded two land rovers for a short trip to the riding stables.

As the group arrived, stable hands had five saddle horses ready. A couple of men excused themselves from the ride. Horses tied along a corral fence swished their tails at flies. The stable wrangler, a lifelong cowboy, had sized up the mounts to each rider and suggested which horses might suit individual preferences.

"Now these two are cutting horses," he said to Eve and Kim, "If they see range cattle along your ride, they might want to take in after them. Reign them in, and they will do everything you ask." Right away, Eve and her mother saw that these were not plodding horses like they had ridden in Florida. They had a little spirit with their ears pointed high and eyes full of excitement. They wanted to go after being tied to the fence! Some of the riders had their favorite mounts. The legal assistant was aboard a horse; its front leg jittering away flies and slacking the bit.

"Better watch out there, cowboy," said Eve, "That horse looks like he may just run away with you."

"No," said the assistant, "He's just a good ole fella, tame as a pup." The riders took off abreast, two in front and three bringing up the rear.

"I'd like to show you some of the immediate property," Syl suggested. Atop a feisty-looking buckskin, she headed off to the southwest as the group followed at a gallop. Riding through mesquite brush and gentle arroyos, everyone had control of their mounts. The riders, descending to a dry creek bed, trotted alongside one another. Syl told about the physical features and history of the landscape.

"One hundred and 75 years ago, this land belonged to the Comanche and Apache tribes. Just below that ridge to the west are old German settlement ruins. The Comanche would raid settlements during a full moon, capturing the women and younger children. They usually rode west toward Palo Duro Canyon, forcing the captives into slavery. It would take days to get to the canyon, riding day and night. If the captives survived, most would adapt to the Comanche culture. They seldom returned to white society, living out their lives as chattel. Among those early tribes in this region, bartering humans was normal. My wrangler back at the stables is Comanche. You couldn't find a sunnier disposition in a man, but don't abuse any of his horses!" Syl smiled as she said this and pointed demonstrably at each rider.

Eve and Syl lingered behind, just the two of them, riding alongside each other. Syl popped a question that took Eve off guard.

"Suppose, hypothetically, that the DNA tests suggest that you were not my niece. How would you handle that?" Eve, unprepared for such a remark, rode on for a few paces.

"Well, it would certainly cast dispersions on my mother." They rode on quietly for a short distance.

"That scenario would suggest that my mother was committed to more than one man in her life; I just don't see it."

"Well, let me ask you this," said Syl.

"How would that unforeseen circumstance change our relationship?" Eve looked at Syl and reigned her horse to a stop. Syl circled and came alongside Eve, placing both hands on the saddle horn.

"I don't think it would change my relationship with you, except for the fact that I would no longer be a Mildenhall. You're a decent human being and a lot like my mother. She never married, the same as you, and I often wondered why. Now, I think I know. Like my mother, you had bigger fish to fry. Mother had one great love in her life, my father, which both of us realize is your late brother, Pete. You, on the other hand, are married to the Mildenhall dynasty. Such an arrangement has served both of you quite well. Tell me if I'm wrong." Syl looked at Eve for a long while and finally spoke.

"For a 20-year-old young woman, you certainly make a lot of sense."

When everyone joined up for the ride home, one group said they had seen the main cattle herd two miles to the south. Syl asked if anyone would like to ride over and chase a few steers. Kim was first to speak.

"I'm a little saddle sore, and I think I'll pass," Eve said she would like to ride over to the Global and talk with the maintenance man.

"I'll go with you," said the legal assistant, "If you don't mind." Eve motioned that he could come along, and the two rode off at a trot.

Horse hooves clattering onto concrete pulled the maintenance worker's attention away from the plane. The riders came to a halt.

"So, you want to see the plane inspection, is that right?" He was addressing Eve. The legal assistant held back as Eve dismounted, put her hands on her hips, and arched her back, following the morning ride.

"I'm glad I didn't have to rely on horseflesh in the trucking business," she said. Parked off to the left was a fuel vehicle with stainless steel tanks and logo, 'Jet Fuel.' She asked the mechanic if he was on staff permanently at the ranch.

"I guess I am," he explained. He was a rover for the Abilene Regional Airport.

"Whenever private parties use an airstrip like this one, we are on retainer for fueling and inspections. The Mildenhalls have a 6,500-foot runway. No problem bringing this baby in," he added. By this time, the legal assistant had dismounted.

"I have a lot of things to check on, last but not least, these two beasts." The maintenance man referred to the twin Rolls Royce BSR 71 jet engines.

"Other than these engines, it's a matter of starting with the main landing gear and strut extension regarding temperature." Pointing out different parts of the aircraft, he went on to talk about checking taxi lights, landing and takeoff lights, strobe lights, and the tire pressure relative to the ambient temperature.

"We inspect the GOX, gas oxygen system, to see that it's charged. We also fuel the aircraft according to the flight plan. You don't want to run out of JP-8 at altitude." He said this with a wink. He walked to a cleanup station a few paces away.

"Well, there you have it," said the legal assistant, "Are you bucking for pilot status in the company?"

"No, I'm not," Eve answered, "But I did pull maintenance with my mother in her flight business. I'm sure you already know that." She gave the legal assistant a look of satisfaction that she knew something that he didn't. The man concluded that he was outclassed and outgunned regarding aircraft inspections, and perhaps he underestimated Eve as well.

"I smell Bar-B-Q; let's go see what's cooking," Eve said. She thanked the maintenance man for his hands-on information then mounted her horse. She and her companion rode a quarter mile to the house and saw a hind quarter roasting on a Bar-B-Q spit. The cook and her teenage sons were working the fire pit. Tying up their mounts, two stable hands mounted the horses and took off toward the stables at a gallop.

"If you want to get out of that riding outfit, would you like to go for a dip in the pool?" asked the legal assistant.

"Only if there's a hot tub to go with it." said Eve, "I'll be back in 20 minutes."

"Yes!" said the man to himself and threw a left hook for emphasis his satisfaction.

All the houseguests were sipping drinks or playing in the water at the pool. The younger boys were lolling in the hot tub. It was an extension of the pool, with water temperatures around 102 degrees. When Eve joined the group, she wore a shimmering solid green one-piece swimsuit. Sipping on a margarita, the legal assistant looked at her with elevator eyes.

"God, you're gorgeous," he said, "If my old school chums could see me now!" Eve laughed and kicked water in his face from the pool's edge. He hoped to push Eve into the pool when he gave playful chase.

"Not so fast," Eve said. She held him at arm's length with the palm of her hand on his chest.

"I want to see you do a full gainer off the high board." Not knowing what a full gainer was, he said, "Ladies first!" Eve walked around him, climbed the 12-foot ladder, and took a position at the back of the diving board. Looking straight ahead, she took three long strides, hopped high, and hit the end of the board. She soared high into the air, legs horizontal and level, bent to touch her toes with both hands, then stretched out full body length backward and hit the water with a small splash. People clapped, and the assistant yelled, "How long has she been doing that?"

"She's been diving since she was six or seven," said Kim from a lounge chair. "You should see her performing on the parallel bars. My girl had a walk-on gymnastics scholarship to CSU, but she dives for fun." When Eve swam to the edge of the pool, people were still captivated by her style. Brushing the hair from her face, she said, "Your turn, cowboy!' The assistant stood, threw off his Hawaiian shirt, and walked to the ladder. Syl, sitting alongside Kim, nudged Kim and said, "This will be good!" The assistant climbed to the top and walked nonstop off the end. He grabbed his knees and did a cannonball into the water with a horrendous splash. People laughed and applauded. When he came up, Eve was also clapping. As he climbed out of the pool, she grabbed him in a bear hug, saying, "You're no Greg Louganis, just try to keep your eyes open next time."

"You know Eve, I've never done anything like that in my life. You inspire me! Let me buy you a drink!" They walked to the end of the pool and situated themselves in the hot tub with the young boys. One of the kids asked Eve, "Were you an Olympian?" "Oh no, no, no, far from it, it takes a lot of time, commitment, and sponsors to be an Olympian, but thanks for the thought."

"What's a sponsor," asked the boy. Eve's companion answered, "It's someone who has faith in you and gives you money to follow your dreams." Noticing Eve chatting in the hot tub, Syl turned to Kim, "I think we have a diamond in the rough here."

"She always amazes me," said Kim. Syl speed-dialed a number on her cell phone and asked, "How long would it take my HR man to get up to the ranch?" A woman's voice on the other end replied, "Tomorrow is Sunday, and there's nothing on his plate."

"Thanks," said Syl, "Run it by him and get back to me when you can."

Chapter 9

MAJOR CHANGES ALL AROUND

December 2015

Eve and Kim had been at the Abilene ranch for riding lessons, but It turned out to be much more. Eve would soon become part of the Mildenhall family and obtain a significant degree of financial independence. It was also the occasion of an annual weekend Bar-B-Que fest with the Mildenhall stockholders.

"You couldn't have come down here at a better time," Syl said to Eve and her mother. Blending into the ambiance, they were royal guests on the 11,000-acre ranch.

"People will want to meet you," said Syl, "Enjoy the moment."

People started arriving by late Saturday afternoon. They weren't all figureheads of Mildenhall Oil but people from behind the scenes. The cook had her two boys work all morning and afternoon. They tended the Bar-B-Que pit with rakes and water spray to keep the charcoals from flaming. Beef and lots of it were on the coals by 4:00 pm. Kim counted five pickup trucks, an assortment of SUVs, and two more planes on the airstrip. The secretary was on hand, directing people.

Several teenagers had jumped into the swimming pool wearing nothing more than underwear. It was a party, Texas-style.

Eve and her mother took a seat in the conference room following the pool party. On hand were Syl's cadre of helpers. All were casually dressed. One wore a T-shirt advertising Nassau, Bahamas.

"We'll make this short," said Syl. "Once you go back to Flagstaff, we're not going to leave you to fend for yourself." She was looking directly at Eve.

"My secretary is in contact with the registrar's office at Northern Arizona University. Mildenhall Oil would like to take you and your mother on financially as a business interest. Does that sound feasible?" Both Kim and Eve nodded in agreement, taken aback by the offer.

"Eve, we will pay your tuition, fees, and anything having to do with your housing on or off-campus. We'll buy a condo; it's up to you. You will also have a credit card, good for incidentals. The credit card amount will have a $500 monthly cap. There will be no accumulation value. Would that be agreeable?" Eve got up walked around the table, thanking Syl and everyone present. The lawyer, not prone to emotion, had a grin from ear to ear.

"I won't disappoint you," Eve said.

There would be stock options for Kim's flight service in Naples. Syl summed it up by saying, "My financial people will lay the groundwork and buy a thousand shares of stock. We will work out the details later next week. In return, we would ask you to make your services available for Mildenhall Oil people who might be active in the area. There won't be many, just vacationers, and it shouldn't be overwhelming. We don't have oil interests in Florida at this time. We would ask that you offer flight service to members of our company at a discount. Does that sound OK with you?"

"That would be great!" Kim said, "I will bring my business partner on board."

"Consider it done," said the secretary. "Just let your partner know that we'll be in touch."

The group dispersed as the day was warming up. Grounds around the ranch house had transformed into a festival atmosphere. A local rock band played south of the house, fifty yards from the parking area.

Several rows of hay bales were in place near the Bar-B-Que area, with tables for condiments. The cook was shooing kids from the kitchen as her two daughters helped with food prep.

A woman seated on the veranda sprang to her feet and ran toward her daughter. The girl, about fifteen, was riding bareback and topless on a dapple mare horse.

"Save that for when you're married!" yelled the woman. The girl was handed a T-shirt by one of the boys who went topless himself. "Come on," said the boy, "Be a sport!"

Drifting toward the revelers, Eve and Kim wore Texas longhorn ball caps. The temperature hovered around 70 degrees, very pleasant. Eve asked if she could help out with the Bar-B-Que. She and Kim were soon turning beef on the large mesh grill. Their cheeks flushed, and sweat dripped off their chins. One of the men took over for Eve and one of the younger boys for Kim.

"Be careful," said one of the boys, "I want mine medium raw." Ice chests were full of soft drinks and beer. The women gladly accepted a beverage from one of the teens sitting on the hay bales. People ate and talked for a couple of hours. Eve and her mother met many neighbors genuinely excited about Eve and Kim's relationship with Sylvia Mildenhall.

"Wow." said Kim, "I guess the cat is out of the bag!"

Following a lot of banter between Mildenhall oil people and several ranch hands, all employees would be back on Sunday for a catered breakfast and a sermon. There were also a few loose ends that Syl wanted to discuss with Eve.

"I thought we had covered about everything," Eve said to her mother. Non-committal, Kim shrugged, saying, "Well, it's a good-sized transition. I'm sure there must be more ground to cover." They left it at that and went upstairs to their room. Most everyone lounged about for a siesta. Farmhands were sprawled in pickup trucks and napped on the veranda. Dust rose by midafternoon as Ranch hands drove away to do chores. "This is a working ranch," said Kim, "You can tell." As festivities wound down, no one went away hungry. The night was fantastic, and sleep came quickly.

Promptly at 7:00 am Sunday, a trumpet blast awakened Eve and her mother. One of the cook's boys was belting out a popular Mexican tune. The women looked at one another from adjacent beds.

"Sounds like a few bars from La Bamba, "said Kim. "I guess that means it's wakeup time. I did hear trucks pulling in; it must be the brunch caterer." Staff people scurried about setting up tables and opening mobile kitchens. Eve touched the window glass.

"It must be 70 degrees out there and warming up!"

An hour after wakeup, people moved outside to greet the day.

"I feel like I've eaten so much," Eve said. "These folks don't live on granola bars and coffee like I've been doing." Syl, dressed in shorts and a halter top, met Eve and her mother in the foyer. She took both their hands, saying, "There's someone here that I would like you to meet." Standing before them was a tall, lean fellow with a Stetson hat in hand and shiny western boots. Not much older than Eve, he waited nervously for Syl to make introductions.

"This is our H.R. man. He flew in this morning from Dallas. He needs to get together with both of you to discuss your titles."

"Titles," Kim repeated the word, "Like job descriptions, that sort of thing?"

"Let me answer that," the man said.

"Job placement with the company is necessary to make sure we're satisfying Uncle Sam for giving financial compensation for your services. There will also be a meeting with John Sebastian. Eve needs to take a placement test so we can process a vocational inventory."

"Well, OK then," Syl said, "Let's eat!"

A line formed off to the left of a mobile kitchen. Present were most folks who flew down from Cheyenne, a few ranch hands, and neighbors. Kim did a nosecount and estimated about sixty people were attending. A podium in the bed of a half-ton flatbed truck sat nearby. Syl's secretary was at the pulpit while people were standing in the food line. He got everyone's attention by ringing a small bell.

"Before we eat this morning," he said, "Let's return thanks for this beautiful day and all these precious souls." The cowboys doffed their hats as he began to speak.

"Gracious heavenly Father, be with us this day. We ask you to bless all your people standing here this morning and the food to nourish our bodies. Keep us from harm and lead us in your ways, amen." There was a resounding amen from everyone. The ranch hands put their hats back on, and the morning chatter resumed.

Kim had not been a frequent churchgoer most of her life, but Eve had been committed to a fellowship of believers. In her early years, she and her friend Trish had attended vacation bible school.

The food line moved quickly. The kitchen cook was in line with the rest of her family.

"It's nice to see that you get a day off," Kim said to the woman.

In response, she nodded, "Si, si."

The H.R. man sidled up alongside Eve and her mother. Looking to people at the tail end of the line, he asked, "Folks, do you mind if I cut in here" No one objected. By a misstep, he bopped into Kim's side.

"Are you packing?" Kim asked.

"Darn right!" came his reply. "We have gunfights down here in Texas the same as anywhere else" This prompted a conversation about company security.

"You may have noticed that Syl doesn't travel alone. There are folks out there in zombie-land who may want to take her down. Some of the others also pack, but I won't say who." Eve, overhearing the conversation between him and her mother, asked, "Where did you get your training?"

"Afghanistan, in the special forces, then I had training at Quantico in D.C. I would have stayed on the force, but I'm damaged goods."

"Nothing serious, I hope," Kim said. "I spent a couple of enlistments as a Chief Warrant officer flying Army Chinooks."

"Oh God, don't get me started. We could be here all day telling war stories," the man said. Eve listened, not moving until someone nudged her and said, "Your turn to order."

"Yeah, OK, well let's see, I'll have a fruit cup and two strips of bacon" Kim and the H.R. man also placed their orders. They walked to the nearby hay bales and sat. One of the catering kids came around offering orange juice or coffee. Kim continued her conversation as Eve admired the guy's presence of mind. He seemed honest and pleasant.

As far as she could tell, the man had a bearing of an old-school pro and was only a few years older than herself. He wasn't hard to look at either. He had the veneer of a poker player and broke out with a smile now and then. The closely cropped hair and sideburns were a combination of styles that Eve had seldom seen.

"So, how did the bad guys hurt you?" asked Kim. A Taliban fighter winged me in a firefight on my hand and forearm. It happened a few klicks south of Kandahar" As he said this, he showed that his left hand was missing two fingers. "They didn't get my gun hand. Otherwise, I wouldn't have made it to the medivac chopper." A moment of silence ensued.

"Eve," he asked, "Could we get together this afternoon about two-ish? I've got some paperwork and testing that we have to accomplish." His piercing blue eyes drilled into hers. "Your mother won't take as long, but for you, I'll need a little more time." Eve, with a warm smile, answered, "I'm all yours. Take as much time as you like!" Kim raised her eyebrows but said nothing. More people were arriving, and the simple conversation turned to crowd noise.

The pastor walked onto the truck bed as people finished brunch, Bible in hand.

"Hi folks, I want to have a word with you this morning. When Sylvia asked me to come out this morning, I asked her, Sylvia, who?" Everyone laughed.

"You know, folks, and it's not surprising that my sermon in a minute," he held up one finger, then continued, ". . . is too short; it also fits the temperament of a working ranch. Out on the cattle drives, a preacher might have even less time. Cowboys couldn't be away from the herd for any length of time. Before we begin, please join me in prayer." People bowed their heads, and again, the hats came off. Eve noticed that the H.R. man's hat also came off as he stood to the left of Kim. The pastor shuffled a few crib notes and began. He took his few words from the book of James 4:7-8. Following a short prayer, he presented a brief sermon.

"Therefore submit yourselves to God. Resist the devil and he will flee from you. Draw near to God, and He will draw near to you. Cleanse your hands, you sinners, and purify your hearts, you double-minded."

The pastor then told the crowd that God asks that you be true to yourselves and Him. Resist evil! In doing so, you will find favor with almighty God.

"Now, if our musicians will tune-up, we will sing the first verse and chorus of Nearer my God to Thee." The guitar players stood up while the drummer beat out the rhythm. When the singing concluded, there were a few amens. Eve noticed that no one needed hymnals. She had recalled the hymn and sang it from memory. The pastor raised his arms and dismissed the crowd with a prayer, "God, we ask you to hold our hearts near and dear to you in the coming week and protect us from the evil one, amen. Go and have a beautiful week!" A few people left the group while others resumed their conversations. Younger kids headed for the stable. More than a dozen men, women, and kids had ridden in on their mounts. Some retired to the pool, while others pitched horseshoes. Eve turned to her mother and the H.R. man, "Remember the sabbath and keep it holy." The words came out softly and with conviction. Her mother gazed to the far horizon and smiled.

"Such a place," she said, "What a wonderful place!"

Most of the guests had passed a few words with Syl by Sunday afternoon.

"You've always been such a gracious host," said a few close neighbors and hugged her openly. A great many of them had pump jacks on their property. Syl had developed the business relationship to extract oil; it paid handsomely for everyone. Most wanted to meet Eve and her mother.

"So glad you came down to Texas so we could get acquainted with Syl's sister-in-law and niece!" They made up their minds that the two were Mildenhall family. They didn't know that DNA tests were in the works. They wouldn't care, and it made little difference if they knew.

The H.R. man took a few steps toward Kim and Eve. "Please come to the computer room, and we'll do those placement inventories. We can plug you into the company with a title and a job description." Both women entered an upstairs room of computers and printers. The PI, John Sebastian, came in and took a seat in a short while. With software forms completed, the vocations of both Kim and Eve came as no surprise.

"Kim, you have the title of Flight specialist – Gulf coast Florida, and for Eve, Public relations - Dallas branch," said the H.R. man. "As of Monday, you will be on the payroll drawing a salary of zero dollars. The compensation package that we reviewed yesterday will be your sole benefit for the immediate future. As we move forward, there will be changes."

"For security reasons," said John Sebastian, "Eve, you will be a Mildenhall, only on paper. As you continue your registration with Northern Arizona University, do it as Evelyn Chambers. It will be for your protection as well as company security. Mildenhall Oil has outsiders looking to infiltrate our resources monetarily and physically. Bad actors attempt this through computer hacking and personal contact. The market cap of the company is very tempting for the bad guys. If anyone should ask, you are Eve Chambers, not Eve Mildenhall. For any suspicious activity, you may encounter, dial this number. May I have your cell phone, please?" Sebastian put a number on her speed dial, Marie Teresa – 928-222-3333. "This goes for anything, someone following you, silent phone calls, anything scary. Help is a phone call away for anything disturbing that you might run into." Sebastian and the H.R. man exchanged glances as Sebastian continued, "If you lose your cell phone, or misplace it in public, get on a separate line and call the same number, we will take it from there. Don't put any email addresses on your computer that has anything to do with the company. If you want to reach Syl, myself, or H.R., group us as Sorority friends. All the compensation coming your way will be deposited directly into your bank accounts. When it's convenient, send me your account numbers."

Eve and her mother would pack for their return trip to Flagstaff through the remainder of the afternoon. As Kim returned from the shower, Eve was reclining on the bed, fully clothed, staring at the ceiling.

"Hey, sugar," her mother said, "We better shake a leg. We have to get back to Flagstaff today!" Eve made little response but shifted her gaze from the ceiling to her mother as she continued drying her hair.

"This all seems to be moving pretty fast, don't you think?" Eve asked. Sitting up on the edge of the bed, she continued. "I feel like

people are pushing too hard. I'm not sure I should go where they say."
Kim stopped what she was doing and sat beside her daughter.

"We all feel that way with the weight of responsibility. It's a matter of
deciding how to proceed with our information. In the end, there will be
personal growth; no pain, no gain." Eve rubbed her temple and thought
about what her mother was telling her.

"I feel like I did on the first day of driving school. How would I get
that giant Freightliner tractor through that tiny gate without wrecking
the fence and getting kicked out of school?"

"We all have those feelings," her mother said. "The first time I
had to land a Huey chopper at the end of my first solo flight, I thought
I might crash and send a fireball ten stories high. Honey, we've both
been given a great road map on what will be happening in the next few
weeks. Just take it one day at a time."

"You're right, mom," said Eve, "I knew you would have an answer.
I'll shower so we can get to the plane."

The Global was waiting and ready, with Bert and Ernie going
through their preflight checks. Most passengers who had come from
Cheyenne on Friday were aboard the plane. Syl's lawyer would remain
at the ranch and wait on DNA results for Eve. As Syl walked with both
women to the Global, she said, "You have gotten a good representation
of the public relations involved with Mildenhall Oil this weekend. Eve,
In your English classes, think about the communication skills you will
be learning. That should be your focus for the next couple of years. If
law school looks favorable, you have my full support. Keep in touch with
me as you would a Sorority sister. Don't let Sebastian or H.R. unnerve
you. It's not as bad as it looks." The three embraced, and Syl stepped
away from the plane.

Ernie stowed the suitcases as Eve, and her mother took their seats.
Shortly they were airborne, heading south. Circling to the northwest,
the Global gained altitude, and G-forces pressed them in their seats.
Once the plane leveled off at cruising altitude, Flagstaff was an hour
and twenty minutes away. Bert checked with the mid-point tower in
the right-hand seat at Puerta de Luna, New Mexico. He came on the
intercom and suggested that Eve and Kim make phone calls to connect
for a ride at Flagstaff. They would be landing in forty minutes. Ernie

said they would be in Cheyenne at 7:15 mountain time for the through passengers. Eve dialed Delmer Cullen, hoping he would pick up.

The Global 5000 private aircraft taxied within thirty yards from Delmer and Laura, seated in the coffee shop.

"Gosh," Laura said, "I wonder who's rich enough to fly around on that!" Delmer's phone chimed as Eve descended from the plane. She was on her cell phone as Delmer answered his phone.

"We're here," said Eve, "Are you at the airport?"

"Wow, I think I see you. Is that you, getting off that Global 5000? We're in the coffee shop." Eve looked toward the glassed shops of the terminal and spotted Del as he waved.

"Gosh, I wonder what the back story is on this," Laura wanted to know.

Along with Eve was a woman Del guessed might be Eve's mother. Another man wearing a suit was walking and talking with Eve as his necktie fluttered in the breeze. Eve turned and waved to Ernie in the pilot's right-hand seat. The pilot gestured toward the cargo hold of the plane. The threesome walked to a small portal as groundcrew offloaded suitcases. Laura stepped forward as passengers came through the terminal doors and warmly greeted Eve.

"I guess you know how to arrive in style!"

"So, Laura," Eve began, "Delmer hasn't said too much about you! We were a bit rushed at the Starbucks a few days ago and didn't have a chance to talk."

"It's all good," came Laura's reply. As Eve warmed up to Laura's presence, she couldn't help but think of the social engineering she had done with Delmer about the girl. The imaginary discourse she had with Del came rushing back, the elevator eyes strategy. Eve knew about her features and the essence of her personality, according to Del. She liked what she saw. Eve decided they would hit it off and thanked Laura for being at the airport to welcome her home.

"Tell you what," Eve said as they walked along, "I feel like I know you, and right now, I could use a friend."

"That's sweet of you," said Laura, "I'm all in."

The man that Eve got off the plane with said, "I've got to get a copy of the 'Wall Street Journal.' I hope Bert and Ernie don't leave me." With this, he turned and stepped away to a magazine kiosk. With a blank stare, Del asked, "Who's that guy?" Eve ignored his question for the moment, saying, "Delmer Cullen and Laura Griffee, this is my mother, Kim Chambers." Kim gave Del a visual once over and smiled warmly toward Laura.

"Happy to meet you. I guess you're friends of my daughter?" Del took over, pulling their suitcases. "We're parked across the departure lane if you're ready to go." By this time, the lawyer had returned.

"See you around," he said to Eve and walked out to reboard the Global. No sooner had he done so than the doors closed, and the plane was taxiing onto a runway.

"That's a lawyer we met in Abilene," Eve said, "He's a talker!"

Del and Laura were more than curious on their ride over to Little America.

"Have a good weekend?" Laura asked among the chatter.

"The best!" Eve said. She wasn't sure how much she should reveal. Kim spoke up, saying, "We had a bit of luck flying out of Abilene and caught a ride with an oil company. If Eve hadn't been so flirtatious, we would still be there. That lawyer liked us and offered us a couple of seats." Saying this, Kim looked out the car window.

"It must be quitting time around here, lots of traffic." They rode toward Little America near the airport. Laura mentioned school schedules and how she and Eve might have classes together. Eve was evasive and didn't answer directly, only confiding that the school year would be challenging.

After checking in at the front desk at the hotel, Kim treated everyone to dinner at the Silver Pines restaurant? The lodge held a masculine, native American atmosphere with a wood-covered central fireplace. The restaurant had dark earth tones and a Navajo ambiance.

"Can I take your luggage to the room?" Del asked.

"Not necessary; we'll just have hospitality do that," Kim answered.

"I'm buying," said Eve, "Anyone for a margarita?" The wine steward came by and asked if they would have wine with dinner.

"Sure," Kim said, "Put a bottle of Veuve Clicquot Brut in an ice bucket right here." She gestured to the space between herself and Del.

"Yellow label?" asked the steward.

"Yes," said Kim, "That would be great!"

"I'm not hungry," said Eve, "Does anyone want to split the Lobster Thermidor?"

"What you can't handle," said her mother, "We'll take to the room; I'll have the same." She handed their menus to the waiter. All the while, Delmer was adding up totals in his head. The two had ordered more than a C-note of food and drinks, with he and Laura still staring at their menus. They finally made their choices and sat smiling at Eve and her mother.

"Such a treat,'" said Laura, "What's the occasion?" Del and Laura were trying to assess the situation.

"I had an offer in Abilene to take my flight business to the next level," Kim answered. For the next half hour, Kim elaborated about the tourist trade in Naples. Florida. She and her business partner would be expanding, and she felt like celebrating.

"Wonderful," said Laura, turning to Eve." Will you be pledging Tri Delts?"

"Perhaps," said Eve, "We'll see." The discussion morphed into finding off-campus housing or living in a Sorority house. Kim learned that Del had lived in Flagstaff all his life. They discussed parts of town that might be a good fit for Eve.

"I don't want to sound stuffy," said Kim, "I want to know what a real estate person wouldn't tell us."

*   *   *

The following morning, Eve had a meeting with her faculty advisor. He was impressed with Eve's level of maturity.

"So, what have you been doing for the last year," he asked? You took time off from your degree program at CSU?" Eve shifted in her chair, explaining that she had taken a job as a long-haul company driver with a Phoenix transportation company.

"You drove a truck?" Her advisor was both impressed and a bit mystified by her answer.

"Yes, I drove a truck over the continental U.S. and parts of Canada. Dealing with warehouse managers and people who do the heavy lifting enhanced my communication skills. There were times when I was thrown into hostile situations and had to be the adult in the room. Responsibility of handling bills of lading and the business end were enlightening." Eve could have said more, but her better judgment told her to stop talking.

"I've seen students take windjammer cruises for the same reason," said her advisor, "That's astounding!" Eve had enough credits to transfer to her current degree program and begin her junior year. Her choice of Law schools could be decided at a later date.

"For now, I think you're on a good track." The two went over Eve's preferred class schedule and talked briefly about housing and how she would handle her living situation.

"I've applied for acceptance with the Tri-Delt sorority, but it remains to be seen if we're a good fit. For the present, I'm staying with friends in Sedona. I'm looking for off-campus housing, and I don't have to take a job at this point. My finances are well covered." As the two parted company, the advisor wished Eve well, suggesting that they meet in a month or two for an update.

Laura Griffee had driven Eve to her appointment with the advisor. Asked if she had gained anything from the meeting, Eve said she had.

"I was relieved when he agreed with my choice of a major. Right now, I have to see the landlord about the place I found." The two drove over to the one hundred block of East Emery Avenue. Eve wanted to see a single-story house two blocks north of the football stadium. There were connecting bike trails to all parts of the campus and a short ride to downtown.

A middle-aged couple was seated on the red stone driveway in a GMC pickup. A tall fellow stepped out to greet Eve. Identifying herself, Eve shook hands with the man as the woman stayed in the passenger seat. Laura also stepped out to see the house and marvel at the outside seating area. The house interior was spacious and furnished with all the amenities of a fully electric kitchen. As they walked about the rooms, the woman had joined the threesome and identified herself. She offered to answer any questions. When it got to the rent issue, Laura braced herself as Eve seemed to pay it little mind.

"We would need a security deposit, with the first and last month's rent. For you to move in, we would need $5000. Next month's rent would be due on the first of the month, $2250. The $500 security deposit will be returned when you move out. Returned that is if there are no damages found on the property." The landlord smiled warmly and presented the lease agreement. They required a six-month lease before Eve could settle into the house.

"We realize that situations change for college students; otherwise, we would require a yearly lease." Their discussion returned to the amenities of the house and the convenience of a bike trail to campus. Eve took out her checkbook, sat at the kitchen table, and wrote a check for $5000.

"I like the fact that it's a single story unit, no one above and no one below." Laura stood against the wall, arms folded, and wondered how Eve could afford such a place. The woman's husband took a seat and mentioned maintenance issues.

"When will you be moving in?" he asked.

"I'll be moving Saturday before classes start, probably December 13th." The woman took out three keys and gave Eve two of them.

"We'll keep one set in case there's an emergency, a water main break, that sort of thing."

"Fair enough," said Eve, and the couple left. They climbed into the GMC and drove away.

"I love this place," Eve said, "So what's on your mind?" Eve could see that her friend had some questions. Laura waited before she spoke. "I didn't know truck driving paid so well! Most college transfers couldn't afford this place. And, what about pledging Tri-delts and taking a room in the Sorority house?"

"I could do both," Eve said. "If necessary, I could sublease this place to another renter."

"Oh," said Laura. Changing the subject, Eve said, "If you have more time, I need a ride to the Revolution bike shop. What do you say?" So, off they went shopping for bicycle transportation.

The shop had a great variety of bicycles inventory. Spending a few minutes talking to a clerk, Eve settled on a Tommaso La Forma. It was a lightweight bike with 27 speeds and 700-centimeter wheels. With Eve astraddle the cycle, the clerk suggested lowering the seat.

"There must be a bit of knee bend at the bottom of your peddle stride. Looks about perfect." The clerk said the bike is suitable for general use, with hybrid tires for winter commutes. When asked its price, the clerk said, "With this aluminum frame, it comes to $899.95. While you're in the store, we could throw in any helmet of your choice at a twenty percent discount." As the two women looked around for helmets, Eve settled on a Giro helmet displaying a $320 price tag.

"I'll take this one," she said and laid it on the counter.

"How about an auto bike rack?" asked the clerk. Eve explained that she had no vehicle at the moment and wouldn't be needing one. He rang up the sale and took Eve's credit card. With the sales tax, the total price comes to $1262.12. The two women stayed for a few minutes while mechanics checked everything and tightened any loose fasteners. Eve and Laura walked around the store looking at other high-tech bikes and their price tags.

"Wow," said Laura, "You could pay about anything you want for a bicycle!"

"You think that's bad," said Eve, "The truck I drove cost the company $180K."

"And what did they pay you?" asked Laura. Eve calculated a few numbers in her head and came up with the sum.

"Somewhere in the neighborhood of one-third of the truck that I drove, $60K a year."

"You must have had some overhead," said Laura. Eve told her about living on the truck and living on the cheap. She had saved a lot of money for tuition and fees over the last few months. She didn't tell Laura that her Aunt Syl paid for her education and housing. Laura assumed that Eve was not telling her the whole story.

"I'll ride the bike over to the house, lock it inside, then take you to lunch for chauffeuring," Eve said. "How does lunch at the Toasted Owl sound?" In thirty minutes, the two were seated just off campus at the café. Time to pick her brain, Laura thought.

*   *   *

SP-4 Gerald Ingalls was well into his Army career south of Miami. Living in a barracks with sixty other enlistees, he threw himself into work on the unit newspaper. There were weekends of scuba diving off the Florida coast. After a couple of weekends of channel diving, pulling lobster from cracks and crevices, the class was ready for ocean diving.

Single scuba tanks with a Hathaway regulator would give him a half-hour of dive time. It was necessary to make decompression stops when ascending from eighty feet off the ocean floor. A Nemrod gas-powered speargun in his possession, Gerald could bag fish. A thirty-pound Grouper could drag you across the ocean floor like a horse on dry land. You could lose your speargun. Well-schooled about the pros and cons of diving, Gerald invited Eve down to Florida. They would go diving with his new group of friends and their wives over the weekend. They would get seriously reacquainted after their time apart. He would also be on his annual leave in February and could spend a significant portion of his time in Flagstaff with the woman he loved.

Chapter 10

LIFE IN THE FAST LANE

January 2015

Eve was about to embark on a whole new campus life and classroom challenges. She had taken on 18 credit hours, a good chunk of school work. As an English major, Eve focused on rhetorical skills along her path to law school. For electives, she would take photojournalism and Chaucer. An avid reader, she knew that educated people developed a broad intellect base. Anything that would help her become proficient in communication was her two-year goal. Having moved into her single-story house off-campus, she had plans for spring break. She would visit Gerald in Florida, but she would address her sorority pledging prospects with Laura for the present.

Laura and Del had an on-again, off-again relationship. Eve invited Laura and a few of her sorority friends to the house for beers and Bar-B-Que for a girls' night out. Eve wanted to see how she would get along with these young women. What she saw didn't surprise her. There is usually a paradigm shift when another person comes to a relationship with two others. Eve wasn't far off in her assessment. She had been out in the world driving over the US and Canada for the last few months.

Laura's sorority sisters were younger than her by a year or more. They possessed a very naive view of the world, and everything revolved around them. Eve could not see herself in the Greek environment except for Laura and one other sorority sister. She had Gerald, and he would indeed become part of her life. As Syl advised, Eve was a Mildenhall and wanted to keep that information under wraps. Another aspect of the girls was that some drank too much and were loud talkers. Some spilled their opinions about sleeping with a boyfriend, and their parents' wealth enamored most. Several girls had been to Europe and other stylish parts of the planet. It didn't fit with Eve that she would become one of them. Laura could see that her friend wasn't impressed by the sorority sisters. They were close enough in their relationship to have an unspoken dialogue. Warm and gracious, Eve wouldn't allow her feelings to steal the atmosphere. The young women were having fun, that was fine, but it wasn't her style.

Laura stayed back with a close friend and helped with the cleanup as they went about their day. The girl with Laura was Navajo, fine-featured, and gracious. Her name was Felicia Yazzie, referred to as Hap by her sorority sisters. It suited the girl as she was congenial and didn't drink like the others. She wore a few pieces of fine Navajo jewelry. In conversations, Hap would weigh her answers before offering an opinion. It became evident that she had occasionally been the subject of scrutiny and presented herself with cautious indignation. She was a peacemaker. When Eve inquired about Hap belonging to the Tri-delt sorority, Laura quickly answered, "Hap is smart." There were only three girls in the sorority who had a perfect 4.0-grade point average, and Hap was one of them.

"So, what did you think about the girls?" asked Laura. Rather than give Laura a direct answer, Eve asked a counter-question.

"Why did you pledge this sorority?" Both Laura and Hap exchanged glances and answered that they kept the sorority grade point average high. As far as friends in the sorority house, they had a few, but mostly, they stuck to themselves. They were suite mates and hung out at the library, hitting the books together.

"I guessed that," Eve said. "Most people might say you two are soul mates compared to the others." Eve steered their conversation to spring break without digging deeper into the subject.

"What are your plans for break?" Laura would be going to southern California with her family, and Hap would spend time with her grandmother east of Ganado, Arizona.

"What about you?" Hap asked, "What are your plans?"

"I'm going to Florida again, scuba diving, and spending a few days in Naples. My mother lives there." She didn't mention anything about Gerald being in the mix.

With school well in session by mid-January, Eve had two classes in common with a few people she knew. Upper-division English classes were much smaller than her first and second years at CSU. There were only twelve students in her Chaucer course. It was like being tutored. Students maneuvered around campus on the trails. Eve could lock up the bike and stuff her helmet in the backpack. She had weekend plans, but they were about to change.

The Clayborne family invited Eve down to Sedona for the weekend. Jill Saunders, twins Owen and Chloe, were also visiting their grandmother. How she would get to Sedona wasn't in question. Two of Sy's cadre dropped by the house in separate vehicles. One was driving a rental car while Syl's legal assistant was behind the wheel of an Alfa Romeo Giulia. Rolling down the window, he said, "Compliments of the boss for making the team!" Not grasping his intention, Eve stood in her driveway between the two automobiles and asked, "I'm DNA approved?" Climbing out of the car, the assistant mentioned that she was indeed a Mildenhall. The lab results had come two days earlier. She rounded up the two men in a threesome bear hug and felt embarrassed as tears rolled down her cheeks.

"Oh, this is great, this is great!" She hadn't been this emotional since the Texas trip three weeks earlier.

"I can't wait to tell my mom; I know she will be excited!" Taking a seat behind the wheel of the Alpha Romeo, she saw that it had an eight-speed transmission. The Rosso Red exterior matched her enthusiasm, and she was ecstatic!

Invited in the house, one man asked how her first week of classes had gone. Eve's thoughts strayed to the car in her driveway, but she answered as best she could.

"I have two five hours, two three-hour classes, and one two-hour class.

"Wow, eighteen hours, that's quite a load," said one of the guys.

"I won't be trying out for gymnastics. That will make things easier."

As the men were leaving in the rental car, Laura pulled onto the driveway, wondering who they were. One of the guys looked vaguely familiar.

"Isn't the older guy the same man we saw at Pallium airport?" Too late to hide her angst, Eve admitted that he was.

"And, who belongs to this neat little red set of wheels?" Laura asked.

"OK, come on in; I'll give you the skinny on a few things." The ruse had gone on long enough, Eve didn't want to alienate Laura with a pack of half-truths, and It was time to come clean. "I'm heading down to Sedona for the weekend. Why don't you come with me? We'll have 45 minutes to talk. Besides, I have to break in the Alpha Romeo." Making their way through Oak Creek canyon toward Sedona, another car was cruising south on I-17 in the same direction.

Lynn and Charles Ingalls had flown into Flagstaff and drove a rental car to their Sedona house. They were out on the town by late afternoon and would stop at the Blossom. They wanted to patch things up with Connie Clayborne. The Ingalls also wanted to hear the latest about Eve. Connie may have some insight into Gerald and Eve's relationship because their son was tight-lipped on the matter.

"I doubt if Connie reveals much; at least we can talk with her," Charles said. Wandering about the shopping area, they spotted Eve browsing in the same place. Lynn clutched Charles' sleeve and stopped him mid-stride.

"Isn't that Eve Chambers?" she asked, "What's she doing with a baby strapped to her bosom?" Eve was sucking on a popsicle and sharing it with a baby.

"Oh my God, you don't suppose?" Lynn said. Drawing the wrong conclusion, Lynn took the baby to be Eve and Gerald's.

"My God, she must have gotten pregnant at the Clayborne wedding last year." They saw Connie Clayborne headed their way as the couple had done an about-face.

"Well, hello," Connie said, "Aren't you two a surprise!" "Come on over; I want you to meet my grandkids."

Connie made introductions all around. "This is Laura Griffee with Chloe and, of course, you remember Eve. She has Owen. These folks, Laura, are Charles and Lynn Ingalls" After marveling at the two babies, the group walked to the east of the shopping area. Lynn expressed a sigh of relief. They strolled through an assortment of shoppers and came to the Creekside Coffee shop.

"Jill and her sister are minding the store," Connie said, "Let me treat you to some refreshment." Connie was eyeing Lynn Ingalls closely. What she had not asked spoke volumes.

Connie had reservations about forcing relationships. Eve and the Ingalls were not on equal footing, even ambivalent to one another. Lynn considered Eve inferior, pure, and simple. Their last meeting was far from amicable. Perhaps Connie could clear the air and bring Eve and Mrs. Ingalls to a sense of reconciliation.

"So, Eve, why don't you bring the Ingalls up to speed on current events," Connie suggested.

Eve had remained subdued as she and Laura walked ahead with the two babies. They managed a short conversation before entering the Creekside Coffey and Bakery.

"What's happening here," Laura was curious to know. "You seem a bit standoffish with the Ingalls."

"It's a long story," answered Eve in a whisper, "They think I'm trying to muscle in on a relationship with their son Gerald."

"Oh, the guy in Florida?"

"Yeah, I guess I should mention to them that I'm going down on spring break to see him."

"I don't know if I would go there just yet," Laura advised.

As they were seated, Mrs. Ingalls asked Eve, "How's life treating you?"

"I'm registered as an English major at Northern Arizona University. It's the first weekend away for my friend Laura and me." Lynn Ingalls looked the two young women over before offering any assessment. Charles spoke up, asking what Eve had chosen for a career path. As she elaborated, Mrs. Ingalls was left to wonder how Eve could afford tuition, fees, and housing. Sensing Lynn's impression of her, Eve added,

"I have a scholarship." It wasn't exactly what she had wanted to say. Now that she had mentioned it, she stopped short on details. Pressing the issue, Mrs. Ingalls leaned forward, elbows on the table, and asked," Scholarship from who?"

"It's an Oil company scholarship for students interested in pre-law," Eve said. Forcing a distraction, Eve lifted her Iced tea and took a sip. Connie came to Eve's rescue and asked if the Ingalls enjoyed their new house on Moki drive. A quiet and shallow conversation ensued.

Back at the Blossom, Eve and her friend plopped the twins back into their carriers. "Connie, I thought I would show Laura around if you don't mind, we'll be back at the house in a couple of hours." After walking with the group toward the Blossom, Mrs. Ingalls said that she and Charles should be running along.

"Can we accompany you? Are you parked nearby," Charles asked Eve and her friend.

"We're out the back door in Connie's parking spots, not far," said Eve. Going through the Blossom's backroom, employee parking was close at hand.

"Well, goodbye for now," said Eve. She offered her hand to Mrs. Ingalls and smiled at Charles. Grasping Eve's hand, Lynn asked, "So, which car is yours?"

"Oh, this little red job here," Eve said, motioning toward the Alfa Romeo. The two young women smiled graciously and said their goodbyes. Eve and her school chum entered the car and left the older couple wondering.

"How can that girl afford a $45K automobile?" asked Lynn.

"Probably a rental," Charles answered.

*   *   *

SP-4 Gerald Ingalls was in the throes of working on a weekend deadline for the 'Defender.' Taking on the job of keeping tabs on the intermural sports schedule for his Army unit, and he was obligated to make all the games at the sports complex. With that and other requirements, Gerald was always on duty. On his days pulling KP, he could land the job of dining room orderly if he showed up early enough. After experiencing the hell job of pots and pans, it was evident that the early bird gets a cushy job in the mess hall. As he walked about the dining area filling salt and pepper shakers, his cell phone chimed. It was Eve.

"I haven't talked to you in a while." she said, "How's it going?" They were talking when the mess sergeant spotted Gerald on his phone.

"I'll have to call you back. I'm getting eyeballed by the mess sergeant." Gerald got off in time for the Sargent to back off and walk away. Later, he would call Eve and suggest they get together somehow. His mother had been making inquiries about his relationship with Eve. He had to find the courage and get the ball rolling that he and Eve could make a lifetime commitment. They loved each other despite the distance between them. Off duty, he made his way to the dayroom. Calling Eve, he said how busy he had been. She was going to school in Arizona, and he was in Florida grinding out his Army enlistment. If he put in for a weekend pass, Eve could arrange her schedule, and the two may be able to meet somewhere.

It was evident. Eve was substandard by Mrs. Ingalls' reckoning; how Gerald's dad felt about her left some room for doubt. Charles wouldn't buck his wife under any circumstance. Eve's accomplishments marked time and distance. She transferred to Northern Arizona and was now part of the Mildenhall family. The clandestine lifestyle was starting to wear on her. She needed to tell Gerald about what had happened over the last month. Eve didn't want to spend the next two years dodging Mrs. Ingalls's skepticism. Eve loved Gerald and simply wanted to have her place in the world with a few close friends. On campus, she had Laura Griffee and Hap. She would confide in them.

Gerald was met with a bombshell the morning after talking to Eve. Written on the Company bulletin board, it was in black and white. There had been rumors, and now it had come to fruition. Twelve fellow enlistees had come down on orders for Camp Lemonnier, Djibouti, Africa. He would be attached to the Army's East African Response Force (EARF). Fundamentally, his role was one of troop morale. American soldiers on foreign assignments could connect with home through stories about their service in the Horn of Africa. Human interest stories would be shared with the folks back home through local newspapers. The military advisory command censored photos and written assignments.

The US government didn't want covert information dispersed to the US, but civilian reporters could write what they pleased. Freedom of the press was a double-edged sword leaving Gerald with minimal clout as a news writer.

Gerald would ship out in thirty days. A silver lining was evident that he would have a thirty-day leave before departing the continental US. Gerald would ask Eve to marry him while on leave. His better judgment told him that he should. First, Gerald wanted to square it with Eve's mother in Naples. He wasn't sure how to accomplish that because he had never met her. Making matters worse, Kim had lost Eve's father, Pete Mildenhall, on Army duty twenty-three years earlier. Gerald couldn't blame Kim if she did not give her blessing for his marriage to her daughter.

*   *   *

Eve was getting along well with her studies. Classroom discussion about figures in literature, particularly Shakespeare, was a great study in human psychology. Absorbed in the significance of people's decisions, her reading list on each class syllabus would require hours of reading. If she wasn't attending to personal matters, eating, sleeping, and maintaining her health Eve was reading. Joining her in discussions and campus life were her close friends.

On the other hand, social functions were an area where they had little in common. The Tri-Delt sorority was frequently doing social engineering in which Eve took no part. Laura and Hap were pleased with sorority life. Eve was a study nerd and liked it that way. When Gerald called and suggested they get together in Sedona, it was a horse of another color. She loved the man and wanted to further their relationship. The meeting place was yet to be determined, but her motivation was to take her relationship with Gerald to a new level. What awaited would not be hard to guess.

Gerald took a military hop on a weekend pass on an older OH-13 bubble chopper. He had friends in an aviation company that flew regular round robin's over southern Florida. As a member of his unit press corps, Gerald could use the operation to write a story for the 'Defender' newspaper. Calling ahead, he set an appointment with Kim

Chambers in Naples. Eve had prepped her mother that Gerald would be landing at the Chopper pad near Fort Myers. Eve couldn't make the trip. She had classes.

As the Chopper touched down at the Fort Myers Heli-pad, Kim was on hand to greet Gerald and his pilot. Kim welcomed Gerald with open arms.

"HI, I'm Gerald," he said. He and Kim formed an immediate bond as they walked to Kim's jeep. She liked what she saw as Gerald had a ready smile and swagger of maturity that was impressive, even for her. Not mincing words, Gerald assured Kim that he and Eve had a long-term relationship going back a couple of years.

"I'm sorry that you and I had not met," Gerald said. They covered a few missing points of their relationship. Why Gerald had not asked Eve to marry him came as a surprise. Kim was adamant that they should marry soon, before his deployment to Africa, if they truly loved each other.

"I made the mistake of waiting for Pete and me to marry; we never did. I wouldn't want my daughter to make the same mistake. Marry my Eve as soon as you can." The apple was ripe, and it had fallen. Not sure how to react, Gerald said, "I haven't asked Eve to marry me yet; I was waiting until I could see her Flagstaff when I'm on leave."

Kim responded, "Get yourself back on that chopper, go to your unit, pack your bags, and boogie on over to Arizona!" The chopper pilot walked to the jeep and asked, "So what's the plan?" Kim read the pilot's name tag and responded.

"The plan is, Captain Schuster, let me buy lunch, then get my future son-in-law back to Homestead Air Force Base. See that he packs his duffle, checks out of his unit, and gets on a plane to Arizona." Gerald assured Kim that he was delighted to follow her orders.

Within eight hours, Gerald's plane pulled up to the Flagstaff terminal. Awaiting him were Laura, Hap and Eve. Entering the airport, he spotted Eve and her two companions. Hap was videotaping Gerald's arrival. Approaching the three women, Gerald dropped his duffle bag and took a knee. Taking Eve's hand, he asked, "Evelyn Chambers, will you marry me?" People witnessing the spectacle applauded when Eve said, "Yes!" Gerald placed the very engagement ring on Eve's finger that her mother Kim had received from Pete Mildenhall twenty-two years earlier.

"Is this my mother's engagement ring?" Eve asked Gerald.

"It is; your mother gave it to me in Naples." Eve clutched the ring on her finger and shed happy tears.

"I wish my mother was here to see this!" Hap was still recording the event on her cellphone.

"It will probably be on the six o'clock news," someone shouted. The commotion continued as friends and strangers alike marveled at the enthusiastic couple. Eve had arranged for a limousine to take all four to her house on Emery Street. Hap had caught the entire procession and immediately sent the video to Kim in Florida, Katie and Alfred, Syl Mildenhall, Jill Summers, Trish Hays, Connie Clayborne, and Gerald's parents. When Mrs. Ingalls' phone pinged in Fort Collins, she said to her husband Charles, "Get over here, you're not going to believe this!"

On receiving the news, Syl Mildenhall dispatched an assistant to Flagstaff. Her ambition was to help the couple with wedding plans when and wherever it was to take place. Gerald was little more than three weeks from traveling on orders to Djibouti, Africa. They would have to work fast! At the Emery, street house were several Tri-Delt friends, Laura, Hap, and Del Cullen. Syl's assistant would arrive the following afternoon. Not sure what plans lay ahead for their wedding, Eve was relieved that her Aunt Syl stepped in to move the ceremony forward on short notice. With Hap and Laura manning a string of phone calls, plans were set in motion for the weddings to occur within a couple of weeks.

"This is for you," Hap said as she handed her cell phone to Eve. On the other end, Aunt Syl asked Eve where she would like the wedding venue. She wanted it to be in either Sedona or at the Abilene ranch.

"Don't worry about a thing. I'll get back to you within the hour," Syl assured her.

It grew late as people left the house so Eve and Gerald might have some privacy. He had no intention of finding other accommodations. Asked if he could share Eve's bedroom, she laughed, "I guess so, but first, you'll have to shower."

"I will if you'll join me. Just give me a minute; I have a few things in my duffle bag," Gerald said. As Eve threw off her clothes and stepped into the shower, there was a commotion in her bedroom. By the time Gerald joined her, Eve was beginning to wonder if he would show up at all.

"I almost started without you," she teased. The two had a few minutes of taking inventory and helping each other scrub.

"You look kind of excited," said Eve, "and it shows!" Toweling off, they entered the bedroom, and Eve was astonished at what she saw. Gerald had strung red rope lights around the bed and was in the process of lighting scented candles.

"My gosh," she said, "looks like the circus has come to town! Are you trying to make a statement?"

"I'm going to turn on all your lights; I thought I'd start with the room," Gerald told her. Eve sat on the bed and rolled onto her side, saying, "I like the way you think! Talk, talk, talk, now, get over here. I want to see what you've got for me."

Awakening the following morning, the smell of frying bacon came from the kitchen. Gerald had two places set at the table, complete with three roses in a crystal vase.

"My, my, you had a lot of stuff in that duffle -bag," Eve said lovingly. She had not removed her engagement ring since Gerald had placed it on her finger. She wore a smile, a pink chenille robe, and the ring. Gerald was scantily dressed and played chef. Before placing omelets, bacon, and a fruit cup on the table, he turned to Eve and said, "My mother called this morning, and she wants to know what we want for a wedding gift. I think she is open to a new understanding about you and me." They attended to practical matters while eating breakfast.

"You have orders for Djibouti, Africa. Where is that exactly?" Eve wanted to know. Gerald explained that Camp Lemonnier was a 600 acre American military base on the Horn of Africa. Strategically, it holds an interest for all major power players of the world. We have Army, Navy, Air Force, and Marine units stationed there. Shipping trade routes converge on the Suez Canal. Fortifications at Djibouti protect them and keep African war tribes from annihilating each other.

As he explained this, Eve took a seat, placed her elbows on the table, and watched Gerald moving about the kitchen.

"While you're in Africa for this six-month deployment, I will be completing my junior year. Do you have any idea where you will go from there?"

"Not sure," Gerald answered, "Wherever Uncle Sugar wants to send us."

"Us? I'm going too?"

"We'll be married, won't we?" Gerald said. He looked at Eve lovingly.

"There are plenty of accommodations for dependents unless it's a war zone."

Eve sat chewing her bacon.

"You know Gerald. I have another year and a half until I get my undergraduate degree, and you have two years remaining on your enlistment. I want to go to law school." Eve would have three years of graduate work and Gerald wasn't sure they could afford more education. He would make E-5 and get a pay raise, but law school seemed out of the question.

"I'll have to bring you up to speed," Eve said. "After getting my BA, I will take the LSAT test before my acceptance to law school. Then there are another three years before I could finish, take the bar exam, and become a lawyer, simple." Gerald sat munching a bagel like a cow chewing a cud staring at Eve.

"Do you have a rich uncle that you're not telling me about?" he asked.

"Even better," said Eve. "There are a few things I need to fill you in on before we tie the knot. I'm very opinionated, and I tend to get grumpy when disrupted, and I wear a size five shoe. They're tough to find!" Gerald looked at her, his eyes dancing.

As a matter of fact," she continued, "I have a rich Aunt, and I come from a wealthy family." Eve let that sink in for the moment. "Money-wise, there wouldn't be a problem." She took another slice of bacon. "You see, Gerald when you marry me, you not only get these puppies." She opened her robe to expose her breasts, "You also get a modest fortune." Gerald pushed his chair away from the table and motioned toward the bedroom, "Let's get back to the sack. I want to fill you in with something of my own, Miss Chambers." Eve stood, wiped her hands on a napkin, and smiled seductively, "You're on, cowboy!"

*   *   *

Later that morning, far away in Florida, Kim Chambers was on her cell phone. She was speaking with the Ingalls in Fort Collins.

"I'm sorry we haven't met," she said, "I was wondering if you and Charles would make it to the wedding?"

"We would if we knew where it was to take place," said Lynn. "So far, we haven't heard much from our son," Kim said that the wedding might be held in either Sedona, the Mildenhall ranch, or the Fort Collins Country Club. It was an inclusive gesture on Kim's part.

"The Mildenhall ranch, what's that?" asked Lynn.

"OK, I think I have some explaining to do," Kim said. She quickly outlined the Abilene ranch location, saying it was home to the Mildenhall family, Eve's aunt. Not sure what all this meant, Lynn had a few questions.

"Our son Gerald is short on information. Who exactly are the Mildenhalls?" Lynn had put the phone on speaker and gestured for Charles to listen in.

Kim explained that she and her daughter Eve had some long-lost relatives. Her sister-in-law, Sylvia Mildenhall, could host the wedding if necessary. Lynn was sure the Fort Collins Country Club had already been booked.

"Well, that leaves Sedona or the Abilene ranch," Kim said.

"You know, we do have a large property in Sedona. Would that be of any use?"

"I was aware of that. Why don't you call Eve? She could discuss it with you," Kim suggested. Lynn Ingalls took the phone from her ear, looked at Charles, and flashed a smile.

"I'll do just that; what's Eve's phone number?"

On the phone with Eve, Lynn Ingalls offered her the Sedona house where she and their son could marry. The ice melted between the two as they warmed to the idea that they could be friends. Mrs. Ingalls coordinated with Trish, Katie, and Alfred. They soon took a flight to

Arizona to help with the wedding plans. The days were short; a small army of helpers had to get organized in a hurry. Though Connie had a business to run, she would give as much time as she could muster. In five days, the Ingalls would see their only son marry. The bride's mother, Kim, couldn't be there until the wedding day. She had a plan that the others were not privy to, but she would soon break her silence.

All hands remained on deck for wedding preparations with only six significant players. Trish ordered the wedding cake and got with Laura and Hap to stage the venue for seating and arrange an outdoor alter. Gerald and his mother did what they could with the guest list. Gerald would choose someone on the fly as his best man with no close friends in Sedona. Eve and her friends hit the books at the Sedona house. They had their first midterm exams until one day before the wedding.

Lynn felt jubilant because she and Eve seemed to be hitting it off so well. Things were shaping up rapidly. The wedding wouldn't be as festive as the Clayborne/Summers weddings, but it would get Eve and Gerald married. That's all that mattered. The spacious backyard of the Sedona house would be the wedding site with Clayborne's pastor officiating.

Kim had a problem because one thing seemed to be missing. She broke her silence to Syl Mildenhall. On the phone, Kim asked if the wedding band of the bridal ring set might be available. Would Sylvia know the whereabouts of the wedding ring? It had been intentionally misplaced two decades earlier by Syl's mother. The only person who might answer that question was Syl. The engagement ring had been located and slipped on Eve's finger at the Flagstaff airport. Where was the wedding band? Pete Mildenhall must have had it in his possession before his untimely death. The thought resonated with Syl. She didn't know but would tend to the matter promptly.

The Cheyenne house and the Abilene Ranch house would be searched top to bottom by staff members. Sylvia's deceased mother must have stuck it away years earlier. The survival assistance officer had sent all of Pete's possessions to the family as policy dictated. Syl would leave no stone unturned until she located the wedding ring.

The next day Kim made flight arrangements from Fort Myers to Flagstaff. Gerald would pick her up at the airport in Eve's Alfa Romero.

Syl had significant business obligations in Dallas and might miss the wedding. It all depended on the delicate timing of Bert and Ernie. They would have to get the Global 5000 to the Dallas/Fort Worth airport on time from previous flight obligations. People continued to assemble in Sedona. When Kim arrived in Flagstaff, a FedEx truck pulled onto the Moki house driveway in Sedona. The missing wedding ring was found and delivered.

The Cook at the Abilene ranch had located the ring with the help of her aging mother. The Mildenhalls had employed the older woman. Over the stable in a locked storage room, Mrs. Mildenhall had stowed memorabilia. The ring was there, and the Cook's mother remembered packing it in a box. It was marked with Pete's name and hadn't been disturbed. The original blue ring box, with the wedding band, was precisely where the older woman knew it should be.

Aunt Syl, along with her lawyers, were wrapping up their Dallas meeting. A limo was waiting at the curb when the Dallas meeting adjourned. The driver would take their party to the Dallas/Fort Worth airport. Bert and Ernie had completed their pre-flight checks, and they flew the team to the Oak Creek Airport in Sedona. The Texas governor and his wife were close friends of Syl Mildenhall. They would also be on board and among the wedding guests. A suite of rooms was waiting at the Enchantment Resort in Sedona.

Chapter 11

CROW-HOPPING THE WORLD

February 2016

The preparations for Eve's wedding were blazing along. On short notice, all dresses were from the Blossom. Eve's maid of honor would be Riley Baxter. Jill Summers, Laura Griffee, Trish Hays, and Hap Yazzie were bridesmaids. Eve had asked Alfred to escort her down the aisle.

"I'm not sure how to say this," said Eve as she approached her great aunt and uncle. "Alfred, you've always been there for me even when you had no idea that you were."

"Ah shucks, missy," Alfred countered in his best John Wayne impersonation. "I knew you were a barn burner when I first laid eyes on you that summer many years ago. Do you remember?"

"I think I remember bringing a baby skunk to the door, and aunt Katie had you help me deposit it back behind the shop where I found it." Katie chimed in, saying, "We knew you had no boundaries. I think you were about eight years old." Alfred looked Eve in the eye as he put a hand on her shoulder.

"Dynamite comes in small packages. You prove a point. People are much better than the sum of their parts. You will make life beautiful for your man and the people you come to know. You have a great capacity for making us feel good about ourselves. If the father you never knew were here today, he would be quite proud. We had you with us for most of the summers while your mother was getting her business up and running," said Alfred adding, "We were lucky to have you!".

"We didn't see much of you through the years," said Katie, "Just an occasional school picture."

"Well, we're together for my wedding day," said Eve with a misty smile, "I couldn't be happier!"

Gerald hadn't chosen a Best man. The groomsmen were Chris Summers, Les Hays, and John Sebastian. Some of the wedding guests were unfamiliar with others in the group. Lynn Ingalls suggested they have an ice breaker in the swimming pool. The one single man, Sebastian, wanted the girls to join them.

"Get into the pool and play with us," he said. Others were setting up the backyard. The wedding was less than twenty hours away.

Two dark limousines pulled into the Moki house driveway. From the airport, Syl and her cadre were in the first vehicle. In the second were the Texas governor and his wife. No one asked the driver's name, and he offered very little information. As new arrivals entered the pool area, John Sebastian and the limo driver locked eyes on one another. John exited the pool, dripping wet, walked toward the man, and the two squared off with smiles and a handshake.

"Good Lord," said Sebastian, "I haven't seen you since Columbia! Hey everyone, this is Gabe. I haven't seen him in a few years!" The two had trained together in their early military careers. With a clipboard of 'honey-dos,' Gerald found that the reconnection of military men piqued his interest. He went over to meet Gabe. Sebastian introduced the two, and Gerald invited them for a Corona and lime. Gabe declined. Gerald held a bond with Sebastian and the newcomer after a year of Army service. Eve, looking out the upstairs window of the guest house, yelled, "Ger, aren't you supposed to be doing something?" "Poor guy," said Sebastian, "Not even married yet and already taking orders." Gerald blew Eve a kiss, "Enough woman," he said, "I'm on it!"

The Texas governor and his wife were in the living room. Lynn, beside herself with pride, motioned for the governor and his wife to take their places in her spacious dining area. Following the governor and his wife, Syl extended her hand toward Lynn.

"I'm Sylvia Mildenhall, Eve's aunt, glad we can finally meet!" Mrs. Ingalls asked if she could get anyone something to drink. They declined.

"This morning after our meeting broke up in Dallas," Syl said, "I wasn't sure if we could make the wedding at all." Lynn wondered how they did make the trip on short order. The governor read her thoughts.

"Syl asked us to join the festivities, So here we are, friends of the bride's family. We have an open schedule for the weekend, and we're happy that we can act normal."

"It's been an exhausting effort around here," said Mrs. Ingalls.

"I don't know where Eve and I would have been without a lot of help." Asked if they were lucky enough to find lodgings on short notice, Syl said that they had. Eve and Trish entered from the kitchen, wondering about all the commotion. Surprised to see her aunt, Eve went straight for Syl, and the two shared a warm rocking bear hug.

"Thank you, Aunt Syl, for the car; I love it! Who is this lovely couple with you" The governor's wife said, "We caught a ride with Syl. It sounds like there's a wedding here tomorrow. Can we come?" They all laughed! Gerald was about to join the group, but Trish motioned him away.

"You're not supposed to see the bride until tomorrow; go out for a bachelor party somewhere across town." Along with his brother in arms, Sebastian and Gerald did just that. Over a couple of beers with Sebastian, Gerald asked if he would be willing to serve as his best man. Sebastian nodded in agreement, saying, "I'm honored, and I'm happy that I had a hand in bringing your lovely fiancé to the ball."

Saturday arrived, and the guests numbered about a hundred people. The large back patio and terrace sat in broken sunlight. Kim and Syl sat side by side. On the left were Charles and Mrs. Ingalls. All the guests were those who could attend on short notice. Most all knew that Gerald would be leaving for Africa within days. The baby grand piano came from the library. Serenading the guests was the governor's wife, playing a theme and variation on Pachelbel's Canon in D Major. Without sheet music, she played from memory.

"I didn't know she was such an accomplished pianist," said Lynn to Charles. Whispering, Syl and Kim were comparing notes about a timeline. Eve had yet to key in her class schedule for the winter semester, which was soon to start. The evening wore on with more than a fair share of jubilation. The guests excused themselves as everyone found their way to accommodations for the night. An explanation came from Sylvia, addressing the subject of Gerald's military responsibility and travel plans.

"We do have Gerald covered; Sebastian talked to him last night," Syl said. "He can travel on orders with us to Abu Dhabi, then catch a hop to Djibouti. From there, he can get to Camp Lemonnier. Sebastian squared it with the U.S. liaison office." As the two conferred, their mood changed to the practical matter of bringing off a wedding the next day.

The stage set for the wedding to take place, all were seated the next day in the spacious backyard of the Moki house. The officiating Pastor asked all to rise as Alfred escorted Eve to the garden arch where Gerald waited. The governor's wife broke into Wagner's Bridal Chorus at the piano. The bridesmaids wore subtle contrasts of rust and gold dresses on her left. The men were in black tuxes, all standing straight as bowling pins. The bride wore a Galina Low Back soft lace wedding gown. Knowing her size, Kim brought it with her on the plane from Coral Gables. The fit was exemplary and didn't hide much of Eve's feminine attributes.

Sebastian nudged Gerald and spoke softly, "Some men have all the luck!" From her place across the aisle, Laura Griffee flashed a smile and winked at Delmer sitting in a second-row seat. When they got to the part where Eve repeated, "Till death do us part," Kim and Syl had difficulty holding it together. The women clutched one another and shed a few soft tears. The Pastor exchanged the vows, saying to Gerald, "You may kiss your bride." It was a gentle exchange of zeal as their kiss sealed the deal.

"For our benediction," said the Pastor, "I'd like to bring your attention to a passage from the New King James Bible. It will offer some words of encouragement to us all. I do this for the reason that Evelyn and Gerald will have a long separation forced upon them. It may help sustain them and all who have ears to hear.

"And we know that all things work together for good to those who love God, to those who are the called according to His purpose." Romans 8:28

Gerald and Eve turned after the Pastors' words to face their guests.

"I present to you Mr. and Mrs. Gerald Ingalls, "The guests stood and applauded, and a few tears glistened on the cheeks of both men and women. Following a short pause, Charles took the microphone and gave directions to the awaited catered lunch. Eve and Gerald walked arm in arm among the rows of guests and stood on the veranda for photos. Eve tossed her wedding bouquet high into the air. Caught by Laura Griffee, she held it like a coveted trophy.

The new couple celebrated their wedding night at the bridal suite of the Adobe Grand Villas bed and breakfast. They returned to the Moki house the following morning as people were putting things in order from the previous day. The Texas envoy had departed, leaving the family to themselves. Gerald would be going in four days, and Eve was to begin her summer semester before her husband's departure. They had very little time to be married before a six-month-long separation.

*   *   *

Wedding guests returned home to their private lives—the bride and groom took residence at the Emery Street house in Flagstaff. Gerald carried Eve over the threshold, setting her down lightly. Retrieving suitcases, Gerald noticed an envelope clipped to the mailbox. 'Enjoy your time together. We won't bother you! Love Laura and Hap!' Drawn on the note were two heart-shaped smiley faces. As Gerald showed the message to Eve, she smiled and said how lucky she was to have such friends.

The Global aircraft would reach Flagstaff on Tuesday and pick up Gerald. Snuggling into one other's arms Monday morning, Eve had to rise and shine. She had a ten o'clock class, and he would pack his gear, ready for life in Africa.

The Global rolled up to the Pullium Airport terminal in Flagstaff with little fanfare. Eve was in Class, having said her goodbye back at the house. Delmer drove Gerald to the airport in Eve's car. The two shook hands, and Gerald told Delmer to hang onto his gal pal Laura Griffee.

"They don't come much better than Laura," he told Delmer, "I can see why my wife and Laura are such great friends."

"Keep your head down," Delmer told Gerald as the two parted company. Ernie waited on Gerald and helped stow his gear on the Mildenhall company airplane. He knew Syl and her secretary, and that was all. The other ten passengers were strangers. As the Global taxied out onto the runway, Syl took the cabin microphone and gave some information about the flight path. They would be flying to Miami for a fuel stop so they could deplane and stretch their legs. They would then fly to their halfway mark, the south coast of Spain. The hotel wasn't anything fancy, but they needed the rest. After Málaga, Spain, the Global would take them to their final destination. The entire party would stay at the Ritz Carlton Hotel in Abu Dhabi. It wouldn't be far from the National Oil company headquarters for their international conference. Gerald felt a bit conspicuous that the Global went out of its way from Dallas to pick him up in Flagstaff.

"I would like you all to meet my almost son-in-law, Gerald Ingalls," Syl said.

"He will be going on from Abu Dhabi to Djibouti and Camp Lemonnier on the Horn of Africa." Hearing this, most of the passengers groaned audibly. Some looked at Gerald dolefully to convey a note of sympathy.

"You will have plenty of time to make introductions, so I'll leave you to it," Syl added.

"Take your seat, Skipper," said Bert from the cockpit. "We're first in line to get off the ground."

Syl sank into a seat next to a roguish-looking guy in a grey flannel suit and tie. Gerald was seated toward the rear, across the aisle from a man in his forties.

"So, the Horn of Africa, huh?" the man said. "How were you so unlucky to draw that assignment?"

"Just lucky, I guess," Gerald answered.

The plane straightened out on the runway for take-off. Bert slid the throttle and roared off the ground faster than most passengers anticipated. Most of the twelve passengers flying to the United Arab Emirates were oil economists. Syl Mildenhall represented the geothermal engineering aspect of the group. She also owned the Global. Representatives on the flight would use their time to pressure cook ideas before the conference with OPEC. It was a cat and mouse game to put faces to the names of U.S. and Arab counterparts. The United States was projected to surpass the rest of the world in oil production. When OPEC increased crude prices, the U.S. would dump crude oil on the world market for stabilization. Leverage was the game's name, and all interested parties knew those manipulations. I win, you win, we all win! Players on the world stage all knew one another and could provide impetus in future committee meetings. His seatmate told Gerald how the world oil market operated. Posturing couldn't take place without military boots on the ground. That would be for the minions of armed U.S. troops at Camp Lemonnier.

The Global aircraft had left Flagstaff on Monday morning. When it touched down in Málaga, Spain, it was 3:00 p.m. local time on Tuesday afternoon. Crossing the Atlantic, most people slept, including one of the three pilots. Two of them in the cockpit would manage the aircraft, while the third could rest. Gerald dozed off somewhere over the Atlantic, awakened by Sy, who traded places with his new acquaintance. The Global was about to land at the Málaga,-Costa del Sol Airport. Syl said if he was up to it, they could catch a taxi over to the promenade port, sit on the beach, and watch the sun go down. The Campanile Hotel was spacious, and the palm trees surrounding the hotel swayed in the sea breeze. A few travelers wandered into the bar while others took in the ambiance of the old port city. The Mediterranean seaside was a ten-minute taxi ride from their lodgings.

Eve's cellphone pinged; it was 3:00 a.m. in Flagstaff. Sleepy and disheveled, she looked at her cell phone to see Syl and Gerald's selfie in a beach setting. The message read, "We're in Málaga, Spain, halfway to Abu Dhabi." She texted back, "I'm a mess; no selfie here. I hope the trip is going well. Love, E."

*   *   *

Boarding the Global for Abu Dhabi, Syl did her routine nosecount and saw that everyone had made it through customs for the last leg of their trip. Morning sun glistened off the Mediterranean as the Global ascended to its cruising altitude and leveled off. Newcomers on the flight learned about people from a nomadic past with an insistence to barter. The U.S. State Department would handle the sticky issues. Syl Mildenhall and her entourage would supply facts and figures for a smooth understanding of the high-stakes game they would play.

The plane touched down precisely at 10:15 p.m. local time, Wednesday. Excellent illumination was apparent with all the private aircraft that had arrived or were yet to land. It was reminiscent of an air show displaying all the latest aviation expediency. Two long black limousines and drivers were on standby, awaiting the Global. Processing on entering The United Arab Emirates amounted to a minor formality. In his dress uniform, Gerald had his traveling orders out for inspection. Surveying Gerald with some trepidation, the customs official seemed perplexed by his presence within the group. Syl said a few words in Arabic, *"Hadha Aizawl abnataya"* (This is my son-in-law). The customs agent smiled and motioned them on. The airport liaison office was open, well-marked, and staffed by a U.S. Navy Commander. Gerald presented his orders, saying he would report to his unit at Camp Lemonnier in two days. The Navy officer date-stamped his paperwork.

"There will be an Air Force C-130 on standby before noon tomorrow," the commander advised him, "You will be issued a boarding pass shortly before take-off." Gerald thanked the officer and walked Syl to the limo to deliver them to the Ritz-Carlton Hotel.

Accommodations at the Ritz were like no other that Gerald had seen, except in movies. "Oil money," said Syl, "Most of the city is like this. They even have a Warner Brothers theme park in Abu. Military personnel comes here for R & R. from Lemonnier, Bulgaria, and Kosovo." Gerald tucked this information away for future reference. He prepared his duffle bag for an early morning departure from the Ritz.

Military men were present in the shared hotel areas, and only a few were U.S. military. He ordered a Perrier lemon twist at the bar and talked to the passengers he had met on the plane.

"If you could stand the heat eight months out of the year, the U.S. State Department hires ex-military," said one of the men. Gerald had some experience working in the Army's S-1 intelligence office, and with further training, he might become valuable to the State Department. For the present, he would remain where he started, as an Army information specialist. With a re-enlistment, he might become a 25 Bravo, I.T. specialist. That was far in the future and would require a 'burst of six' (six-year re-enlistment). For the moment, he considered civilian life with Eve. If she were to become a lawyer, what would he do? Thoughts raced through his mind as the hour grew late. It all amounts to who you know. He knew a few influential people. Gerald would start with John Sebastian for advice and counsel.

Sebastian had come to the Abu Dhabi airport to see Gerald off, wishing him good luck with his new assignment. Before leaving the Ritz Carlton, Syl said her goodbyes and clutched Gerald's hand in a death grip before he boarded a taxi. "You'll be fine," she said and kissed him on the cheek. Sebastian assured Syl that Gerald would be A-OK. Gerald was not going to a war zone.

A US Air Force C-130 touched down on the tarmac at Abu Dhabi by 10:15 Thursday morning. SP-4 Gerald Ingalls was lined up, boarding pass in hand, with other soldiers going to Camp Lemonnier. Several were American military personnel, while two others were members of the French Army. The red webbed seating of the aircraft interior was not plush like the Global 5000. A few sacks of mail were with the soldiers, with a jet engine chained to the fuselage floor. It had been out for repairs at an American Air Base. The internal combustion engines of the C-130 sounded like thrashing machines, and any conversation was hopeless. The passengers remained silent, focusing instead on their immediate prospects. The plane revved its four props and took to the sky, as a U.S. Airman came on the intercom saying they would be airborne for a little over three hours. The engine chained to the floor lurched back and forth like a mechanical King Kong testing its trusses. Chains slacked and drew leverage only three feet away with tons of pent-up energy. Gerald thought, 'maybe I won't die today.' The chains held, and several men fell asleep despite the engine noise.

On touch down at the Djibouti-Ambouli airport, a U.S. Army Staff sergeant was waiting for the men. By way of two black hawk helicopters, the men, bag, and baggage were crow-hopped several miles south to the landing pad at Camp Lemonnier. The French soldiers took off on foot while a troop carrier awaited the Americans. Sp-4 Ingalls was one of three new arrivals at the camp. The others were returning from R & R.

"Ah, new blood," said the driver of a canvas-covered truck. "I've got twenty-eight days and a wake-up. Welcome to the underworld!" It was always the same with new arrivals, old-timers, rubbing it in with the new guys. Gerald smiled at the driver and said," Feels like the Arizona desert, no problem!"

The very air of Camp Lemonnier was thick with dust whipped by winds off the Bab-el-Mandeb straits. This American Army post had a new commission at an old French garrison site. Since the construction of the Suez Canal in 1868, sea trade routes have taken on profound significance. Ships would no longer sail south around the southern tip of Africa. The Chinese also had a recent foothold in the area. They were keen on the region, as were the Americans, British, Italians, and the rest of central Europe. The 600-acre American military post was self-contained. Water wells were pumping from underground aquifers. The Americans have been guardians of the gate since 2002, protecting U.S. interests and sea trade. They also helped quash piracy off Africa's east coast. The Sovereign Republic of Djibouti, Africa, is a high-end landlord. The Americans paid one hundred million dollars in annual rent, and the Chinese paid sixty million. It remains Djibouti's only reputable source of revenue other than salt.

Sp-4 Ingalls would be here to help maintain troop morale. There would be intermural sports and human interest stories to write. No newspaper existed; he would convey his stories online both here and back in the U.S. Written electronic news would pass through the U.S. Advisory command before release. Operations would also need his impetus in reports to S-1 Army intelligence. Some functions were classified, and others were not. Winning the hearts and minds of the local populace was necessary for any region since conflicts began. SP-4 Ingalls was in Africa to see that credible information became available locally and abroad. In-processing ran a few days. For the moment, he must adjust his eyes and mind to the new and exciting vibe.

When Gerald's chopper landed at the camp on Friday afternoon, it was 3 a.m. in Flagstaff, fourteen thousand miles to the west. He would call Eve in four hours before she would bicycle to Class at NAU. Gerald should never refer to his whereabouts. He would ask Eve the local time and give her his local time. Eve would know that her husband was on the horn of Africa performing his duties. When Eve's phone chimed at seven-thirty a.m., Gerald had just finished supper at the dining hall.

"Hello, my love," he said when Eve answered. She was anxious to know about his trip and if he needed anything. They had not spoken by cellphone since his stopover in Spain.

"Things are a bit different here, we are self-contained, and there is no place to go, even if I could," he said. The weather was muggy and about eighty degrees. Winds off the east coast keep the humidity high.

"Do you miss me? I sure miss you," he said, stating the obvious. Eve spoke on her headset while cycling to her first Class in English Lit.

"I do miss you, Ger, more than you know. I sleep in one of your used T-shirts." Gerald mentioned that he could do better than that if she could somehow visit London or Abu Dhabi in the coming months.

"Just have Aunt Syl take you on one of her business trips," Parking her bike at the English department building, Eve said she would look into it.

"I gotta run," she said, "Class starts in five minutes, and I want my usual front-row seat. Bye Ger, love you, don't get ambushed over there." They signed off as Gerald walked along with other men going through orientation.

Chapter 12

STIRRING THE POT

June 2016

During the long intervals away from Gerald, Eve held the future in the palm of her hand. No power on earth would change the fact that they would survive. Months of truck-driving over the nation's highways solo had tempered Eve. She did reminisce about those she loved. After a few days, only blips of memory surfaced about Gerald. She might even forget what he looked like, but she never forgot his mannerisms or the love they held for each other.

Eve and Gerald were on different career paths, but they could plan together one day. For the present, she could maneuver at her discretion. Eve had empathy for people in her immediate network of friends at NAU. Eve had Laura, and she had Hap; that was enough for her present situation. When her husband returned from Africa, they could establish the vibes that made life the stuff of dreams. She loved Gerald, and he loved her. They would endure the hardships.

*　*　*

At home in Fort Collins, Trish and Les Hays had settled into the routine of married life. Investments they had made in common with the bank president had not yet accrued much wealth. The potential was there, but it would take more time to yield an adequate net profit. They had considered a substantial financial gift to Eve and Gerald, but their wedding came sooner than expected. Another nagging thought surfaced. It was a brief encounter and mind-numbing for Trish, but it happened. There was little room for regret following an interval of life-altering indiscretion.

After her and Les's marriage in Naples, Florida, Flynn visited Trish at the Indian Hills home. He ran into trouble when a warrant was issued for his arrest. He trashed his apartment and needed a place to stay. All Trish could do at the time was refer Flynn to Social Services. He was penniless and had lost his CSU football scholarship due to non-attendance. What came next was spontaneous when she allowed him into her life after fifteen months of separation. Events leading up to their reconciliation were predictable.

Flynn was an interesting dichotomy of positive energy and dangerous extravagance when they lived with Eve and Gerald at the Remington street house. He was fun to be with but also pushed the limits of sound judgment. Once while rock jumping at Horsetooth Reservoir, he plunged thirty feet, hitting the water between submerged boulders that might have killed him. Winter camping at Chimney hollow campground on another occasion was a total nightmare.

A Florida girl taking part in such an experience was unthinkable, but Flynn talked Trish into doing it. He saved her life by building a snow cave, lining it with their sleeping bags, and spending the night miles away from civilization. They provided warmth to one another by clinging tightly together through twenty-degree overnight temperatures.

"I would never let anything happen to you," Flynn told Trish, and she believed him. She took comfort in the fact that they shared the experience and made her realize how she loved him in an unsustainable way. Flynn was risky. The bond they shared was stretched too far and broken when Flynn highjacked his future by crawling away from personal responsibility. "You're just a good-time Charley," she had told him on occasion. Their relationship was finally severed when

Flynn couldn't break away from a party animal lifestyle. After intimate encounters with Flynn, she took the high road and latched onto her co-worker at the bank where she worked. Flynn was left to flounder in the sorrow that he lost someone he may have wanted to be with for a lifetime. At Trish's new home in Fort Collins, their passion rekindled. Trish could not receive from her husband Les Hays what Flynn might provide. Her defenses fell away, and Trish willingly succumbed to one last fling with her old boyfriend.

Visiting Trish at her home months after their break-up, they both felt the heat of the casual sex they had shared at the Remington street house months before. It started as a slow passionate dance in her kitchen. When Flynn reached under Trish's blouse and the warm palm of his hand caressed her stomach, she gasped but yielded to his touch. Her eyes glazed, and she melted into her former boyfriend, whispering, "Right here, right now." Clutching each other, they were the only two people on earth. She was ready, and Flynn was willing to accommodate the woman he could never have for a lifetime. The only sounds in the room were sighs, gasps, and noise from a cat clock on the wall. The tick-tock-tick-tock, with the cat's tail swishing and its eyes moving right and left in unison, was the only witness to their passion. The two un-rapped each other in a feverish frenzy, and Flynn soon became a surrogate daddy.

Trish eased herself onto the kitchen table and adjusted her legs as they possessed one another in a simple, fast, frantic proclamation. It was spontaneous, and it was complete. As their heat dissipated, she established a sense of restraint, smiled, and softly whispered that Flynn must leave.

"I don't want to see you around here again, she said. Silently, the two rearranged themselves as Flynn drew Trish near to himself. Their lips met as a seal of lament for Flynn. Anxiously and silently, Trish motioned that he should leave and do it quickly. 'Love on the run,' Trish thought. She handed Flynn an envelope containing $748 in cash. It was all the cash she had in the house. It was a penance for her, but Flynn thanked her profusely and rode away on a mountain bike. He had lost his driver's license. Trish considered that Flynn's only means of transportation, the bicycle, was probably stolen. That was a couple of months ago. Since then, Flynn fell off the grid and vanished like a dark cloud at sunset. Trish phoned Eve in Flagstaff, warning her that Flynn might hit her up for money.

"I'm sorry I didn't tell you a couple of months ago," Trish explained, "I should have prayed to the Saint of Lost Causes on Flynn's behalf." Eve advised Trish not to worry; Flynn would land on his feet and get his life together. Trish failed to mention the sexual foray with their old housemate.

*   *   *

Flynn boarded an Air France flight. He traveled from Denver's International Airport to the Charles De Gaulle Airport in Paris with Trish's money. On arrival, he would avoid visiting local attractions and hastened to the gate of the French Foreign Legion. He hailed a cab and told the driver, Fontenay-sous-Bois, Île-de-France. The driver gave him a blank stare but drove several miles to the address. On arrival, the driver accepted his fare and gestured toward a large wooden gate of a stone fortress—an old wooden structure of an eye-level peep-hole that opened inward. Clutching a small tote bag of his belongings, Flynn kicked at the gate with the toe of his boot. A voice from inside asked who he was and what he wanted.

"I'm an American. I want to join the Legion," he said. The gate opened inward. Flynn met with a uniformed legionnaire in a white *kep*i. He was escorted to an austere room with a wide lectern and bench against one wall. The legionnaire gestured toward the wooden bench.

In minutes, the cadence of two men echoed down a stone hallway toward the room where he sat. An officer told Flynn to empty his pockets and produce identification on entering. The questioning was in English. Inspecting the contents of Flynn's pockets, he asked, "Why do you want to join the French Foreign Legion?" Flynn answered, "I have nothing to keep me in the U.S., and I've had some trouble with the law. Asked what kind of trouble Flynn had gotten into, he answered that he had stolen people's identities, dabbled in forgery, and taken part in ruffing people up on occasion. The officer asked Flynn if there were any murders or rapes on his rap sheet.

"No sir!" he answered. The leading officer had a few words with his sergeant and left the room. According to Flynn's statement, the sergeant took out a form from behind the podium and began filling out information.

"Sign here." There was no bartering, no welcome aboard, and no words of acknowledgment. The sergeant gestured toward the bench once more, where Flynn took a seat. The officer re-entered with a piece of paper and told Flynn, "From this day forward, you are Robert Collins. If you accept the name and sign, you must agree to a five-year contract with the French Foreign Legion, is that understood?" Flynn nodded.

"Once your five-year contract is honored, you can assume your old identity or keep your new one; it's up to you." Acknowledging the officer, Flynn signed the paper. He was escorted to an adjacent building and told to change out of his civilian clothes. Flynn had become a legionnaire in the making. Flynn no longer existed on paper, but he would keep 'Flynn' as a nickname.

Robert "Flynn" Collins, in his first weeks of training with the French Foreign Legion, had taken solace with the Legion of the damned. Recruits were not to think but to act. The members of the brotherhood were from all parts of the world. When U.S. Army soldiers would exit the mess hall, they would do pushups. When the French Foreign Legion recruits left a mess hall, they attacked each other in ground fighting. Flynn fought with his fellow recruits at night or day, rolling and tumbling around on the ground. Twenty-year-old men kicking up dust was expected and sanctioned as part of the training. Thirty-six hours without sleep was typical. Mud, water, and uphill jogs were all part of the grind. French as a first language was mandatory. The men were comrades in arms in the barracks for a few hours' sleep. Overseen by the ever-watching eyes of drill instructors, they fought, ran obstacle courses, swam fully clothed, and received punishment for any infraction of regulations. Backtalk was unknown. Do or die for France, and the man next to you, was the mantra on everyone's lips.

And die they did, 36,000 since the inception of the French Foreign Legion. Over a thousand Americans had joined the FFL since it was formed in 1831 by King Louis-Phillippe. The last significant battle loss was Dien Bien Phu against the Viet Minh of southeast Asia. An unmarked grave awaited those killed in battle. If you were an officer, you received a marker. That was the deal. Take it or leave it.

When Flynn could finally don his white kepi with the rest of his graduating Class, it amounted to the same ritual as the US Marines attaching the Eagle, Globe, and Anchor emblem to their collars. Esprit de corps was alive and well among the ranks. Then, his orders came for further training at the Djibouti Sea Camp.

Training and living an austere life were expected, fortified by regulation, and forged in honor. If Flynn lived five years, he could either take an extended commitment with the Legion or drop out and stay in France as a citizen. He could return to the U.S.; it was his choice. He made it through all the rigors thrown his way. After sea camp training, his first duty station was in Chad at a French prison housing Boko Haram terrorists. It was a smelly thankless job that hardened him to the rigors of stamping out the opposition and following orders from command headquarters.

The Legion fought terrorists in any part of the world. Flynn held a sense of pride in ridding the world of human vermin who insulted the weak with deadly force. Five months into his five-year commitment, he was sent to Camp Lemonnier on the Horn of Africa at twenty-four years of age. Photos of burning corpses and the killing of Christians by Boko Haram were part of his training. Flynn's brotherhood became eradicators, men who kill cockroaches and smash the heads of snakes. He fulfilled a commitment when he first put a burst of three rounds into an enemy combatant. He was protecting a woman he had left back in the U.S. The personification of that protection rested with Trish Hays.

*   *   *

Months before Eve and Gerald's wedding in Flagstaff, Trish and Les Hays attempted to start a family. Les went through the motions with little regard for reproductive sex, yet Trish could not conceive a child. Often, she would call his office saying the basal thermometer had bumped, "Get home and give me some sugar!" She was reluctant to see a specialist saying, "We'll do this on our own or not at all!" Les went along with the deception, knowing Trish would never conceive a child by him. Three years before they married, Les had a vasectomy but had not told his wife. He would forsake children and live, hoping that Trish would eventually give up on starting a family. Less didn't want children. He wanted to be free of all encumbrances that children might bring. Or so he thought. He wanted financial stability and a trophy wife. Les was confident that Trish would, one day, throw in the towel and invest her passions elsewhere. She wouldn't give up and was relentless in her pursuit of getting pregnant. After a few weeks of sex with her husband, Trish was confident something was amiss with Les's reproductive plumbing.

Following Flynn's visit with her, she had missed a couple of periods, all unknown to her husband. Before things became apparent to God and the rest of humanity, Trish called her old friend Eve. She caught her at home, packing for a departure to Boulder, Colorado, and a scheduled internship.

"Eve," Trish said, "I have something to tell you. Are you sitting down?" Eve was scurrying about her house saying," OK, but make it quick. I have a red-eye flight to catch." Trish didn't beat around the bush.

"Remember me telling you about Flynn and his visit to me a few months ago?" Eve recalled that she had, and asked, "Is he hitting you up for more money?" Trish said that he was not, but there was something else Eve should know.

"When we both lived at the Remington house two years ago, you ran off and went truck driving," Trish said.

"Yes, please don't remind me!" said Eve. Trish explained that she and Flynn had a thing for each other. "When you were off heading to God knows where Flynn and I were in my room playing house. To make a long story short, Flynn visited me recently, and we conceived a child together. I was pregnant with his baby at your wedding."

Eve, trying to remain tranquil, dropped into a chair. "Oh no, you mean you gave him money just to get lost after the two of you conceived a child?" Following a short silence, Trish answered meekly, "Think of it as a service fee."

"Oh, Trish, are you nuts?" Eve asked.

"No, I was just desperate," Trish answered.

Chapter 13

HOLD THE FORT

November 2016

Eve Ingalls remained focused and applied herself to her studies. She took summer and fall classes with little thought of taking a break. She didn't know the meaning of the phrase, 'take a break.' It was non-existent in the transportations industry as a driver. She applied the same mentality to her coursework at N.A.U. Making good use of her time on three fronts, Eve would maintain momentum in her courses by honoring the sacrifices that aunt Syl had committed to her. Tuition and fees were over $27K annually. Eve would not slack and discredit people who made her education possible.

She would also communicate with her husband, who lived half a world away. Third, with her direction and focus, Eve would take prerequisites for law school. After getting her B.A. in English Language Arts, she would apply for law school at Miami University.

Her faculty advisor gave Eve recommendations and the process to help achieve her goals. He made three suggestions. The Honors English program would look good on her reference sheet, and she would also take electives in the skill of legal writing. Her essays were excellent, and she could convince any judge with the watertight briefs she wrote. Another aspect of her education would allow her creativity to develop. Courses in fine arts would be therapeutic. Her advisor suggested that Eve take oil painting, stained glass, woodworking, or some other medium of expression. Finally, he hit on something that would help Eve further her degree program with faculty and staff. She couldn't pass up on his final suggestion as he explained it.

A faculty accreditation committee of the University would soon have meetings concerning the general studies program. Eve could be in attendance at those meetings, acting as a student secretary. The University was losing body count because there were too many mandatory classes in general studies. They required far too many subjects that all students must successfully pass before receiving their diplomas. Prospective students from all over the state and beyond were opting out for other institutions of higher learning. All University departments were losing FTE (Full-time equivalency). Eve could give her opinion as a student representative. Her advisor tactfully suggested that Eve, being a nontraditional student, the faculty committee would value her opinions. She could make sense of their thoughts and present a more comprehensive outlook. She latched onto the opportunity and threw herself into the fray. The first meeting came on a Monday, several weeks before the end of the fall semester.

Gerald listened on his phone at Lemonnier as Eve explained her immediate plans in Arizona. "If I hear another of these department heads use the term parameters, I think I'll throttle him." She let loose on some of the arguments they threw out to protect the FTE of their respective departments. "It's like breaking up tantrums among toddlers who can't share their toys," she said. "So, what's up with my hubby these days?" Gerald was equally specific, telling Eve about his time and trials.

"I do a lot of intermural sports reporting. I'll be heading out on an operation, but no one tells me what and where. I'll find out when it happens. It sounds exciting, and I'd like to see a different set of faces. Our unit news N.C.O. was an editor for the 'Des Moines Register' and knew his business. I don't want to let anyone down. I'll pull my extra duties and keep my nose clean." Gerald was always careful not to catch his wife when she was in class, considering the ten-hour time difference. That limited his phone calls to a very narrow window. Eve could expect him to check in once or twice a week on weekday evenings. If he called from his duty in Djibouti shortly after five in the morning his time, she would be at home expecting her phone to chime at seven o'clock the previous evening.

"I love you, babe, and miss you terribly," he would say when signing off.

"I miss you too, Ger," Eve mentioned that commercial flights from Phoenix to Abu Dhabi were around $1,200, and she wouldn't expect Aunt Syl to assist her in flying to the far side of the world. The Global is in some lease agreements with other businesses. Mildenhall Oil couldn't leave a 54 million dollar aircraft sitting around, and it had to help pay its way. Commercial round-trip flights between Phoenix and Abu Dhabi took more than twenty hours.

"Why don't I meet you in Spain sometime before the summer semester," Gerald suggested. Eve said she would "Take it under advisement using lawyer speech." Gerald laughed, "Save the legalese for when we meet, counselor. When I think of you, I sweat testosterone." Eve responded that she would know how to cool him off.

*   *   *

On returning from an Oil producer conference in Abu Dhabi, the Mildenhall team was ecstatic. They had secured their place on the world stage. They would be shakers and movers by 2017, as the U.S. would soon lead in worldwide oil production. Whenever the OPEC oil-producing conglomerate cut production to raise the prices, U.S. producers could dump products onto the world market. Syl Mildenhall would turn her attention to guaranteeing stockholders that their investments were paying off. Eve would soon begin her senior year at N.A.U. Syl wanted her to experience a few rewards. Syl threw out a few ideas to help Eve along her career path. Pulling in I.O.U.'s from business partners, Syl suggested a few opportunities for her niece.

Following Eve's help in cutting requirements in the general studies program at N.A.U., she could also act as student liaison for the Dallas oil conference. Syl's secretary contacted the provost of N.A.U. Leader and champion for scholarly pursuits, the provost and his cronies were long-time associates for promoting economic stability in the west. The provost had been one of Syl's suitors in bygone years and had asked for her hand in marriage on two occasions. Syl convinced him that she was married to her oil company, and she didn't have the time or the energy to pursue a marriage commitment. Shaken but not stirred, the man remained an advocate for everything Syl Mildenhall touched, and he would be present at the Dallas oil conference.

It became evident that the U.S. government's philosophy might change with a new president. All this made little difference to the oil conglomerates. There would be a need for fossil fuels well into the next millennia. Still, it was a nagging prospect, and Sylvia wanted someone in the room who she could trust. That person, in her estimation, would be her niece, who might land a significant internship in the process. There were several internships that Syl could leverage into for Eve's senior year.

With the help of her faculty advisor, Eve could fill a role in a company providing data and analytics for the oil industry. There was also the office of Banner Resources to consider, a company dealing in Global Oil properties. Mildenhall Oil had plats all over the southern states, Wyoming and Colorado. There were seventy B.R. company offices in thirty-five countries that gathered information in every corner of the globe. They have a hand in credit ratings, assessments, and analyses that governments, companies, and individuals find valuable. Conveniently, there were several offices in the western states where Eve could spend several weeks of internship. Syl would recommend considering the B.R. Global Platts office in Boulder, Colorado.

The Dallas symposium would be a good springboard. Eve was on the payroll in public relations for the Dallas branch. Her Aunt Syl had figuratively pinned applets on Eve's shoulders as she came to the podium. She was summoned late in the evening to say a few words. Eve wore a Badgley Mischka white cocktail dress. Her hair was parted down the middle and pulled back above the ears. Many attendees considered Eve as star power. Large screen monitors on each side of the podium made a statement. It was evident by all accounts that Eve Ingalls would be going places. In proper poise, she gave assurance to the five hundred in attendance that she was grateful for the opportunity that her Aunt Syl Mildenhall had given her. There was spontaneous applause; Eve was an 'it' girl.

Following the Dallas conference, Sylvia sent her attorney to Flagstaff after Eve returned home. He would consult with Eve's faculty advisor about her placement in the internship that Syl had suggested.

"I've had only two classes in economics," Eve said, "I don't see how that would qualify me for such an assignment!"

"Eve, this wouldn't be a hands-on job," said her advisor, "You would simply be observing, and it would be an excellent asset for your business acumen.

Her advisor was on board with the high-stakes game. Syl Mildenhall had been approached about running the Department of Energy during the Bush administration. She declined the offer. That didn't stifle enthusiasm for Mildenhall Oil and the prestige of the University where Eve attended.

You have enough credits to graduate after the spring semester because of your summer sessions. For a 40 hour week with the Boulder B.R. Office, you would receive three credit hours with N.A.U. You would be an intern for no more than several weeks. That would leave a sixteen-hour spring credit commitment for you to graduate." Syl's lawyer looked at Eve, saying, "For the team Eve, for the team."

*   *   *

Far away, a conflict had been brewing in central Africa. At a meeting in Nyandeni, South Sudan, opposition leaders voted to boycott the National Liberation Council. A coup attempt was about to take place. Ethnic instability had been commonplace on the outskirts of Juba City, the capital of South Sudan. Armed factions forced intertribal warfare, and the city of Bor, located in the Jonglei State, was seized by the (SSLA) South Sudan Liberation Army. In a nearby skirmish, the United Nations compound at Akobo Jonglei fell. The United Nations Secretary-General was concerned because the U.N. staff was constantly receiving threats.

The U.S. president and his secretaries of state and defense advised that United States citizens leave South Sudan. Armed conflicts escalated. A humanitarian assistance operation got underway from Camp Lemonnier. Sp-4 Ingalls would be among infantry units on orders to defend U.S. interests in Juba City.

Conflicts were intensifying a short distance from the camp. Elements of a combined task force scrambled to protect the American Embassy in Juba City. Specifically, they would receive orders to evacuate U.S. Citizens and crucial personnel and protect the physical assets. A U.S. Army brigade of one hundred fifty-three American soldiers was ready for an evacuation effort within thirty-six hours. A platoon of US Marines was on the ground at Entebbe, Uganda. Warnings went out that incoming C-130 flights could not land in Juba City. The airstrip pockmarked with mortar and rocket craters was of no use. An Army Signal Corps detachment was soon on station to provide eyes and ears for the American effort. Within three weeks, the airstrip had been repaired. Sixty embassy staff members, along with the embassy personnel, were evacuated. One hundred twenty American dependents went sent back to the states.

SP-4 Ingalls was on hand to record all these activities through his camera lens and with news briefs. Events unfolded with moments of anguish and trepidation. There was so much to do!

Once the Black Hawk choppers had set down, Gerald and his unit were eight miles from the American Embassy. The pilots brought them in at high noon to an incredibly hostile environment. With little situational awareness, the troops are being circled by truckloads of African soldiers; firearms aimed skyward. Entirely out of touch as to who was on their side and who the hostiles might be, time dragged. Finally, a convoy of land cruisers arrived to carry the task force and equipment to the American Embassy compound. Gerald, a light traveler, had only his DSLR Nikon camera and his ever-present M2-40 Lima rifle slung on his shoulder. He wore the standard sand-colored tactical vest, which sent rivulets of sweat running down his back. There was a great deal of camaraderie. Gerald and a big mean gang with whom he had sworn an oath was ready. He was there to help protect and defend his buddies and record the process. For the moment, it was a psychological thriller about what might happen next. The convoy of troops finally moved out for an eight-mile ride to the American Embassy.

Troops arrived at the Embassy compound through dusty streets accompanied by the ever-present smell of diesel engine exhaust. A contingent of Marine security guards and the Ambassador herself greeted the convoy. Delighted to see the troops arrive, she soon passed her bull horn to military contractors and US Marines who would provide a briefing. Intelligence operatives told the men that twenty-five thousand enemy SPLA soldiers were marching their way, along with the White Army. They were trolls with machine guns and hatred for everyone; Christians, Muslims, and Americans.

'Swell, 'thought Gerald as he continually snapped photos of the layout surrounding himself and the other American troops.

*   *   *

Eve's plane landed in Denver, Colorado, shortly before 1:00 a.m. on a Saturday. She had a ride waiting at ground transportation. Off to Boulder in the early hours, traffic was light. From the airport, her limo driver took the shortest route to Highway 36, the Boulder road. Once in town, they got off at Arapahoe Avenue, setting a westward course near downtown. They entered an older neighborhood a few blocks west of the C.U. campus.

The house was set back along tree-lined streets with manicured lawns. The two-story garden-level home was typical of off-campus housing, but this one had a few upgrades. A Vespa scooter sat on the front walkway. Eve thought there must be a reason, doubting that she would ride a scooter to the B.R. offices. On a narrow driveway off to the right of the house, she spotted her Alpha Romero with Arizona plates. She wasn't aware that her car had been air-shipped to Boulder.

In the limo, the driver introduced herself as Maxine Donahoe.

"So, here we are, Eve, welcome to your home away from home. Everyone calls me M.D., and I'll be your Girl Friday while we're in Boulder." The presence of M.D. came as a surprise to Eve. She hadn't considered that the limo driver would be staying on with her.

"Your Aunt Syl wants you to concentrate on the task at hand. Think of me as Kato who worked for Inspector Clouseau," said M.D. Eve wasn't sure of that reference and didn't ask.

It all came rushing in, security for Syl's little red-headed niece. The Vespa belonged to a housekeeper, who was inside shampooing carpets.

'Everyone knows what's going on except me,' she thought. The home interior was immaculate with polished hardwood floors and a kitchen that made her little nook in Flagstaff look like an add-on.

"Your suite is upstairs, ready for you to relax and get settled; I'll see you in the morning," M.D. told her. Eve asked where her housemate would be and learned that M.D. had private rooms off the kitchen. The housekeeper would be heading home after she finished with the cleaning. Too tired to ask more questions, Eve went up the carpeted stairs to her suite. She had most of the weekend before her.

Eve came down from her room to the kitchen before noon on Saturday. Noticing that the limo was gone, she inquired where it might be.

"The rental agency picked it up forty-five minutes ago," M.D. answered.

"How will you get around while I'm working?" Eve wanted to know.

"I'll take the Hop, Skip and Jump, Boulder's bus service. On weekends, we can travel in your car."

"No problem," Eve answered, "But let's get something straight; I don't need a nursemaid." Dropping the towel, she was drying her hands-on; M.D. looked at Eve.

"You don't need a nursemaid. What you do need is someone to shadow you. Syl pays me more than you want to know for doing that. I won't follow you everywhere, but there are limits."

"Such as?" asked Eve.

"Well, for beginners, the coming-out event in Dallas put you on a lot of radar screens. I've been scoping the bad guys for more than twenty-five years. It's alright being a little naive, but it can also be dangerous." Eve wanted to know why anyone would be interested in her.

"Haven't you seen the movie, 'Molly's Game'? I can think of forty reasons why bad guys out there want to get you alone. It's all part of the game."

"How would you stop these bad guys from jumping both of us?" Eve asked. M.D. smiled as she walked toward Eve.

"I have a third-degree black belt, and a 9mm Ruger LC9s strapped to my ankle. Why don't we go to the gun range, and I'll show you how to use it."

"Not necessary," Eve said, "My mother has the same qualifications and schooled me on them before I graduated from high school. Between the two of us, I think we could kick butt."

"Well, OK then," M.D. said, "I'm glad we cleared that up."

On Monday, M.D. drove Eve to the Banner Resources office on Walnut street. Approaching the reception desk, Eve asked for the senior project manager. The receptionist punched a couple of numbers on her call center.

"Jerome, there's a young lady at the desk asking for you." The project manager and a gaggle of men came to the front foyer. One of them stepped forward.

"Hi, you must be Eve Ingalls?" He struggled not to give Eve the elevator eyes treatment, "Come with me, and I'll show you around. You will be working with a team for a couple of days, and then I'll assign you to carbon markets analysis." Along the hall, they passed a photo of the current workers. There were approximately thirty-five people, even numbers of men and women.

"We have our cafeteria," he said, "But we often go out for lunch." At the end of the hallway, there was a double door with a sign above, Conference room 1.

"You can park your paperwork here. I'll get ahold of your team leader; please take a seat."

Momentarily, the team leader entered the room with his secretary.

"So, you'll be doing an internship with us from Northern Arizona University?" An obese balding man in his forties, he was all business.

"You're an English major looking toward law school, is that correct?" Eve nodded.

"We're mostly bean counters here; why B.R.?" he wanted to know. Eve explained that she worked with commercial and customer engagement teams, executed commercialization plans, communicated value propositions, and provided ongoing support to the customer base through emails and multi-media. It was strictly a reference to her time on the Curriculum Committee at Northern Arizona, and it sounded impressive. She kept a straight face; the supervisor and his secretary bought it, hook, line, and sinker.

"Is that all?" the man laughed nervously. Then he looked at the ceiling, saying, "Thank you, God!" The secretary asked Eve, "Who recommended you to us?"

"My Faculty advisor made the suggestion," Eve said confidently. "And my Aunt Syl wants me to learn the inner workings of worldwide Oil Platz."

"Aunt Syl, and who's she?" the secretary wanted to know.

"Sylvia Mildenhall of Mildenhall oil," Eve responded.

"Oh, my," the team leader said. He sat straight like someone had jabbed him in the back with a pitchfork.

"Get the rest of the team in here; they've got to meet this young lady!"

For several hours, people were filtering in and out of conference room 1. The associates explained the proper inner workings of B.R. They were all about reducing gas emissions and addressing worldwide sustainability formats. The organizational objective was to bring transparency to segments of the corporate world seeking to decarbonize.

"We help in a way, so companies don't go broke and remain in business through daily market research," said another analyst. By late afternoon, Eve heard from all but a few of the team members.

The project manager stuck his head in the door, "Eve, why don't you go home early and digest all that we've been throwing at you." No less than four guys offered to take her to wherever she lived. She smiled, got on her cell phone, and called M.D. to pick her up. Two guys hung around the foyer and watched as she got into the passenger side of an Alfa Romero.

"Mercy," said one, "How would you like to crawl in the sack with that? I could teach her a few tricks!" His associate nudged him, "She probably knows a few more tricks than you do. See that set of rocks on her ring finger?"

"But she smells so damn good," said the first man.

"She's married!" shouted the receptionist from her desk.

*   *   *

Around the American Embassy in Juba City, South Sudan, hundreds of sandbags were filled and placed at strategic locations. The Army troops set M-60 gun emplacements for firing, harassment, and interdiction. Gunfire was rampant from sections of the city day and night. With strong fortifications in place, the gathering of supplies came next. One squadron confiscated anything of value from the surrounding shacks and utility closets. Spools of fine metal wire would come in handy for defensive measures. At choke points, soldiers set traps to discourage a frontal attack. As professional sportsmen, the theme was to take what the opposition had given and use it against them. Placed along with the wiring to fire them were dozens of Claymore mines.

Imagination was the key to success as Gerald snapped photos of the process. For himself and his buddies, preparation was crucial. The troops were severely outnumbered, according to intelligence reports. A measure of faith rekindled many of the soldiers. Talk of personal salvation became a topic of discussion in the quieter moments. They waited, but they also worked. Squads of soldiers were setting a defensive posture for avenues of approach with trip flares for nighttime illumination. Tanks of raw gasoline were in place and wired for detonation. Once accomplished, a third and final task was to destroy any sensitive information stored on hard drives or hard copies of classified information inside the Embassy. With any defensive position, soldiers could catch sleep while others worked. It was an ongoing effort day and night for survival. Gerald would operate an M203 grenade launcher, the thumper, attached to his rifle in the event of a ground attack.

The deployment turned out to be longer than anticipated. 'Isn't that just ducky,' Gerald thought. Three days of deployment turned into two weeks. At long last, estimates for enemy contact were twelve hours away. Soldiers patrolled fortifications, waited, joked, and fretted about the what-ifs of conflict. Everyone was on a first-name basis. Rank insignia dissolved as the cream of natural leaders rose to the challenge. They were brothers in arms.

At 3:00 a.m. on the seventeenth day of deployment, the White Army wiped out the U.N. Compound located a mile from the Embassy. It was a vindication for harboring refugees of the wrong tribe. The embassy compound guarded at such a high level was left untouched. The American presence was primarily an evacuation force. Regardless, the Embassy fortification remained under guard for another forty-one days. Their Army infantry unit sent to defend an American existence in Juba City was ready for action. No action ensued, but they held the fort.

* * *

Eve had simmered down her outfits back in Boulder after her initial interview at the B.R. Office. On Friday, she wore a granny dress. Women in the office would watch the men as they ogled Eve. They painted her with their eyes. It was getting old to the point of embarrassment for her, and it might cause a rift. Gone were the long red tresses about her shoulders and down to her mid-back. She wore her hair up, slicked, and pulled back, but it didn't help. She didn't like men ogling her and ignored inappropriate remarks. When two of the guys came close to overstepping the line, she would tell them.

"Fellas, I've driven a semi-tractor trailer over the U.S. and Canada for more than a year, and I've heard it all, men wanting to check my oil with their dipsticks." At the beginning of her third week, things cooled because Eve had more talent than some people working there.

She mastered the dialogue and turned out analytical reports to the Low Carbon Market Footprints manager. The work was fast-paced in a highly collaborative environment. There were data visualization platforms, conferences, events, and several customer engagement forums where she took part. Before reaching the end of her tenure, Eve was considered a strong team player by all her colleagues. She could think critically, act decisively, and deliver results.

"Why don't you forget law school and come to work for us," said the project manager.

"Don't think I haven't thought about it, but my mind's made up," Eve replied. "I must work with Mildenhall Oil and slug out the sticky relationships we have with our stockholders." Then, during the last two days of her work in Colorado, she spoke at the Denver oil conference.

Eve would deliver a keynote address on what she had learned throughout her internship. She prepped by using M.D. as an audience and gathered her concepts two days before the event. Finally, there she was, like in Dallas, speaking before three hundred participants.

The Denver office building on Larimer street rose to thirteen stories, with the Banner Resources suite taking up the entire second floor. It wouldn't allow ample parking or seating for a massive influx of people. The meeting would take place a few blocks away at the Colorado Conference Center. The giant blue bear statue peeking into the glassed wall second floor made it unique. Preparations had been in play for weeks. As Eve entered the underground parking with her entourage, she sensed correctly that the atmosphere was more than a convention of bean counters. Her remarks at center stage would be a stepping stone for her future.

Exxon Mobile, Royal Dutch, Chevron Corporation, and Aramco Americas had table displays along the mezzanine. It was all about oil energy and who could bring the next hundred years, setting a precedent. Who could bring about positive changes to the industry? Banner Resources Oil Platz is a force to bring about clean energy worldwide. Eve would be the penultimate speaker with notes on her iPhone in the latter portion of the program. She would be the face and stimulus of bringing younger generations onto the world energy stage. Mildenhall Oil groomed her for this very role. Unfortunately, her Aunt Syl would not be in attendance. Eve was stepping from under the wing of her mentor and confidant; she wouldn't disappoint.

An after-party at the Copper Palace Hotel brought scores of conventioneers. Many were staying at the palace, taking elevators to the ballroom. Eve kicked off her shoes and walked on the plush carpet, working the room. She brought smiles and laudatory congratulations for the address she had given a couple of hours before. The Project manager's wife spotted her and sidled up. Seeing Eve shoeless, she also kicked off her shoes, telling her husband, "Do something with these, would you!" The band was accompanying a popular songstress, and drinks were on the house. From her left, one of the men asked Eve, "Where's your husband? I'd like to meet him!"

"Oh, he's around here somewhere," Eve lied. Her eyes were a bit glassy, and her glass was near empty. The man knew full well that Gerald was on the other side of the world. A junior C.E.O. from Planters Oil Energy, the man, was not used to having women ignore him. His tailored suit and flashy looks spoke vociferously, 'I'm here, come and get me!'

When Eve moved away for a refill, the C.E.O. shadowed her.

"So, you're the face of Mildenhall Oil, now?" he asked. Eve turned, looked him in the eye, and responded, "Only for today!"

"You know," he said, "You and I could have more privacy with some of my people upstairs."

"Sounds like fun," she answered, "I'll call my husband and ask if I can attend!" As she said this, Eve smiled and winked.

"That would be a long-distance call because he's in Djibouti, Africa," said the C.E.O. She wagged her finger, "Ah, ah, ah, don't try to be a bad influence; it might backfire." Filling her glass from the Margarita fountain, she sashayed across the mezzanine to M.D.

"Keep an eye on Mr. Slick, the guy wearing the flashy sideburns; he's looking to get laid," Eve said.

"There are at least four more I've spotted trolling; shall we call it a night?" M.D. asked.

"No, let's stick around for a while; the fun's just starting," Eve answered. They both joined the celebration as the night was young. Soon, Eve was cutting loose on the dance floor to the tune of Rihanna's 'Love on the Brain' with the young C.E.O. she had met. M.D. thought, 'Girls just want to have fun.'

The Project manager's wife, gyrating against her husband, expected more people to get sassy and let their hair down. Throughout the evening, her glass was seldom empty. "Let's get out of here and get back to the house. I feel sick," she said. All who came to Denver would not return to Boulder from the Valet parking kiosk. Boulder people entered the limo except for Eve and M.D.

"Did you mention to Eve that we were leaving?" someone asked. Slurring her speech, the P.M.'s wife answered, "They're big girls; they can figure it out!" A few in the limo were apprehensive about leaving Eve and M.D. behind but forgot as the vehicle accelerated away. They had other things to consider. The PM's wife was about to vomit on the men's Cormac Woven wingtip shoes.

"You don't give up, do you?" Eve said to her presumed escort, the Planter's Oil guy.

"Ah, come on," he said, "It's just a few of us going to the spa. You can bring your chaperone!"

"She's not my chaperone," Eve retorted, "Maxine is my housemate; she has a third-degree black belt and likes kicking men where it will hurt the most."

"I'll keep that in mind," the man said. A man and woman split through the couple heading for the elevators.

"That's my roommate and his date. They're going where we're going." The C.E.O. turned and motioned for M.D. to come along. The hotel's penthouse suite had a small lap pool, a hot tub, and a palapa bar on the edge of the deep end.

"I don't have a swim outfit," Eve said.

"Neither do I." The guy shed his trousers and upper garments. Down to his socks and skivvies, Eve asked, "Help me with this zipper." As he turned and attempted to bring down the long zipper of her dress, Eve grabbed his hand, and the two jogged for the deep end of the pool. Nonstop, they both went headlong into the water.

The guy wasn't ready for the cold pool that awaited them. It was such a shock that he inhaled a large gulp of water and began coughing. Eve summoned M.D. to help drag him from the water. The pool assistant whipped out his Iphone and began recording the incident. Eve assumed it was for insurance purposes to protect the hotel. She and M.D. rolled the guy onto his stomach, and she applied artificial respiration. The Iphone camera of the pool assistant captured it all. Eve was astraddle the guy and pressing on his back. Her dress was up to her waist; as she lifted his elbows, water gushing from his mouth. He soon began to cough and breathe. He looked up at Eve and mustered a smile.

"I think that's enough fun for tonight," M.D. said. Eve, fully clothed, rose to her feet. She was sopping wet with long red tresses cascading onto her shoulders. The pool assistant, his Iphone still in action, raced to the towel table and one-handed, threw half a dozen towels toward the threesome. Then, he disappeared through the glass doors from the pool. Eve and M.D. didn't give it much thought. They all began to laugh and to shiver. Eve looked around for the pool assistant, who had disappeared.

"That's strange," she said, "I wonder where the guy went."

Gathering themselves, Eve reasoned that she and M.D. should get back to Boulder. She got on her cell phone, and a passenger van arrived minutes later. The women found hotel robes and rode down a freight elevator to a service exit, wet and cold. People in the ballroom were questioning why one of their star speakers had left.

A subordinate from the B.R. office came to pick up the two women.

"Looks like you two made a big splash at the conference," he tried to joke.

"You could say that," came M.D.'s reply. Arriving at the Boulder house, they thanked the driver and collected their wet clothes. Inside, M.D. pulled a bottle of Jameson Irish Whiskey from a kitchen cabinet as Eve retrieved two tumblers.

"Say when," M.D. said.

"Two fingers and lots of ice," Eve replied. The two sat and sipped the fruity whiskey, still dressed in robes from the Copper Palace.

"You suppose they'll accuse us of stealing these robes," M.D. snickered.

"It would be a perfect ending to the day," Eve said as they clicked their glasses.

Early Sunday, Eve was awakened by a loud thump from the Boulder newspaper hitting the front door.

"That little fart sure makes a lot of noise," M.D. yelled from the kitchen. Eve retrieved their newspaper from the porch.

"Well, would you look at this!" she said. On page three was Eve's photo, sitting on top of a man in his skivvies. The caption read, 'Man nearly drowns at Denver's Copper Palace hotel.' "No, no, no, no," she said and read the story aloud.

"A wild party following Denver's Western Regional Oil Conference ends in near-drowning. An oil executive was dragged from the Palace Hotel pool as drunken revelers saved the man's life. The Public relations director of Dallas, Mildenhall Oil, rendered life support. Neither of the oil executives could be reached for comment.

"Oh no, no, no!" Eve repeated. The phone rang!

"Yeah," said M.D., "Yeah, she's right here." M.D. handed Eve her cell phone.

"It's your Aunt Syl!" Taking the phone, she stood saying nothing.

"Eve, are you there?" Syl asked. Eve rendered a soft, "Hello."

"Well, I'm happy you weren't wearing holey underpants, nice tush!" The story had gone online and in local newspapers.

"I can explain," Eve said. In the background, on Syl's end, she could hear stifled laughter.

"Welcome to the big leagues' kid!" Sylvia wasn't as upset by the altercation as Eve thought she might be.

"First off, Aunt Syl, I wasn't drunk!"

"I know, I know," answered Syl, "These things happen; we'll talk about it when you get back to Flagstaff. I'm sure you will get a good grade for the internship; ha, ha, and, ha. Please tell M.D. I need to speak to her again!" M.D. took the phone, went to the living room, and sank onto the couch. From the kitchen, Eve heard a muffled conversation for several minutes. Finally, M.D. tossed the phone aside, staring at the opposite wall. Eve approached apprehensively and asked, "You didn't get canned, did you?"

"No, nothing like that," M.D. answered.

Chapter 14

THE TIES THAT BIND

March 2017

When Gerald was in Juba city, Flynn bumped along with his fellow Legionnaires on a covert operation. They were usually patrolling in Mali. They were deployed to the savanna south of Juba City as bad luck would have it. There, they worked in concert with other NATO allies. Rolling along in an A.P.C. looking for G.A.T.s (Groups of Armed Terrorists), they hit a snag. Legion vehicles were always off the beaten path, maneuvering through the vast savanna. On a logistical course, Flynn's A.P.C. hit a land mine. The blast bounced Flynn and two others off the interior walls of their vehicle. Two of his squad lay injured, along with Flynn. The squad sergeant radioed for a medical evacuation. An American medivac chopper was dispatched from Lemonnier to pick up the wounded and return them to the MASH (Mobile Army Surgical Hospital) Unit. Within an hour, the French operatives were resting easily.

Flynn, reluctant to reveal his real name to U.S. Army doctors, had a bed near his injured buddies. Two of the three had broken arms, while Flynn had deep lacerations on his torso that demanded internal and external stitches. He would also need a couple of weeks of recovery, and he slept a lot. A navy Corpsman was on-call to meet Flynn's needs and check on him regularly.

Awakening from a deep slumber, he heard the notes of an old tune. It emitted from an M3 P player on his food tray. Fully awake, the Corpsman and a familiar face came into view.

"I thought that would get your attention," said Gerald. The tune, an old favorite, 'Willow,' sung by Taylor Swift, opened Flynn's eyes. With the Corpsman stood Gerald, hands-on-hips, surveying Flynn's face. The two locked eyes and Flynn spoke.

"Qu'est ce que tu fais ici?" asked Flynn. Gerald looked at the Corpsman, and she stared back, unknowingly.

"What did he say?" asked Gerald. One of the guys in another bed answered in broken English, "What the hell are you doing here?" Gerald looked back at Flynn, unnerved.

"I was thinking the same damn thing about you, old buddy!"

******

"You got a phone call from Gerald about an hour ago," said M.D. in Boulder. Before Eve could react, M.D. added, "He said it could wait until you got up, something about Flynn, the guy you've been telling me about." Eve had come into the kitchen from her bedroom. She got on her phone and dialed her husband.

"You'll never guess who I ran into," Gerald said as the conversation crackled off orbiting satellites.

"This better be good," said Eve, "I haven't had my morning coffee."

"Our old housemate, Flynn, went off and joined the French Foreign Legion!" Letting that sink in for a bit, Gerald continued.

"He speaks French and pretty good too." For the next hour, they conversed about what might have brought Flynn to jump off the deep end and leave the U.S.

"Did you tell him he's going to be a daddy?" Eve then filled her husband in on the latest. "Trish is pregnant, and she said it's Flynn's."

"Oh my God, how can that be?" Gerald asked.

"Duh," said Eve, "How do you think it happened, stud? They had a brief fling in Fort Collins, and then he shipped out for Paris."

"Let's save that for another time, Ger. Right now, I want to know how you're doing after all the military activity in Africa. It's been all over the news!" Gerald gave her a synopsis of the mission and how he and his fellow troops had protected the U.S. Embassy in Juba City.

"Was it scary?" Eve asked.

"Well, yes and no," Gerald responded. "We had all kinds of air support, and the opposition didn't want to decimate one of their jewel cities. At least, that's what I drew from the experience. The U.S. Air force would have laid the place to rubble if necessary."

Eve asked Gerald not to mention the Flynn thing to anyone back home because it was a little secret between herself and Trish. Gerald told his wife that Flynn had a new identity by joining the Legion. "Do you want me to mention anything to Flynn about Trish's condition?" he asked. Eve hesitated for a moment.

"You may as well be honest. Just break it to Flynn gently, she said."

M.D. pointed at her wristwatch from across the room, and lip spoke that they had to leave.

"Ger, I have to get off. M.D. and I are going to the Denver office today; Banner Resources wants me to see the Denver layout. I'll be spending a few days there."

"OK, let's set a date, Evie, the next time you call, and maybe we could have a rendezvous in Spain. I need you, mind and body!"

*   *   *

As Trish finished setting up the interior of their Fort Collins home, she grew restless. She had been on her computer chasing commodity trades and doing little else. When Les arrived home on a Friday, he suggested that they go out for supper and get away from work for a few hours. Trish reluctantly signed off her two computers and freshened up for a night out. While Trish looked over the restaurant menu, Filet Mignon sounded suitable for Les. She suddenly started to tear up.

"I have something to tell you," she exclaimed. As Les handed their menus to the waiter, the candlelight revealed that his wife was about to lose it. Her eyes welled up with tears and would soon wet her cheeks.

"What's the matter Babe?" asked Les. Her remarks came softly, in a way Les had never seen her express herself.

"I haven't been wearing a diaphragm for quite a while, and I lied to you. I wanted to get pregnant, but it seemed that I couldn't, and now I am." Losing their appetites, the two forgot about eating and got up to leave. People watched as they went toward the door. Trish headed for the front entrance as Les followed close behind. A woman who witnessed the commotion suggested to her friend, "Well, I guess he wasn't the one, and she finally got around to telling him." Both women chuckled and sipped their Chardonnay.

Once at home, Trish cooled emotionally and wanted to talk to Eve in the privacy of her bedroom. She was on her phone, upset and making no sense.

"Remember how upset you were trying to navigate New York City?" she asked Eve. "My whole life is like that!" We were trying to have a baby but couldn't. Then Flynn deposited himself on my doorstep.

"You haven't told Les, have you?" asked Eve soberly.

"Noooooo," Trish moaned in a wheezy whisper. "How could I? It could be a deal-breaker!"

"Well, you've got to tell him something!" Eve strongly suggested.

"I told him that I stopped wearing my diaphragm. When I start to show, he'll think it's his."

"That's your plan?" Eve asked, as though it would never work.

"That's my plan, and I'm sticking to it," Trish answered.

There was a gentle rap on the bedroom door. Les opened the door slightly and asked if Trish was feeling better after talking with Eve. "I feel much better now," she said and punched off her cell phone.

*   *   *

Within three months, when Trish started showing, Les thought she might have been consuming too many carbs. As it became more evident that Trish was carrying a child, Les considered his options. If he were to tell Trish that he had a vasectomy before they met, she would go ballistic. Instead, he would keep his mouth shut. The thought of losing her was too much of a risk! He would play the game on her terms.

"Well, I guess I'm going to be a daddy," he said one morning over his newspaper. Trish responded, "That's right," as she spread orange marmalade on her toast.

"I guess our little friend, the basal thermometer, paid off. You caught me at the right time." Trish sipped her macchiato and said nothing more. Les backed and leaned into the kitchen counter.

"Is there anything you and I need to discuss?"

"Not really," Trish said, "There is a Lamaze class that I would like to take when I get a little further along." She looked up at him with mournful eyes and cracked a smile. "My OB/GYN says she would like you to come in on my next visit."

"Well, OK," Les said, as he gathered his Iphone and walked toward the door. "One other thing, did you talk with someone about family planning at the clinic? You haven't said."

"You're right, Les; I haven't said. I did get inseminated, but not in the usual sense."

They didn't share information and indiscretions when it came to baby talk. It was the way they approached such matters. The less said, the better. Afraid to say more, Les turned to leave. As the front door closed, Trish turned to the back of her newspaper and found the 'Dear Amy' section. 'You people have nothing on me,' she thought; 'you're just a bunch of amateurs.'

Les had gone. 'Yeah, I got inseminated alright,' she said to herself, 'by Flynn.'

*   *   *

Katie and Alfred set about tidying up their mountain home acreage. There were pine needles to clear from rain gutters, and dead branches from the ponderosa trees needed trimming. It was all part of fire mitigation for them and their neighbors. Fires were an imminent threat in the mountains, and lightning strikes were often the cause. They had packed necessary belongings and keepsakes on three occasions when fires threatened within the last twenty years. Evacuation orders had been in place but not mandated.

Most people want to stay and protect their homes, and water pressure is lost when mountain residents have the same idea. It's easier to evacuate and allow professional firefighters access to private property. If people vacate their homes, the County sheriff's department will not allow them to return until the threat is gone. On the coast of Florida and in the Gulf of Mexico, hurricanes were a seasonal threat. For Katie and Alfred, it was forest fires.

As Alfred cleaned their rain gutters, his ladder toppled over, sending him to the ground with a clatter. He hit his head and hurt his left shoulder. Considering the emergency, Katie drove her husband to the doctor. After seeing his primary care physician, Alfred spent two days in the I.C.U. at the Medical Center of the Rockies. Katie got the word out that Alfred was in bad shape.

Eve was busy at the Boulder Banner Resources office and wanted to know if her mother could somehow assist Katie. Kim secured a plane ticket and flew from Fort Myers to Denver. She had time on her hands. From D.I.A., Kim drove to her great aunt and uncle's home in a rented pickup truck. It was the right thing to do, help with Alfred's recovery. As Kim arrived on the property, the ladder was still on the ground where Alfred had fallen. She hadn't seen her relatives for a while, and their rustic home was a welcome sight. Alfred had returned home from the hospital and sat in his recliner. He was on orders to take it easy for a few days. He was also on restriction from driving. Katie needed a driver and soon. Kim felt obligated to return family favors, and it was not a burden.

Eve had grown up without a father, and it was always a concern for Aunt Katie. Now that Eve was married and on her Boulder internship, they seldom saw one another.

Years earlier, when Kim was at crucial stages getting her business off the ground, Katie and Alfred took Eve for the summer months. Alfred taught her how to drive, and they maintained a close relationship through the years. She learned the rudiments of woodworking, especially French polish, finishing work on her projects. Sometimes, they would travel to New Mexico and Arizona. While in Santa Fe, they would stop by Artesanos to pick up and hand-painted Mexican tiles for their wood projects.

Eve held fond memories of the southwestern states. She loved the area and considered it her home away from Florida. That was several years before, and times had changed. Then the accident with Alfred happened. Eve realized the treasure she had of knowing Alfred and Katie. She was adamant that her mother help the older couple.

When Katie received the call from Eve asking for a place to stay while she attended truck driving training, their relationships had taken on a new meaning. They developed a reconnection, and life became attractive for everyone. When her Uncle Alfred walked Eve down the garden path at her wedding, their relationship rekindled. The older folks were quite fond of the man Eve had chosen for a husband. Gerald was an Army man, and Alfred was a Vietnam Army veteran. They had much to discuss, military life ramifications, and long separations from their wives and loved ones. The cycle of life had come full circle, and family ties bloomed. When he fell off the ladder cleaning his rain gutters, it was natural that Kim would step in and render some assistance. Alfred had to attend Adult Rehab from his fall. Within a couple of weeks, Kim returned to her Flight business and continued the air charter service.

Katie and Alfred, ever grateful, went about their lives with a new outlook. They wanted to leave their estate to Eve and her husband, so they contacted a Family lawyer and drew up their will and codicils, leaving everything to Eve and Gerald Ingalls.

Chapter 15

FULL DISCLOSURES

June 2017

In the MASH unit at Lemonnier, SP-5 Gerald Ingalls told Flynn that he and Trish had a toddler back in the states. The news came as no surprise to Flynn. He looked at Gerald and asked, "Is she still with that guy from the bank?" Before Gerald could answer, Flynn added, "She wanted a baby; I gave her one." Flynn drew his attention away from Gerald for the moment and shifted in his bed. "What's its name?"

"Dax, she named him Dax. Eve says he's a solid little guy with curly hair; he gets into everything. And yes, she's still with Les Hays, who she met at First National."

"If there's any way to tell her," Flynn drew a fist and tapped softly on his bed, "I want her to know that her happiness is all that matters to me. Could you tell her that?"

"She's solid," said Gerald, "She has money, she has a munchkin, and Les is solid too. I'll tell her that you're happy for her."

Ten days into his treatment, the conversation came with moments of optimism as Flynn recovered from his wounds. He would never have a long-term arrangement with Trish, but he learned from Gerald that she was in high spirits. Her sunny disposition resonated with Eve and all her friends. As Flynn healed and faced the return to his regiment, he gave Gerald a snappy open-handed salute and processed out of the MASH Unit.

"I'm not sure how we will keep in touch," Gerald said, "Somehow, we'll make it work."

Gerald soon went before the promotion board and passed his oral exams for making E-5. He would not make E-6 unless he went through with reenlistment. A life-long military career was not his ambition. He would stick to his guns and process out of the Army when Eve would begin her second year of law school, but that was all speculation. She was about to finish her internship at the Banner Resources office in Boulder.

Eve returned to the B.R. offices Monday morning. She would collect personal items from her desk and get a signed statement from the senior project manager. She and M.D. went together, parking at the Broadway street garage. They were entering the B.R. office as all the office personnel stood around applauding. With her husband stood the project manager's wife. She held a framed photo of Eve sitting atop the Planters Oil CEO.

"Would you autograph this for me?" she asked. Not sure what to do, Eve looked around the group and finally said, "Oh, certainly!"

"This is for my high school daughter," said the manager's wife, "You're one of my daughter's folk heroes!" Eve signed the 12" X 18" framed photo with a flourish. As others gathered around to offer congratulations on a job well done, one of the men said, "Just one thing Eve when doing artificial respiration, you're supposed to kneel in front of a drowning victim, not straddle their butt!"

"Very funny; I'll save that for next time," she said.

Later, Eve's boss signed the paperwork in the manager's office, saying that she had satisfactorily completed her internship.

"So, what's next for you?" he wanted to know. Eve explained that she had another short summer session in Northern Arizona.

"I have been accepted at Miami University," she said. They shook hands, and the two women prepared to leave.

"If you're ever in the neighborhood, do stop by; you're not one we'll soon forget!" "Thank you, I think," Eve said as she and M.D. headed for the front door.

The next day Lynn Ingalls called Eve from Sedona.

"Ya know, honey, I was checking out at Basha's grocery store. Your picture is all over the tabloids! I bought one, so I could sneak it home and show Charles." After a silence, Lynn gave a summation of what the article said.

"The caption says, 'Mermaid saves Oil tycoon from drowning.' I'm sure it's you, but they airbrushed a set of fins off the back of your cocktail dress, lots of cleavages."

"Yeah, it's the same for all our grocery stores, too," Eve said. "There was an after-party at the Denver Oil Conference, and one of the guys tried to go skinny dipping in the pool. I saved him." The conversation took on another mood.

"What are you going to tell Gerald?"

"Well, for starters, I wasn't drunk like the article says, and I wasn't alone with the guy. He went into seventy-degree water, and he panicked. My driver Maxine Donahoe and I pulled him out. How's the Sedona weather," Eve asked, in an awkward attempt to change the subject.

*   *   *

At the Lemonnier post exchange, Gerald saw the same tabloid. Circulation of the magazines was over 30 thousand, which included most U.S. Military exchanges overseas. It was right next to ARAMCO Magazine, with his wife's glossy photo in full display on the front cover. His wife Eve was straddling a nearly naked man with sideburns in a very provocative position.

"Yeah, that's my Evie," he chuckled. When he called his wife at five a.m., it was 10:00 p.m. local time in Boulder. She responded and explained what had happened. The following morning at reveille, Sp-5 Ingalls came to the front of the formation. His platoon sergeant said, "Report to the Post commander as soon as we break formation!"

Gerald forgot about being nervous, sitting next to the adjutant's desk before seeing the base commander. He had rehearsed the conversation, mindful of what might take place. The door opened, and a lieutenant said, "You can go in now!" A tabloid magazine was on the Commander's desk with Gerald's wife on full display with the nearly naked man.

"Take a seat and tell me about it," the Commander said. Gerald laid out the essence of what his wife had told him the night before.

"OK, here's the problem," said the Commander as he sat back and filled his pipe.

"Once the civilian press gets ahold of the fact that your wife has a husband on duty at Camp Lemonnier, we'll have all manner of inquiries of what we're trying to accomplish. That's not acceptable!" Wide-eyed, Gerald wondered what he was supposed to do about it!

"I am aware," the Commander said, "A lie can travel halfway around the world before the truth can get its shoes on; the trouble is, neither one of us want to see your wife's photo plastered on every CLU (container living unit) wall. I will give it about three days. I'm going on record, putting you in for a transfer. Where would you like to go for permanent TDY?" The Commander blew pipe smoke toward the ceiling and waited for Gerald's response.

Gerald sat for a moment, then answered.

"I would rather remain here and perform my duties through the Information office as I have been doing. As for my wife, in my view, she did nothing wrong, sir. She was not inebriated, and she was fully dressed, and, in the end, she may well have saved a man's life. I'm very proud of her, sir!" The Commander tamped down his pipe and relit.

"I'll tell you what, Specialist Ingalls, I've been following your byline in the Stars and Stripes and here at basecamp. You have been performing your duties two ranks above your pay grade. Would you object if I put you in for a jump step promotion to Sergeant First Class?" Gerald fidgeted in his chair.

"Let me explain," the Commander continued, "I understand that you performed well during the evacuation of Juba City. I also know that you were deployed on a navy vessel for interdiction against Somali pirates two weeks ago. You came under fire on that mission in a combat situation. You deserve a Combat Infantryman's' badge (CIB). As for your wife's exposure, that doesn't distress me, but I am concerned about the ridicule that you may get. You should move to NCO quarters."

Gerald gathered his thoughts. "Yes, sir, that would be a welcome change." Then he changed the subject.

"As for the Stars and Stripes story, I was on that battle cruiser, standing next to a Phalanx CIWS when it cut loose on the pirate vessel. The Somalis aboard their boat were firing on us. I heard live rounds hitting the water, plunking against the hull, and cracking overhead. I fired my Lima toward the pirate vessel."

"There you go," said the Commander, "I have written endorsements of that, case closed." The Commander punched a button on his communication system.

"Lieutenant, could you get in here?" The Lieutenant circled the Commander's desk and had a few words with his CO. He brought a form on-screen at the computer and filled out the necessary information. In two minutes, he said to Sp-5 Ingalls.

"Would you come around here and punch the enter key?" Gerald jumped to his feet and went to the computer.

"When you hit this key," said the Lieutenant, "You're a Sergeant First Class with a CIB, Comprende?" The Commander stood and extended a hand toward him. The new SFC (Sergeant First Class) Ingalls shook hands and saluted.

"Go with the Lieutenant, and he will tell you what you must do to keep that rank through the duration of your enlistment. And another thing, give your wife our best." SFC Ingalls saluted again and followed the Lieutenant out of the Commander's office.

*   *   *

Following the summer Oil Conference in Denver, Eve called to make arrangements for a moving company to come in, pack up household items and have them drop-shipped to the Emery street house in Flagstaff.

"Let's you and I take a road trip," she said to M.D. "Stick with me; you and I have a few things to discuss." They stood aside as three ladies and a man packed up everything, including most of their clothes. A Yellow freight truck pulled to the curb and loaded their household goods. The housekeeper would clean up the place and call her supervisor.

Before she could begin, Eve placed five one hundred dollar bills into the woman's hand.

"Muchisimas gracias," said the housekeeper, and the two embraced.

"Do you think we can make it to Flagstaff? We may run into snow?" M.D. inquired.

"You'll have to trust me," Eve said, "If we run into complications, we'll chain up or hang loose somewhere along the route. I was a truck driver, remember." They planned to travel westbound on I-70 into Utah then south toward Moab on Highway 191.

"It's the scenic route," said Eve, "I've had my fill of interstate driving. I called Syl and told her that I was adopting you. Any objections?"

"Sure, why not? You're the boss," said M.D. As they sped along I-70, the weather held as they made a stop in Dillon. At Ruby Tuesdays, they had a late lunch, then continued to Grand Junction, spending a night at The Candlewood Suites.

In the complimentary breakfast nook, Eve told M.D. that she wished they could take it easy on the road once in a while with all the driving she had done with Jill Summers and Riley Baxter.

"I drove with each of them for weeks. Then after training, I signed on with the transportation company. We could never do this, have a nice trip, take our time and share conversation. One of us drove while the other slept, but this is bliss!" In Moab, Utah, they took another break, settling on coffee and lemon cake at Starbucks.

"M.D., you got sort of quiet after talking to Syl a few days ago. Is there anything that we need to discuss?"

"My Ex died," she said matter of factly.

"I'm so, so sorry!" Eve said, "You should have said something!"

"Being married to me was like trying to catch a forty mile an hour freight train. We were together so Mitch could father a couple of kids; I was always off somewhere when I wasn't pregnant. He raised them. They are grown now with children of their own."

"Oh, my gosh!" Eve said, "Shouldn't you be somewhere besides here?" M.D. explained that she hardly knew her grandkids.

"You have grandchildren you don't know? What are their names?" Eve asked.

"The two older ones with my son are Brook, and her younger brother is Ralph, George, something like that. I don't know the names of Shelly's two; I've never laid eyes on them. I have to go to the john!" M.D. rose abruptly from her seat and walked away. Eve sat bewildered by what her companion had said. When M.D. didn't return to the table, Eve looked for her.

"Let's just go, shall we," said M.D. sitting in the car. "I don't feel like discussing my private life!"

They traveled down to Bluff, Utah, in silence. When Eve got out to stretch, M.D. awoke from a fitful sleep.

"There's nothing here," Eve said. "Would you like to drive?" They switched places and motored on to Ganada, Arizona. Eve got out to pump gas while M.D. went to the convenience store. When she returned, Eve was on her cell phone.

"OK, could you meet us here? We're at the Speedway store junction 191 and 264; great, we'll see you when you get here." She was smiling as she ended the call.

"We're staying here tonight. My friend Hap from NAU lives nearby with her grandmother." Soon, an older model Mercury Marquis came alongside them on the gravel parking lot.

"I'd know your car anywhere," said Hap from behind the wheel. M.D. noted that she was a couple of years younger than Eve.

"Maxine Donahoe, this is Felicia Yazzie, Hap for short. I never caught the name of your grandmother," Eve said. Hap gestured to an ancient Navajo woman wearing an enormous black Stetson hat sitting in the passenger seat. M.D. thought she might be a dummy as she hadn't moved a hair's breadth.

"This is my grandmother Awena. It means sunrise." Hearing her name, the older woman turned and looked at the two strangers.

"Just follow me; we're about twelve miles from the house." As they waited for Hap to take the lead, M.D. turned to Eve with a probing look.

"What are we doing here?" Eve cut the tension by taking no notice and said nothing.

*   *   *

Trish Hays had an infant son and was ready for another child. Problems remained that her husband Les couldn't develop a sperm count. Trish arranged a fertilization clinic appointment. Checking their bloodwork panels, clinicians realized that Les Hays was not the father of Dax, the firstborn son. Blood matches between Les and Dax were not genetically consistent. The attending physician showed little alarm. This kind of thing occasionally happened during the last thirty years of his medical practice. When the Doc's lead nurse presented the results of the bloodwork, he responded, "Here we go again." It would be tricky for the medical team to couch their findings with Trish and Les. They would start by consulting with each of them separately, beginning with Les.

Les was nervous as a cat in a dog race as his appointment came around. He thought about findings that may surface, though he was not sure. Entering the waiting room, he slithered into a chair, making no contact at the reception desk. The clerk noticed Les from behind the counter and handed him a laptop questionnaire to complete.

"The doc can see you in about twenty minutes," she said. He came to the part about being suicidal on the questionnaire, nearly selecting the eight of ten choices on the scale. 'Crap,' he thought, 'Why do they ask such things? It's not like anyone would be honest.' He gave it a one on the check-mark boxes. Les rehearsed a few scenarios formulating a response when the doctor would ask questions. He went to the scale for weight and height measurements. He sat for the blood pressure check the air saturation test and answered a few questions in the examination room.

"Mr. Hays?" asked the clinician, "Why is the doctor seeing you today?"

"Paternity, no, no, I mean for a general check-up," he stammered.

The Doc swept through the door like he was there to greet an old friend.

"How are you doing?" he asked smiling, as he washed his hands. Les would play it coy and evasive. The Doc sat at the computer counsel, going over the bloodwork and precursory exams. Finally, he pushed his roller stool directly in front of Les.

"Mr. Hays," he said, "We both know that you are not the father of Dax. You had a vasectomy four years ago." There it was, out in the open for discussion.

"Yeah, that's true, but my wife doesn't know that," he said meekly.

"I have to be honest with both you and your wife."

"Trish will leave me if she knows the truth!" Les said.

"Hmmm, we'll play along with you if you believe your marriage hangs in the balance," the Doc said.

"Would you consider a reversal of the surgery?" asked the Doc. Les declined.

"There is another part to this deception Mr. Hays. We must rationalize how Trish became pregnant with Dax." There it was like a three-pound hammer had walloped the countertop.

"I don't think she had an affair. I did ask how she became pregnant! She told me she had insemination performed. She didn't say where or anything about a donor program."

"We have no record of that," said the Doc, "She may well have gone to another clinic. Let's leave it at that. We'll proceed with a sperm count test on you, already knowing the result." He let this sink in before continuing. "Then, we will give you and your wife some information on the sperm donor program. Does that sit well with you?" asked the Doc.

"It does," Les responded, and he was very much relieved.

While Les was at his appointment, Trish was on her phone trying to reach Eve. Somewhere between Boulder and Flagstaff, Eve had no phone reception. Trish was eager to make contact with someone who could locate Flynn. There was a fertilization facility in Paris at Centre Chirugical Ambroise-Pare. 'Wasn't Paris home to the French Foreign Legion,' she reasoned? Unsuccessful in her attempt to reach Eve, she would let the matter rest for an hour or two.

Trish's appointment with her doctor came three days following Les's appointment. She wasn't nervous. When the med-tech took her vitals, it was like school chums comparing report cards. The two were in deep discussion as the Doc entered the exam room. Trish gave the short version of how she had conceived Dax and wanted the same father for baby number two.

"The Doc may suggest IUI insemination at the clinic," said the tech.

"There's a catch," said Trish, "The donor that I want is in West Africa fighting Boko Haram terrorists."

"Well, that certainly complicates matters, let's give it some thought," the tech said. Trish countered that she had already given it a lot of thought as her doctor came into the room.

"Thought about what?" he asked.

"Well, you might as well know," Trish said, "I had a boyfriend from two years ago who fathered Dax. Les doesn't know, and I'd like to keep it from him."

"Do you want me to leave the room so you two can discuss this?" asked the tech.

"Hell no, stay where you are," Trish said. "I need to have another child from the same father. I'm thinking continuity. I don't want to compare apples and pinecones, and I want all apples."

"Could you please fill me in on what you're asking?" the Doc said. The assistant elaborated on what Trish had told her, including the part about the guy in West Africa. The Doc sat, taking it all in.

"If you can find the man, we'll take it from there," he finally said. Trish drove home from the clinic, leaving the Doc and his assistant wondering how to coordinate logistics.

*　*　*

When Trish finally got ahold of Eve, she and M.D. were on I-40 cruising toward Flagstaff. "I've been trying to reach you," Trish said. "Is there any way you can have Gerald get in touch with Flynn?"

"I think you're breaking up," said Eve, "I heard you say something about Flynn."

"I did!" Trish said in a panic. Eve listened as the car approached Winslow, Arizona.

"Wait a minute; I have to put something on the CD player!" Eve rummaged for her Eagles CD. "It's a compulsion of mine, 'Take it Easy' must be playing whenever I pass Winslow." Trish went on explaining about her crucial indulgence. "Uh-huh, yeah, OK, I get it, I'll be in touch," Eve said into the phone.

"Accept my heartfelt appreciation," Trish said, "We both have our agendas; yours is just a bit simpler than mine." M.D., watching the road as she drove, turned now and then, sneaking a peek at Eve as she communicated with her friend. Off her phone, Eve said, "I have to do something for Trish." "Like what?" M.D. asked.

"I have to get sperm from Flynn, fighting Boko Haram terrorists in West Africa, and get it to her."

"Oh, is that all!" M.D. snickered. "Considering my connections with Sebastian and the CIA, it would be a cake-walk!" They exchanged glances and laughed uproariously.

"You can't be serious," M.D. said, wiping away tears. "That's the first time I've ever heard you laugh uncontrollably," said Eve. "How does it feel?"

"Feels great. I should do it more," replied M.D.

They drove on west on I-40 with a new degree of friendship that surfaced between the two women. Pulling up to the Emery house, both women began unloading.

"I want to thank you," M.D. said, "for setting me straight. You were right; it isn't all about me! I've made some huge ripples in my life. Thanks to you, I'll learn how to survive the ripples. I promise you I won't drown. Just hang with me!" The two shared a moment of silence then Eve suggested a truce.

"You can talk to me about anything, and I'm here for you!" said Eve, "Just promise me, Maxine Donahoe, that you will stop beating up on yourself. Tomorrow is a new day."

In Ganada, while staying with the Yazzie family, Eve and M.D. hit on a physical and mental treasure trove. Eve stocked up on southwestern items made by Hap and her family. They had a flourishing business. Pottery, turquoise earrings, hand-woven rugs, and tapestries were displayed throughout the house. Awena Yazzie had created several wall hangings, and Hap was an artisan of silver and turquoise jewelry. M.D. bought gifts for her son and daughter's families.

It was a purging that M.D. appreciated, and she thanked Eve for stopping at Ganada for a visit. On the drive along I-40, they discussed that M.D. would shadow Eve as she attended Law school in Coral Gables. M.D. would soon learn that her children were owners of a thriving upholstery business in Perrine and not far from Miami University. She and Eve would take up residence a short drive from M.D.'s long-lost family.

Chapter 16

THE PLOT THICKENS

July 2017

Eve and school friends Hap and Laura sat at a large table sipping hard cider at her in-law's Sedona guest house. They were comparing class schedules for the summer session. Eve popped a question that startled Laura.

"I haven't heard much from Delmer lately," Eve said, "Are you two still an item?" She directed her question toward Laura, who appeared close-minded on the subject.

"To be honest," Laura replied, "We haven't seen much of each other lately. He's got a thing for Bev Berquist. Her family runs the Chevy dealership in Flag. Besides that, Del is, well, he's, Del if you get my drift. He doesn't turn my crank to use Del's form of the vernacular."

"I could tell you a little story about that, but I think I'll save it for later," Eve said.

"I'll hold you to it!" said Laura.

* * *

Temperatures on the horn of Africa hovered around eighty degrees as SFC Ingalls walked across the quadrangle with friends in the press section. Eve had phoned him late in the afternoon when he was off duty. They discussed the distance between them and tossed out ideas about getting together. Eve's in-laws wanted to visit Paris.

"What do you say we make a reservation for the Regence Etoile, right downtown surrounded by restaurants?"

"Wow, you have been thinking about this!" Gerald said.

"Your parents have stayed at the Regence Etoile and think it would be an excellent choice! The moon will be full, and I will be ready to mix it up with you for a baby!"

"Baby?" Gerald asked, "And the moon too?" After some pause for effect, Eve suggested, "Our baby, the one that could begin life in the City of Light!"

"I'm all in, and I have some leave time coming to get the job done," Gerald assured her.

"That's what I was thinking, and If at first, we don't succeed, we'll try, try again. I don't have my first classes until mid-July."

"Make your reservations," Gerald suggested, "I'll put in for my leave tomorrow morning."

*   *   *

Three pings in succession, the women's cell phones bore a text selfie of Del Cullen and Bev Berquist in front of Cesar's Palace, Las Vegas. Bev, with a raised hand, displayed a set of bridal rings. The message read, 'We're in Vegas, we got married!'

"That little shit!" Laura said, "He practices his spiel on me for more than a year, and I kept putting him off! He dates Berquist for three weeks, takes her to Vegas, and marries her?! That little shit!" Eve and Hap didn't touch the tête-à-tête as Laura continued with a few choice four-letter words. Eve asked, "Refills anyone?" They drank the hard cider in silence as Laura vented.

"I guess I should mention it," Eve said, "I feel responsible for leading Del on to you in the first place."

"How's that?" Laura wanted to know. She appeared to be thoroughly disgusted and ready to dig her nails into anything that moved.

"A couple of years ago, he tried to get in my boat," said Eve, "I gave him some advice on how to meet other girls."

"Oh no," Laura said, "Was that the elevator eyes thing?"

"Yes," said Eve, "Did he try it on you?"

"He did, but the elevator eyes stopped at my breasts; that's when I slapped his face! That's not all. After Jill and Chris's wedding, we ran over to the Ara Bella and got a room; 118 I believe it was."

"Oh my gosh," Eve said, "Gerald and I were above you in 218!"

"Oh, so that was you and Gerald rattling the light fixtures?" asked Laura. Both women smiled at one another, then started to laugh. Hap, innocent as the Easter bunny said, "Isn't love grand?"

That evening, Eve phoned Gerald. "Delmer Cullen got married," she said.

"So, Del finally got hitched to Laura; great!" he said.

"No, he married someone else," Eve said, "What!" Gerald asked, "Who?"

"You don't know her," Eve said, "She isn't a friend from NAU. She works at her father's Chevy dealership here in Flag." The conversation lingered about how strange it was, that life could turn on a dime. There were no guarantees.

"So, how's Laura taking all this?" Gerald wanted to know.

"She's putting on a good front, but underneath, I know she's hurting!"

"Not to change the subject, but your parents and I are flying out of Sky Harbor two days from now. You and I have a baby-making date in Paris. Speaking of that, have you been in contact with Trish Hays? She has her mind set on insemination from Flynn."

"How does she plan to bring that off?" Gerald wanted to know.

"I'm not sure," Eve said, "With Trish, anything's possible."

* * *

After talking to Eve, Gerald wondered how he could apply pressure to the FFL's 3rd Regiment and have one of their very own supply a sperm specimen to an American woman half a world away. Then it hit him, John Sebastian, the guy who could arrange anything short of flying a Piper Cub to the moon. Sebastian was as easy to reach as Eve had always been. 'Cell phones,' he thought, 'what a miraculous achievement in technology!'

"I've got a covert assignment that I need your help with," Gerald started to say as he contacted Sebastian. "Could you arrange a chain of custody courier for a package from Paris, France, to Fort Collins?"

"Containing what?" Sebastian asked.

"Here's where it gets tricky." Gerald laid out the operation exactly as Eve had related it to him. "All we need to do is get Flynn out of the Mali desert and to Paris, where the specimen could be collected."

"Suppose the man says no even if we can find him?" asked Sebastian.

"Once he knows what's going on, I don't think he will refuse," said Gerald.

"OK, give me a couple of days to flesh it out," said Sebastian, "It sounds like a challenge but doable. I love a challenge! We could tell him to do it for France; then, everyone would be on board! Hell yes, the Frogs would probably order him to Paris!"

Later that day, Sebastian called in a few markers. He knew operatives were working out of Bamako, the Mali Republic capitol. A contact attached to the French foreign service told Sebastian the operation would be easy if they played their cards right.

"Elements of the FFL, 3rd Regiment always march in the Bastille Day Military Parade, the Defile Militaire du 14 Juillet. They've been doing it since 1880," said the contact.

"How difficult would it be to have a Robert Flynn Collins on that duty roster?" asked Sebastian.

"I'll grease a few palms and get back to you." said his contact.

*   *   *

With arrangements made, there would be a timing strategy to consider. Eve called and told Trish that she would likely get her wish in late July.

"You mean this month?" Trish wanted to know. "Flynn will be in Paris for the Bastille Day Military Parade," Eve said.

"That would be perfect!" said Trish. Eve hesitated, carefully guarding her words.

"Difficult things are easy; the impossible takes a little longer." She said. "Don't hold your breath. It's a wonder that we could bring this thing off at all!" Trish was equally responsive, saying, "I'll contact my clinic and bring them up to speed. Nine months from July, Dax will be out of diapers; I like it!"

*   *   *

Flynn's Regiment had been patrolling along Africa's west coastal waters. The squad sergeant presented Flynn with a citation stating that he must be in Paris on Bastille Day. An asterisk led to another endorsement about taking part in a covert operation while Flynn was in the French capital.

Wondering what that could mean, he rested uneasily for a few days. His cell phone chimed with the identifying caller SFC Gerald Ingalls, Special Ops. The ensuing conversation lasted several minutes. Gerald said he would be the contact man for Flynn's Covert Operation in Paris.

"You? Why you?" Flynn wanted to know. It was a delicate matter, and Gerald explained the logistics using insightful and well-chosen words.

"Semen specimen, is that all?" Flynn asked.

"That's it." said Gerald, "Get your groove on for Trish Hays."

*   *   *

Eve and her in-laws had booked their flight to Paris. They flew from the Phoenix Sky Harbor Airport to Boston. They remained isolated at Logan airport for hours until connecting flights joined other transatlantic passengers. They were in a festive mood. The Delta flight on a Boeing 767 wide-body taxied toward takeoff. Cold rain slanted off portal windows and soon swept away as the aircraft gained takeoff speed and lifted. The wheel wells clunked shut for a six-and-a-half-hour flight to de Gaulle airport. An infant, small enough to be held in the seat with its mother, was cooing and soon fell asleep on the mother's bosom. Eve was eyeing the blending of mother and child.

"Don't worry dear, your turn is coming," said her mother-in-law. The two held hands and spoke softly. They were in love with the same man; one was his wife, and the other was Gerald's mother.

"I have so many plans, and I truly love your son," said Eve.

"When you two start having babies, it will be a fun-loving free-for-all; just you wait!" The sun shone brilliantly on a carpet of white as the plane broke through a carpet of clouds. Daylight faded to the west as flight attendants distributed neck pillows and blankets. Sleep was elusive. Eve would begin a new chapter for herself, her husband, and the family.

Gerald had taken a US Airforce C-130 flight from Djibouti to a NATO base near Sofia, Bulgaria. Transferring planes, the KLM flight to Paris, he arrived as his family left Boston for their long journey across the Atlantic. Gerald took ground transportation to the Regence Etoile, secured their two-room suite, showered, and made the place homey. He ordered room service and catnapped into the wee hours after midnight.

Eve fell asleep on the Atlantic crossing and dreamed. *She pulled her old flatbed truck loaded with people exposed to the elements. At high speed, those on the flatbed trailer were falling off, one by one, lost in a fog. All that remained were Hap and a few family members shouting for her to stop! She couldn't hear them but could see them in the rearview mirrors as wind and cold rain lashed at their faces and hair.* She was shaken awake.

Charles Ingalls came into view. Her father-in-law was jostling Eve's shoulder, asking softly, "Bad dream?" Coming fully aware, she said it was her lost dream. Charles inquired what her dream might have meant. Eve thought it had to do with the changes coming, law school, Aunt Syl, Gerald, and the pressure on herself. She looked at her father-in-law and pulled him close.

"Maybe I'm just a perfectionist, demanding too much of myself!" Charles consoled her, saying that people always put too much pressure on themselves.

"You and Gerald are going to be fine! You have your whole life ahead of you," he said. At that moment, Charles Ingalls became the closest man who would ever be a father figure to Eve. She liked the feeling, and she slept peacefully, her head on his shoulder.

Passengers awoke as the Airbus landed in early morning darkness and rain. Eve had always wondered what the signage meant at airports, ogL/27R, the terminology that meant nothing to passengers and everything to airline pilots. Did pilots see such things in their nightmares? She wondered. The plane nudged to a stop at the terminal as a cacophony of seatbelts snapped shut, and passengers rose from their seats. The progression of people heading down the aisles seemed endless. Then finally, "You ready?" Charles asked, "You first."

It was unlikely that Gerald would be at arrivals, considering the early morning hour. Terminal personnel had many questions as the Ingalls trooped through customs showing passports to no less than three attendants at different stations. Finally, one woman in uniform asked Eve, "Will you be in France long?" Eve stifled her response, not saying she would be in France long enough to get pregnant. Instead, she chose the higher ground saying, "Vacances" (vacation).

Even at the dark morning hour, Paris was still quite vibrant. The Ingalls' suite of rooms was on the fourteenth floor of an ultramodern high-rise. Views of both the Arc de Triomphe and Eiffel tower rose above the city several miles to the northwest. Both colossal structures were in a golden luminance of light. Gerald had met them at the door of their suite as Eve lightly knocked.

The first view of Paris from their room brought the younger couple to a tender embrace. Charles helped the Chasseur deposit baggage into the rooms. As Lynn crossed the bathroom entryway, she caught a mirror reflection of her son and daughter-in-law enfolded in ravenous passion.

"I think we should leave," Lynn whispered to Charles, "Looks like Eve and Gerald want to get reacquainted!" The two crept silently through the common doorway to their suite.

Lynn and Charles sat at a table for four in the Mayo Restaurant the following morning.

"My gosh," said Charles, "Do you suppose they will eventually come up for air?"

"Butter me one of those delicious-looking baguettes," Lynn said, "It's been months; Gerald and Eve will come down when they're good and ready. Right now, they need each other."

The Concierge suggested a brisk promenade among the neighboring shops for Charles and Lynn. They took the elevator to their fourteenth-floor suite by late afternoon, where remnants of food scraps on silver service were in front of Gerald and Eve's hallway door.

"Looks like they're taking nourishment," said Charles, "I'm sure they need it." Soon, they heard the shower running in the adjacent suite as they made plans for a couple of excursions. A knock at the suite door came at two o'clock in the afternoon. Gerald, in casual attire, stood, ready for the day, putting on a sheepish grin.

"Eve will be along in a half hour or so," he said. No sooner had he said this when there came an unexpected knock at the door.

Through the peephole stood a familiar clean-shaven face. It was Flynn! Along with him was a security officer who escorted Flynn to their door. On opening their door, the security officer said. "Adjudant-Chef Collins says he knows you." It was pretty obvious when Gerald took Flynn's hand, shaking it in disbelief.

"Oui!" Gerald said. The young men fell into conversation. In his dress FFL uniform and white Kepi under his arm, Flynn looked lean, tan, and muscular. He bore the rank of a Legionnaire who leads an infantry platoon. Following introductions, Flynn appeared unabashed against Charles' gaze.

"I'm trying to make the connection here," Charles said to them.

"Oh, you remember Flynn, our housemate in Fort Collins?" Then it swept over the older couple that this was the party animal who hung out with Gerald back in their wild days of Fort Collins.

"My Gosh," said Charles, "The French Foreign Legion?"

"Oiu monsieur," replied Flynn. After more banter, Gerald stated the obvious, "I wasn't expecting you!"

"I'm here on a covert operation." Said Flynn with a wink.

"Oh my God," said Gerald, "Have you already? "Before completing his question, Flynn said, "Yes, mission accomplished. I'll tell you about it later."

Eve came looking like a modern, rosy-cheeked Aphrodite through the adjacent suite door. The avalanche of words repeated itself. A nitrogen shipper tank containing four straws of Flynn's seed was barcoded and en route to the Fort Collins/ Loveland Airport that morning.

"You can thank UPS cargo, everything is shipshape," said Flynn. Eve and Gerald smiled at the older Ingalls. They were pretty curious about the conversation, trying to remain aloof. Stepping into the hall, Eve said, "We'll be just a minute," and she shut the door. The minute turned into more than an hour as the trio, Eve, Gerald, and Flynn, went to the Mayo Restaurant on the mezzanine.

"The plan was to meet at the Bastille Day Parade; you jumped the gun," said Gerald. Flynn informed his old friends that his Capitaine got wind of the ruse. He enlisted sixteen handpicked men to accompany Flynn to Paris and do their sovereign duty for France.

"When you get in touch with Trish Hays, tell her that the horse has left the barn," said Flynn.

"Just like that, you did this; I can't believe it!" Eve said, wide-eyed. Flynn mentioned that he had some inspiration. He pulled a folded photo of Eve straddling the Oil Exec in Denver from his uniform breast pocket.

"Oh my God said Eve, you mean you?" Before Eve completed her thought, Flynn said, "I just fantasized that I was the Oil Exec, but I was laying on my back instead of my stomach." Silence ensued.

"Can we just move along!" said Gerald. Flynn elaborated that thousands of American women seek semen donations from European men. Eve and Gerald looked at one another as Eve said, "Gerald and I prefer the old-fashioned method, Bucko!"

"Damn straight toots," replied her husband. As they laughed off the subject, Eve was curious about legal matters that Flynn might face.

"How about legal parentage?" she asked. Flynn said he had to sign a waiver of legal parentage at the donor center. On a note to accompany the sample, he did insist they include a message. 'Arielle, name her Arielle; if it's a girl, it means 'Lion of God.'

"If you could relay that to Trish as a backup, I would appreciate it."

The elder Ingalls entered the restaurant and spotted the threesome.

"May we join you?" asked Lynn.

"How about you, Flynn, in the here and now, do you have a girlfriend?" Eve persisted.

"I have a girlfriend I met on leave in Abu Dhabi last year. She is a sophomore majoring in Media Culture Communication at the NYU branch in Abu. I have a little more than two years remaining on my FFL contract, and then we plan to become an old married couple living in Europe after she graduates."

"So, what does a Foreign Legion Capitaine do after chasing Boko Haram around Africa?" Gerald asked.

"I've already applied for a position with the French Foreign Service. I have French citizenship by way of spilled blood. It came by that land mine wound I received south of Juba City. I'm currently on track to become an OCONUS Cat II French/Arabic Linguist. I have to brush up on my PowerPoint." He glanced around the table.

"Any more questions?" Flynn asked. The waiter came around offering menus to the new arrivals. Lynn and Charles declined, and Lynn insisted that they visit the Louvre.

*   *   *

At the Abilene ranch, Syl received a text ping from Eve. 'We saw the Louvre, threw kisses off the Eiffel Tower, and had a delectable 13' Haut Brion with Beef Tournedos at The Lasserre. By the way, Gerald and I anticipate an announcement!' Syl thought, 'Gee, I wonder what that could be,' then laughed. Texting her response, she sent notes about her progress in Coral Gables. Eve and M.D. would have a place to live, beginning for the fall semester at Law school.

*   *   *

Kim and M.D. had a meaningful rendezvous with M.D.'s family in Perrine. There were five grandchildren that she got to know. The children would refer to Maxine Donahoe as Mother M. Her daughter. Shelly was a bit standoffish at first. Her mother's strong personality fit with the notion that both women were alpha dogs, but the two warmed to one other quickly.

"I never knew why you and dad didn't live together," said her daughter.

M.D. answered that she loved Mitch, "I was always away on assignment somewhere in the continental US while your dad would be at home seeing to you and your brother. I tried to be more involved by joining the PTA, but it was an exercise in futility."

Once on a drug bust in Dallas, her cell phone rang, nearly blowing the operation. On the other end of the call was her eight-year-old son, wanting to know when she would come home. The situation prompted a sit-down reprimand from Maxine's AIC (agent in charge). The incident nearly cost her the job she had spent years training to do.

"How did one of your kids have access to your encrypted cell phone on a covert operation?" the AIC had asked. M.D. tried to explain that she gave the phone number to her young son in case of an emergency. The situation grew worse. Agents on field assignments cooked together, trained together and had heart affairs. It would be nothing physical though soul-binding and challenging to reconcile.

"When I would be home," said M.D., "I would be mourning for the kinship that I had with my fellow agents, and it was consuming me. Finally, I just stopped coming home, and your dad had his plans too. Mitch was only human. Single mothers knew one another and would have get-togethers, tossing around ideas on raising kids and the plethora of events that came with being a double parent. Mitch was an intelligent, good-looking guy; the rest became history.

"People can have a great capacity for love. The key to a great life is properly placing that love and respect. I've mourned the loss of relationships with different agent teams. I caught your father inauspicious circumstances on several occasions; I was with the FBI after all." M.D. gathered her thoughts and continued.

"When your father accused me of spying on him, we separated. I always sent a considerable portion of my earnings to our bank that your father could draw on. You and your brother wanted for nothing." M.D. paused, looked around at her grown family, and continued.

"I was selfish, I know," she said softly, "I regret not spending more time with you, but it just became a way of life. Then, Mitch died suddenly."

M.D. smiled in the attempt to fill her family in on personal responsibilities, knowing that it lacked substance. Then M.D. changed the subject.

"When you finally meet Evelyn Ingalls, my boss, and companion, you will adore her!"

"Are you her maid?" asked her grandson.

"I'm her protection first and foremost, but don't ever repeat that," she said with a wink.

"Why does she need a bodyguard?" asked her grown son. She told about Eve's husband, an Army sergeant serving in Africa. Eve would be alone. If someone weren't living with her. "Eve comes from a very wealthy family, and her Aunt Sylvia hired me to be her protector and housemate."

"Do you know karate?" asked another grandson.

"Yes, I do; as a matter of fact, I taught classes at the FBI training academy in Quantico, but don't tell anyone." Mother M smiled as she said, "Women should know how to protect themselves. It's nothing new."

*   *   *

Eve had a glow about her on the return flight from Paris that showed. Sitting in first class, she told her mother-in-law about the plan for the last semester at NAU. She also said how romantic the trip had been, elaborating around the edges of family planning.

"If I didn't know any better, I'd say you're pregnant," Lynn said with a raised eyebrow. Eve had a bright and ambitious response, "How could you possibly know that?" Lynn responded that Eve had a certain glow about her; she was a bit glassy-eyed and smelled like sweet, warm milk. Eve laughed. "You can tell all that just by sitting next to me?"

"You can correct me if you have a couple of months of the normal life cycle," chided Lynn. Eve took Lynn's arm, entwining it in her own, and smacked her lips against Lynn's temple.

"You're going to make a great grandma; you know that?"

Arriving at Sky Harbor in Phoenix, the Ingalls' party loaded up and headed toward Sedona. Before getting out of Phoenix, Eve called Trish and told her about their Paris encounter with Flynn.

"You can expect to hear about an LN2 canister showing up at your fertility clinic any day," Eve advised her.

"They already have it," said Trish, "It arrived yesterday. I love the name Arielle that Flynn suggested!"

Eve wanted to know how she planned to bring the clandestine operation off with Les; he didn't have the whole story.

"It will be easy, said Trish, "The professionalism of her fertility clinic would only say that the specimen was from an unknown European donor."

"Uh-huh, "Eve said, "But you and I know the truth! How are Gerald and I supposed to weigh in?"

"We'll cross that bridge when we come to it," said Trish. "Right now, I'm supposed to monitor my temperature and give pee samples to the clinic. Other than that, it's a matter of waiting for ovulation."

"Sounds like you're ready for this!" said Eve.

"I'm ready, Les is ready, and the baby room is ready, Woo-woo!" The phone reception crackled as the travelers climbed out of the Phoenix basin on I-17 and headed toward Sedona.

"Love you, kid!" said Eve.

"Back at you!" Trish responded.

*   *   *

Eve and M.D. returned to the Flagstaff, Emery street house following a weekend celebration in Sedona. They were bubbly about M.D.'s newfound family ties in Florida. They looked forward to resettling in Coral Gables in the late summer. Eve would have an easy schedule of class time to meet graduation requirements. The LSAT had come in April, and she passed with flying colors.

Eve had one five-hour class and four-hour, plus industrial arts for the final summer semester. She would be taking Linguistics, Topics of film and media, and the Art of French-Polish Cabinetry as her elective. Her upper-division classes were in round table formats. As a rule, only eight to twelve people would be in class along with the professor. She thought it might present some problems at first but was willing to wait and see what shook out. In her prior years at NAU, one of her professors took Eve aside and suggested that she take her place in the back of the lecture room. Wondering why, she asked, "Why would I do that?" The professor came back with a stunning revelation.

"Miss, don't be coy with me. You are 'D-E-C' in case you haven't noticed."

"D-E-C," Eve repeated the term.

"It's what we in the trade consider distracting eye candy. Some of your fellow students will be paying more attention to you than to me!" Well, there it was; Eve was categorized as a distraction and had never heard the term 'D-E-C.' There was no place for her to hide in the round table lecture configuration. The boys would have to put their ineptitude aside.

Linguistics was interesting, and Eve wondered why she had not taken the class before. The English language was not as phonetically correct as Spanish, but it was close. Topics of film and media turned out to be a history of cinema and how it influenced American culture. It might have some application in a courtroom setting, or so Eve thought. The industrial arts class on French Polish Cabinetry would extend what her great Uncle Alfred taught her in his Carter Lake woodshop. It would be something fun and creative. It would take her mind away from the nuts and bolts of other classwork.

Above all, time was on her side, and there was a bun in the oven.

Chapter 17

DANCING WITH THE DEVIL

August 2017

"Papa, we got the job done!" These were the first words out of her mouth when Eve contacted her husband. She and Gerald congratulated each other and set a timeline for parental goals. She already had a sign in the back window of her Alpha Romeo, 'Baby on board!'

Gerald had only six months remaining on his Army enlistment. Once he rotated back to state-side duty, he would be a short-timer. Online briefings taught Gerald how to act as a mid-rank field-grade NCO. His honorable discharge would come in February of 2018. Juggling military duties with Eve and a newborn child would be an exciting transition. His wife would be in law school, and he could discover new challenges in the civilian world. A future in the State department was always a possibility.

Sebastian would lay the groundwork for Gerald to work in the foreign service following his discharge from the Army. There were no specific requirements about education level, academic major, or proficiency in a foreign language. All this aside, Gerald would have the Army's guarantee of four years of higher education. The G.I. bill was on the table if he could manage his time with proficiency and decorum. Gerald and Eve aimed to pursue the Miami University course catalog in the coming months and nail down his career path. On the phone to his wife, Gerald laid out the next few weeks with his wife.

"If we could manage the timing aspects," he said, "It would be a cake-walk if we could get the ball rolling"

"You will be on orders for an Army post near Miami? That sounds like an answer to prayer," Eve said.

"Yes, it's almost too good," said Gerald, "But there it is; John Sebastian had something to do with it. All that aside, the baby thing is all I've been thinking about these last few days. Be careful and know that you two are in my thoughts, Evie; you and the munchkin you're carrying." It was all speculation as Gerald still had a few weeks to wrap up his duty assignment at Lemonnier.

Several courses of study interested Gerald when he got out of the Army. Political science and Central European, East European, and Eurasian studies. He did have a rudimentary knowledge of the Afar Somali language group, Danakil, Adali, and Odali. He had acquired some local language proficiency on assignments near Lemonnier. The MASH unit would set up medical inoculation sites, and Gerald would take photos of the local African kids getting vaccinated. He could move around the Horn of Africa and live on the economy while on assignment. Gerald soon found out that he could not be friends with his subordinates; he must be a leader and enforcer. With any profession, people are better led and not pushed. He learned to delegate authority with the help of the Officer in charge of the press section.

Gerald's OIC (Officer in charge) was a graduate of Texas Southern University. She had applied for a direct commission as a second lieutenant and trained at the Army Information School like Gerald. Their working relationship and background gave the two a starting point in the wacky world of journalism. Military writers were the ugly red-headed stepchild of civilian journalism. The Public Affairs Office (PAO) would clear all news copy meant for public readership.

Gerald's boss was good to work with and down to earth in assessing Gerald's problems.

"You gotta slap that boy upside of the head," she would say when he couldn't get a solid response when giving an order to one of the men.

They were talking about SP-5 Ron Bacon. His friends called him 'Pig.' He worked at the five-watt radio station that broadcast a short distance to the camp perimeter.

A celebrity would be performing as part of the USO tours that frequented overseas military bases. Among them would be a starlet/vocalist, Jackie Emerson.

"All you gotta do for the interview Pig is get her to say, 'Hi, I'm Jackie Emerson, drive safely'! How hard could that be?" It was troubling that Pig wouldn't commit to such a gravy assignment. The starlet, Emerson, made most soldiers sweat testosterone when laying eyes on her, yet, Pig wouldn't budge.

"I'm not going to be doing that!" he would say to SFC Ingalls.

After reveille one morning, the Lieutenant approached Gerald in the mess hall at the NCO table. She pulled a chair out from the table, turned it backward, and straddled it, taking a seat.

"I've got an assignment for you, Sergeant Ingalls! I want you to do a story with photos on Pig interviewing Jackie Emerson."

"I'm listening," said Gerald.

"On Pig's D.D. form 22 66, I see that he's from rural Butte Montana. Do the story and send it to 'The Montana Standard newspaper. You will find the name of the features editor in the online Ayres directory. If that doesn't make him budge, put him on detail." The Lieutenant told Gerald to have a good day and returned to the officers' table.

"Just put a boot in his ass! "said another NCO sitting across from Gerald.

Two Chinook choppers arrived from Djibouti two days later with entertainers on board, with Jackie Emerson. Escorted to the Company dining hall, there would be a photoshoot with the starlet and other dignitaries with the troops. Gerald had taken Pig along to help carry lighting equipment to the shoot. Milling among the entertainers was a young man, the group publicist. Gerald shook hands with the guy asking how he and his assistant could help.

"This place reminds me a lot of Montana," said the publicist, "Dry, big sky and no shade!" Pig piped up, saying, "Montana, huh, that's where I'm from!" The two commiserated on life in Montana. Miss Emerson came alongside the two.

"Could you please tell someone that I could use some water!" she said. Pig, bold as brass, says, "I can get you, water ma'am!" With his camera at the ready, Gerald snapped a dozen photos of Pig helping Miss Emerson.

"You're my hero, "she said. She clutched Pig to herself, kissing him on the cheek. Still in her grasp, he looked down at her.

"Would you be available for a short interview after the photoshoot?" he asked.

"Sure," Emerson said, "Just tell me where and when!"

"Our radio station is in building 970, two doors east."

"Which way is east?" Miss Emmerson asked. Taking her hand, Pig said. "Come with me!" Gerald had shot a dozen photos of the two. He turned to the publicist, saying, "Well, I guess that settles that!"

"She's one of the most down-to-earth people you'd ever want to meet," said the publicist.

"Appears so," said Gerald, "I didn't have to say a word, and my associate is getting his interview."

*   *   *

Trish and Les's appointment with the fertility clinic would address IUI insemination. She insisted that her husband should go with her to the clinic. Les knew they were starting the process of getting his wife to conceive a child. He had no idea that the doner, Flynn, was known to his wife. An anonymous donor was all he heard when it came up in a discussion. Trish's temperature and labs would see her ovulate in early September.

The LN2 canister would keep Flynn's specimen potent for weeks with an eighty percent fertilization guarantee. There seemed to be no hurry in the process. From now on, it was up to Trish and her cycle readiness for the insemination procedure. With a September pregnancy, she would deliver sometime in June of 2018. The firstborn son Dax would be walking and out of diaper mode.

Les Hays anticipated a new baby with enthusiasm. Anyone could be a father to his way of thinking; not every man would be a good daddy. He and Dax were couch buddies, spending hours together during the week. He read several books on Trish's body changes when she carried Arielle.

"Suppose it's another boy," he would ask Trish on occasion. Trish would always say, "It won't be another boy; I won't allow it!"

"Well, all right then," Les would say, ending the discussion.

*   *   *

"Would there be room for three kids in your sandbox?" asked Eve in a phone call. She informed Trish that she and Gerald were expecting a bambino.

"I don't see why not. Are you pregnant?" asked Trish with some surprise.

"High as a kite," Eve answered, "Gerald knows; I call him with weekly updates."

"Wow, that's huge, both of us, mid-twenties, soon to have three munchkins between us! Who would have thought? So, tell me all about it!" insisted Trish. "Was it the Paris trip?"

"You can bet on it. Gerald and I hardly left our hotel room. His parents knew what we were up to and left us alone. We were on a mission! I'm here to tell you that 'honeymoon-itis' is real! We were making up for lost time!"

"I have something I want to share with you," Trish said, "It's been gnawing at me for some time, and I need to come clean."

"Well, there's no time like the present!" said Eve. There was a protracted interval as Trish gathered her thoughts.

"Well, it's like this; it could be a deal-breaker on our relationship. I'm not sure if I'm ready to risk it quite yet."

"Oh, now you've gone and done it, leaving me to hang on a hypothetical!" said Eve.

"I'll give you this much," Trish said, "It involves money, not sex or anything like that." "Such a relief," Eve said, then she cut Trish short for more conversation.

"I've got to run. We'll talk later in the week." Eve was running late and bicycled to her two o'clock class. Disappointed but not deterred, Trish would table her admission of stealing from Eve's in-laws.

*   *   *

Bicycling to class on Wednesday, Eve was on her headset phone with Gerald. A 'Baby on board, sign attached to her bicycle seat. Along her way, she surmised that she might have to live out of the country if Gerald was sent to a foreign service site away from the U.S. American missionaries, ex-patriots, and working-class people lived on foreign soil with their families, and so could they if it became necessary. It was a sign of the times for the adventurous and strong-willed. Maxine Donahoe often came up in conversations between Eve and Gerald. She asked Gerald about M.D. in her next phone call.

"What would she do? We're like sisters!" said Eve.

"We'd take her with us to Florida!" Gerald said. We'll cross that bridge when we come to it. M.D. may decide to stay in southern Florida with her son and daughter's families. The best-laid schemes of mice and men go awry," Eve said, quoting Robert Burns. As she rode along, the discussion morphed into concerns about cash flow.

Eve was on the clock with Mildenhall Oil for a generous monthly subsidy. Gerald would have his tuition and fees paid by the Army following his discharge.

"We'll get by," Eve said faintly into her headset.

"You don't sound like your ole' self, anything wrong?" Gerald asked. There were intermittent pauses with muffled sighs from Eve. Reestablishing the conversation, she said, "I had to stop and barf. I've had morning sickness for several days now."

Eve had a regular route to her first eight o'clock class in Linguistics. She would bike to a massive flower pot outside the Language Arts building and vomit. School chums knew enough to avoid the area; Eve's regular spittoon for her morning hurl. M.D. wasn't far behind where she could stick with her companion, get her squared away, and on to class. The morning sickness would go on for the first trimester and then some.

"I don't even have the satisfaction of a hangover," Eve would say to M.D.

"It will be over soon," she was reminded, "Just think of the little munchkin you will have at the end of your distress." The coaxing and encouraging did some good, but Eve pined away for her husband. At her lowest times, she was grateful to have M.D. Eve saw that her assignments were completed and turned in on time. The industrial arts class was a Godsend! It gave Eve some downtime from all the reading and classroom lecturing.

Eve was ahead of her woodworking class because of her instruction as a young girl in Uncle Alfred's woodshop. Her French polish finish went on her project to the envy of others. The tabletop had an iridescent, three-dimensional glow, like the neck of a mallard duck. It gleamed! In the same class were Laura and Hap. Laura worked on the undercarriage, and Hap saw the steam bending of hickory legs for the table they were building. On completion, the project would go to Hap's showroom in Ganada.

Once in a while, Aunt Syl would drop by Flagstaff with her legal secretary. They would mark the passing of time toward Eve's commencement. Then reality would set Eve feeling distressed. Graduation was coming, and her husband would miss it.

"Yes, Gerald will miss your graduation, but he won't miss the celebration," her Aunt Syl would remind her.

The table project in shop class turned out to be useful, well designed, and practical. It was 30" high, 48" long, and 13" deep. They constructed it from African and South American hardwoods, walnut, and steam-bent hickory legs. A blue ceramic tile, set on point, was inlaid at the center, and there was a matching lower shelf. Their instructor gave them an A-minus because it was a team effort. Eve thought to argue that they should have received an A, but Hap squashed the idea.

"Save it for the courtroom counselor," she advised, "Besides, you've got a baby bump, no stress!"

*   *   *

Presenting the table to Hap's grandmother was a tribal affair. The matriarch, easy to smile, had a field day! The Yazzie family attended the spring weekend with fry bread, honey, wheat sprouts, and a delectable meat dish.

The rambling single-story adobe-style home where Hap grew up had no less than forty cars and pickups in front of the house all afternoon. When the grandmother learned of Eve's condition, she felt her abdomen and said, "Niyaazh!" Looking around apprehensively, Eve saw Hap staring at her.

"A son, Awena says you're going to have a son!"

Eve turned to the grandmother and embraced her fully in front of the younger kids who had gathered around. As late afternoon sun sent streaks across the red stone arroyos, it was time to leave.

"Why don't you come to our place for the night so we can decompress" suggested M.D. "I'll drink to that," Laura said. Eve wanted to know the meat dish with the turkey flavor served with red chilis and cumin.

"Prairie dog," Hap replied.

*   *   *

Flynn was out on patrol in central Africa with two armored cars and fourteen troops under his command. The vehicles bumped along in the open desert, looking for any sign of enemy combatants. Off to the south, a heavily loaded Toyota pickup, its suspension inverted with weight, held several women, a couple of goats, but no men.

"Nous ferions mieux de verifier ca," (We better check this out) said Flynn to his men. They rolled to a stop alongside the pickup, and troops exited the vehicle taking up positions. With a lite inspection of the passengers, Collins demanded, "Ou sont tes hommes?" (Where are your menfolk?). The women looked at one another apprehensively, gesturing toward the direction of travel. On further inspection, they found that the vehicle's undercarriage was laden with boxes of small arms, rifles, and rounds of ammunition. As Flynn ordered his men to confiscate the munitions, the women wailed! Their men were in danger of being killed or captured by rival tribes. The turf war over desolate landscapes always puzzled Flynn. With the nearest water wells miles away, why would there be so much fighting? It was decided they allow the women to travel on, sans the weapons cache. As the A.C.'s fired up their diesel engines and stayed on course, the Toyota pickup truck made a U-turn reversing direction.

"Tete de voyageur!" (trouble ahead) Collins said to the troops, "Reste attentif!" (stay alert).

The A.C.'s came under heavy fire from small arms and RPG rocket grenades by evening. Enemy combatants were among a series of low-profile buildings set against a darkening sky. At a range of two hundred meters, the legion gunner opened up with the 90mm Sagaie, providing grazing cover for the FFL troops. Legionnaires fanned out to the left and right flanks, diving for cover. The air whip-lashed with the solid roar of tracer rounds as the heavy firefight ensued.

Minutes later, a small white flag of surrender appeared from the village. Communication crackled on the headsets as Flynn yelled for a cease-fire. He guided a five-person squad toward the direction of the surrender flag. Setting up an L.P. (listening post), they dug in.

"Pourrait etre un piege," (could be a trap) Flynn told the men as they took cover. The dust settled from the horrific dust storm created by the guns. The second fighting vehicle was set up at a flank position and sighted on the white flag. They waited and spied for enemy combatants with night scopes. A heavily armed V-22 Osprey aircraft arrived on station and landed by dawn. Onboard was SFC Gerald Ingalls with his camera, Lima rifle, and a heavily armed squad of U.S. marines.

The Osprey commander told Flynn that the terrorists had melted into the jungle during the early morning hours before daylight. The opposition forces of Boko Haram had fled, and there was no tactical air support to pursue them.

"You're bleeding!" barked one of the Osprey gunners as he stepped toward Flynn. An Army medic looked at Flynn's head as he doffed his field cap. Blood surged down the right side of Flynn's face saturating his ear and running onto his shoulder. The medic strongly insisted it could be a brain bleed and added that she had another man down with a sucking chest wound.

Whipping a field phone to his ear, the C.O. said, "We need medivac, guide on my coordinates!" His next order was for the Marines and their FFL NATO allies to comb the village for casualties. The morning sun was rising faster than anticipated; there was much to do.

Flynn caught the eye of SFC Ingalls, saying, "Toi encore?" (You again?), then fell against the medic as both slithered to the ground. The energetic field doc lay sprawled under Flynn's right leg.

"Not so fast, general; you'll have to wine and dine me first!" The medic scrambled to her feet, looking down at the prone warrior. The FFL unit fell into formation and did a nose count. Flynn and a corporal lay wounded after the battle. They needed medical attention, and they needed it soon.

As the medivac choppers arrived, the medic insisted that she may have to tap Flynn's skull.

"Too much pressure on his brain, and this guy could go into seizures!" she said.

"Hold on, hold on," shouted Gerald above the roar of the Osprey props, "The MASH unit is only twenty minutes away!" The medic looked at Gerald, "He may not have twenty minutes!" Flynn regained consciousness and looked at the two saying, "I'll chance to make it to the field hospital!" While he remained conscious, the medic asked him, "Do you know what day this is and where you are?" He answered, "C'est mardi et je suis dans le desert." She looked at Gerald, "What the hell did he say?"

"He said he's in love with you and wants you to have his children." Staring daggers at Gerald, he rephrased his answer, "It's Tuesday, and he's in the desert." The wounded FFL grunts were loaded onto the medivac and flown northeast to Lemonnier.

"I should report you to your C.O. for sexual harassment," teased the medic to Gerald, "but not today!"

*   *   *

In Pig's billet at Camp Lemonnier, the sleepy soldier rose out of his bunk for reveille. The Squad Sergeant took a nose count and relayed several orders for the day.

"Before we dismiss, I want you to get on your computers and bring up the 'Montana Standard' newspaper in Butte. We have a celebrity in our midst!" After breakfast in the dining hall, two of Pig's buddies came to his table; they sat and congratulated him on the story, page three of his hometown newspaper. Opening his email, Pig found several messages from home about him and Jackie Emerson. A trio of photos under page three masthead displayed Pig, with Miss Emerson, a second of her kissing him on the cheek, and the third photo of them holding hands outside the Lemonnier dining hall. The caption read, 'Local boy meets celebrity Jackie Emerson in Africa.' Facebook hits came from people who remembered him from high school. His mother's photo was also prominently displayed. She wore a wide smile with the caption. "That's my boy!"

As SFC Ingalls looked at the photo review of Pig, he thought, 'That's why I'm here, to bolster the morale of our troops.' The photo session would bring more Camp Lemonnier Army personnel to the Information Office for their fifteen minutes of fame. Well, almost.

Some of the guys were reluctant to give attention to themselves from half a world away. Gerald was among them and shared their feelings. If he received too much publicity, it translated that he and many other men had wives and girlfriends back home alone.

*   *   *

The incident transpired to a fiasco between M.D. and a lowlife man who attempted to make a move on Eve in Flagstaff. It started innocuously enough. An acquaintance of Laura Griffee overheard her say something about Eve living in the Emery street house while Gerald was in Africa. A man smitten with Eve made the wrong assumption that she might need his attention. The attention amounted to the world-class line, "Let's get together. What your husband doesn't know won't hurt him." It came in an anonymous phone call. Unfortunately for the would-be suiter, M.D. had answered the phone. Not realizing this, the guy spouted his line. M.D., not amused, suggested she and the guy get together for a coffee and see what might transpire. As she told Eve, it came as a shock that someone would be bold enough to move into her personal life while Gerald was out of the picture.

"So, what did you tell him?" asked Eve. She looked up from her computer wearing blue blocker glasses, a chenille robe, and bunny slippers.

"I told him that Friday, 5:00 p.m. at Starbucks would be fine and that I'd be wearing tactical gear and carrying a can of mace." The next evening, the guy came on a bit bolder.

"Come on, babe; your husband has been away so long, you're out of practice. I can help!" This time, Eve had answered the phone. She hung up, but the phone calls persisted. The fourth time the call came, Eve and M.D. expected the phone call. This time he said, "I hate to see a woman like you practicing monogamous sex, don't you agree?"

"OK big boy, I'll be at the Paramount Café tomorrow at 8:00 p.m., bring a friend!" Then Eve silenced her phone. Earlier, she had called the phone number she was given by John Sebastian when she might feel threatened. Sebastian set it all up and checked out the location where the meeting was to take place. The stage set, Eve was at a table in the corner and M.D. at an adjacent table with her back to Eve. The guy walked up and sat at the table across from Eve. He slipped Eve a key card for room 422 at the Holiday Inn. Bold as brass, he said, "You're even better looking than I thought!" Playing it coy and evasive, Eve let the guy dig himself in a little deeper.

"Where's your friend?" she asked. "I thought this was going to be a menage a trois." As she said these words a bit loud, out walked Sebastian from the kitchen along with two burly men. M.D. slid her chair around and faced the guy.

"You know, sport, I don't like people pushing in on my territory." With this, she gave Eve a big wet kiss on the lips. The two men with Sebastian sat on either side of the guy and gave him fair warning. They were speaking softly enough that Eve couldn't make out their conversation. The guy stood, backing away from the scene. Sebastian took pictures of the guy getting into his car his license plate and handed him a note. As the sting broke up, Eve asked Sebastian what he had written in the message.

"Nothing you would want to know," he answered.

Chapter 18

HOMECOMING

September 2017

Trish paid a surprise visit to Eve and M.D. in Flagstaff as they were packing boxes for the move to Florida. Unexpected, there was an air of foreboding as Trish knocked on Eve's door.

"Well-well," Eve said her old chum, "What brings you to Flag? You didn't say you were coming."

"I was in the neighborhood," Trish said as the two sat in the kitchen.

"Yeah, right, you were in the neighborhood; tell me another." M.D. came into the room with her backpack and chimed into the conversation.

"And who might this be?" She asked.

"Sorry, I guess you haven't met my housemate," Eve said, referring to M.D.

"Oh yeah, the one who wears tactical gear and carries a can of mace around, I've heard about you!" Walking to the door, M.D. turned and said, "I'll be a couple of hours; I have to meet Sebastian." Both women at the table waved and nodded as M.D. left. Trish wanted to talk to Eve in person, and it couldn't wait.

"So, how you feeling," both asked in unison, then laughed.

"I'm doing fine. Baby Henry is due in March. I feel like there's a waddle in my steps; how about you? "asked Eve. She was more than a little curious why Trish would make such a long trip unannounced.

Trish talked about IUI insemination. "It's kind of like making love to a soda straw in a roomful of people, and I don't recommend it! My due date, is in June." With these milestones marked on their calendars, Trish brought up the sore subject of money.

"Remember," asked Trish, "When I was working at First National in Fort Collins, and you hosted at the Silver Grill?" Trish told her friend about the heist she made from a safety deposit box. Eve had her elbows glued to the table, both hands over her mouth.

"You robbed a safety deposit box?" she asked.

"Well," Trish said, "It wasn't just any safety deposit box; it was the Ingalls', Charles, and Lynn's. But there's more." She told Eve about the envelope with $100K and Gerald's name on it. Hard to follow, Eve had Trish repeat some elements of her story. Trish, Les, and the bank president were attempting to make up for the Ingalls' loss.

"It's not like we need the funds, but where is the money now," Eve whispered aloud.

"Well, I gave fifteen hundred dollars to you for driver school, and you paid Katie and Alfred for your lodging with some of the money."

"Humm, so now I'm mixed up in this too?"

"Well yeah," Trish said, "but I didn't tell you the true source of the money. I told you that I won it gambling in Black Hawk. That was a lie."

"So, what are you proposing?" Eve asked.

"The Ingalls don't know that I did the deed. They think someone stole the money from a holding company in Cincinnati."

"You lost me again," Eve said. For the next half hour, Eve was enlightened about the end game of Trish's underhanded theft. Eve furrowed her brow and got up from the table.

"I'm making coffee," she said, "You want some?"

"Sure," said Trish," Answer this; why on earth would you want to name your baby 'Henry'?" Eve looked up from her coffee-making activities and asked, "Why are you changing the subject?" Trish responded, "It's what I do when things get messy, I just thought you should know about my mischief." Eve returned to the table, taking a similar posture as she had before.

"After I tell Gerald, I'm sure he will have an opinion on the matter," said Eve, "He and I don't keep secrets from one another. It can wait until I move to Coral Gables and he comes home on leave. I will say this much; we will level with Gerald's parents and take it from there."

*   *   *

Propwash scattered debris as the Blackhawk touched down at the Lemonnier field hospital. When the C.O. called in a Nine Line (emergency), the Army medic with Flynn assisted on the flight. SFC Ingalls was aboard the chopper as well.

"This guy and I go back to a stateside friendship," he said into the headset. He was referring to Flynn, who had regained a degree of consciousness. The medic looked at him and shrugged, saying nothing. She checked Flynn's eye dilation a couple of times during their twenty-minute flight.

"He should be fine," she finally said, and Gerald nodded. The sucking chest wound patient would do OK as well. The medic had applied a large field compress to the wound, and the soldier displayed no symptoms of unequal chest size or bulging neck veins. Looking at Flynn's hands, they had good color, nothing blue.

"No one's going to die today," the medic said to Gerald. In the field hospital, Gerald caught the medic's arm.

"I'm sorry for what I said back there; I have a wife, sorry if I offended you!"

"No harm, no foul," she said, "I'll take good care of your buddy. Why is he in the Legion?" she asked.

"I'll bring you up to speed about Robert Flynn Collins as soon as I report to the Legion Commandant about his men.

"We have two of your people at the Lemonnier field hospital," he told Flynn's commander by field phone. "I will get back to you following medical evaluations." The phone conversation went over several exchanges before reaching the FFL Commandant.

"Qui sont-ils?" asked the Commander. Guessing that he wanted the identities of his soldiers, Gerald complied with the names of Flynn and the other man. He flinched, wondering if he got it right about the man with Flynn; his Russian was abysmal.

Later in the press compound, Gerald downloaded his aerial photos onto a computer. He wondered why pockets of armed resistance were moving south from the morning skirmish. Several conclusions came to his attention while he briefed a cadre of S-1 field officers.

Enemy contact had demanded the attention of NATO forces while something else was brewing. And so, it was. Reports came over the wire services that three hundred schoolgirls had been captured in Lagos, Nigeria. Attacks against the NATO task force south of Djibouti had been a coverup. Intelligence sources and satellite surveillance came to the same conclusion. Boko Haram and their captives melted into the sub-Saharan landscape.

Africa is a vast country, and NATO forces had control of a small percentage of the territory. 'It's like playing Wham-O,' Gerald thought, Quell one disturbance, and a much larger one pops up two thousand miles away. These futile exercises had almost cost Flynn his life on two occasions. He would try and talk his Legionnaire buddy into retirement. The 'spilled blood' clause in Flynn's contract with the FFL would likely be honored if he pushed the paperwork. Perhaps the medic and Flynn's doctors would convince him to end his military obligation. He had the option to continue life somewhere in Europe, the United Arab Emirates, anywhere but Africa as an expendable grunt.

*   *   *

Far away in Arizona, Sebastian and his network would have a get-together in Flagstaff. M.D. met Sebastian on the same afternoon that Trish had dropped by the Emery street house. In her turning class, she had several pots ready to fire. The bug bit her at the Yazzie home in Ganada. Her pieces lacked the finery created by Hap, but it was a start. Leaving them in her cubby, she bicycled over to meet Sebastian. Removing her bike helmet at the midtown Starbucks, she saw John Sebastian in his usual floral-colored shirt and shorts.

"I knew what you would want, so I ordered for both of us," he began. The two sat dead center in the coffee shop, M.D. faced one door, and Sebastian sat facing the rear door.

"Old habits die hard, don't they?" he said.

"Sure do," M.D. responded, "So what's up? I know you didn't need a Caramel Macchiato." "That's what I've always liked about you, M.D.; you come right to the point," Sebastian asked how things had gone, living with Eve and safeguarding her through the months. For the most part, things were going well, but M.D. missed the rush of collaring the bad guys and living out of backpacks with the team. They debriefed about the sting operation with the sex predator trying to hit on Eve.

"That was quite a performance, you smacking Eve on the lips, anything to it?"

"It was all theatre," M.D. replied, "Just rubbing it into the perp." Sebastian brought up a few significant factors about M.D.'s future.

"You know, you're pushing early retirement. Is that on your radar?" M.D. said she would like to hang on to her assignment with Eve stick around until Henry was born. Sebastian, a bit astonished, said, "Henry, why Henry; strange name for a newborn these days."

"Everyone asks that; Eve and Gerald have their reasons. I think it has something to do with Gerald's lineage."

"Here's the deal," Sebastian said, "Syl Mildenhall underwrites your current assignment. She asked me to pull strings so you would have the position. Are you getting bored, and do you want to get back into the game?" M.D. pondered her future for several seconds before responding.

"You know, John, if I follow Eve down to south Florida, it's always open season on the kingpins. It would be a great cover for teamwork; I would be in the shadows."

"I can't argue with that." said Sebastian, "And do us both a favor, don't tell Eve about our conversation. We don't want her feeling pressure that you might leave. Sebastian's thoughts strayed to Gerald and his contemporaries in Africa.

"I'd like to hook Gerald up with a few contacts that could launch his future; stay in touch." The two separated, M.D. exiting the front door, and Sebastian went out the back door.

*　　*　　*

A Navy corpsman and the Army medic were consulting about Flynn's care. He would only be in the MASH unit a few more days, then booted back to his FFL Regiment.

"Do you know anything about his stateside background?" asked the medic.

"When he was in here a while back, he mentioned something about his life in Colorado," answered the corpsman.

"When we brought him in, he said something about a girlfriend in Abu Dhabi. Should we try to reach her and let her know about Flynn?"

"You like this guy, don't you?" asked the corpsman.

"No, I just thought someone should know he's in our unit and could process back to civilian life."

"It's against protocol to get involved with these guys," said the corpsman, "Especially the FFL grunts. I wouldn't take anything too serious about what he may have said in delirium. Most of these guys go to Abu to do their butt sniffing, he may have a girlfriend, and then again, he may not. The guys have a reputation for being coy and evasive."

The Army medic went about her business, changing dressings, perusing patient charts, and bringing meals. Flynn asked on the second day of his treatment when he could leave.

"You have to do a couple of outpatient days of testing to see if you're capable of driving a vehicle and handling your weaponry." Flynn stared into the ceiling rafters, sighed audibly, and soon fell asleep.

After a couple of hours, Gerald came alongside his friend and took a chair. Looking at the medic, he asked, "Can you wake him? I need to talk some sense into this idiot." She shook Flynn's shoulder softly, "Time to wake up and chit chat," she said. One of the docs came over and stood by Flynn's bedside for the briefing. Flynn came around suddenly, waking with a start, pushing up to a sitting position while the medic arranged his pillows.

The doc stood by as Gerald asked Flynn a few questions.

"What day is this?" Flynn focused his eyes, "Tuesday, I think."

"Where are you?" the medic asked.

"I'm at the Emirates Palace in Abu, with my woman," he responded. Looking at Flynn cynically, the medic responded, "He's fine!" Gerald chimed in, following more words about Flynn's general condition with the doc.

"Remember the second time you fell when we were rock climbing in the Poudre Canyon?" Flynn fixated on the distant past, "Yeah, so?" "Remember what I told you back then?" Gerald inquired.

"You told me I could fall once, maybe fall twice and live, but the third time it would kill me."

"Well, don't you think you've fulfilled your obligation with the FFL? You've been in this MASH unit twice; next time, it could be in a body bag! Take stock, and put an end to your adventure!" Gerald thought he may have gotten his point across; the rest was up to Flynn. The medic looked on with apprehension, hoping that Flynn would muster out of the FFL.

*   *   *

Eve was busy in the Miami University library. It was her ambition to formulate study habits before classes started. She read books on studying, emphasizing preparation for the Bar Exam. Time was on her side, but the baby inside her had a different schedule.

"Henry, stop that," she would say as she felt life within her, "We're in the library!" People would look up, noticing her apparent pregnancy, and smile. Gerald's DEROS (date of expected return from overseas) would grant him a thirty-day leave. Free of living at a distance from his wife and their expected child, he would develop a strategy for the remainder of his enlistment. He was fortunate that he would soon be on duty at the Doral Garrison a few miles east of Miami. 'It was Sebastian's doing, he thought and left it at that. Why mess it up!

At Lemonnier, life moved along faster than Gerald had anticipated. He planned to travel on orders to his new duty assignment. Aunt Syl suggested that he could get a hop to Abu Dhabi, where she was conferencing with contemporaries. Gerald could catch a flight back to the U.S. with Syl on the Global aircraft. He asked if a friend could join the flight. Ronald Bacon (Pig) was also returning to stateside duty. Syl agreed, and the two men would come aboard the Global 5000 for the flight home. Syl approached the two soldiers at the Abu Dhabi airport, dressed in a wide floppy sun hat, flowery dress, and dark glasses. She looked very out of place, yet she carried herself like she was right at home.

*   *   *

Flynn processed from duty with the Foreign Legion, but he wouldn't be returning to the U.S. A few FFL veterans extended invitations for him to stay in Europe and pursue their futures as a group. A former Sagaie gunner on the A.C.'s suggested, "If you want to give it a go, you can come to work for my family." He lived in Brandon, England, in the county of Suffolk, which was mainly farmland and forest. London was a short drive away, with transportation on the tubes, very accessible. Flynn accepted the idea and caught a flight to Heathrow. He also promised to stay in touch with Eve and Gerald as they pursued their plans in south Florida.

*   *   *

Málaga, Spain, was six hours away as the Global took flight. Syl booked rooms at the Grand Hotel Miramar G.L. Seated next to Ron Bacon on the global, Gerald was on familiar turf. The two settled into discussing stateside duty, especially living in Colorado at Fort Carson.

"I do have my thirty-day leave before I report to Carson," Ron said, "But you will be on duty at the Doral garrison; that's not too shabby." Gerald hesitated, then said there were strings attached. He would have to get his paperwork in order with Eve's help and find his way around Miami University. The plan was to take a few classes after hours from his military duties. "I have my family waiting, Eve with a baby on board and Maxine Donahoe, our housemate. The three of us will be a total of four souls by next March.

"You have daddy written all over you," Ron said, "You're in for a fantastic future."

"And you will be fine too," said Gerald, "You had all that positive press when you met Jackie Emmerson."

"Yeah, I developed a few e-mail pals from that experience, and I plan to follow up," Ron said with a sheepish grin. Shortly after 1 p.m. local time in Spain, the Global touched down to sixty degrees and lite rain. Their stay was short-lived as everyone was anxious to get home to the U.S. By noon the following day, the Global was airborne and six thousand miles from Miami.

Due to routine maintenance on the Global, pilots Burt and Ernie would get in a few rounds of golf at Doral Gulf Club. Gerald, excited to see his family, had been on his cell phone. He was eager to see Eve and feel her tummy. Trailing through customs, the group collected baggage and found ground transportation to Eve and M.D.'s condominium. Ron Bacon would go his separate way to Montana.

"Pig, don't get into any trouble at Fort Carson," Gerald said as the two shook hands. It was bitter-sweet that the two would probably never cross paths again. Such was Army life. The mix of people meeting Gerald included the extended family, but he only had eyes for his wife Eve. Finally, there she was, bloomed with the addition of Henry in her midsection.

"Gosh, I have to lean over to kiss you," Gerald said," There's someone between us." Eve placed Gerald's hand on her tummy.

"Wait for a second," she said, "Here it comes!" The ripple of Henry's elbows or knees graced the interior walls of Eve's abdomen.

"Did you feel that?" she asked Gerald. "That's your son saying that he's delighted to meet you!"

On the third day of their reunion, there came a sobering message for Syl. Her kitchen lady called from the Abilene ranch with bad news. It was about the woman's mother.

"Mi madre esta muy enferma," (My mother she is very sick). Taking the phone from Eve, Syl was emotionally distraught as she listened to the call from Texas. Eve looked on with empathy and stayed by Syl's side after reading her aunt's body language. She asked Gerald to call Bert and get the plane ready.

"I have to get to the Abilene ranch. Maria Sanchez is on her deathbed," said Syl. She explained that Maria, a mother figure, had liver cancer. She hurriedly prepared to travel. Gerald drove her to Miami International as Bert and Ernie were ready for departure.

"This is going to be tuff," Syl said to Gerald. By late afternoon, the Global touched down at the Abilene Ranch airstrip. The ranch foreman met her at the plane hangar. Tears glistening, he said that Maria had passed that morning, September 28th.

"Maria's daughter and the rest of the family are upstairs with her now," he said. Silence reigned for the moment. Releasing a tearful sigh, "We'd better get up there." Syl said. There were more than a dozen people in the bedroom. The Sanchez family and a few nieces and nephews were grieving. The family pastor stood close with a Catholic priest, who was performing the last rites of the Church. Thankful that Syl was there, young and old, joined hands with her or touched her arms and shoulders. The bond was both instant and compassionate among all those in the room. As two of the younger children began to fidget, people broke into separate groups, silently discussing what would come next. The ranch foreman addressed the group saying that he had called the county coroner. Procedures were in place that would take Marie to Elmwood mortuary in Abilene.

*   *   *

Six months later, after Peter-Henry's birth, Eve attempted to teach their infant son to nurse while Gerald sat exhausted at the beside. He had been up nearly twenty-four hours assisting Eve between contractions and was now generally fixated about not leaving his wife's side. Baby Pete-Henry didn't know how to nurse, and his mother's milk hadn't come in right away. Nonetheless, Eve was brushing her nipple against the infant's cheek and tiny nose, trying to get a response. A nurse came in, took the baby, and said they would try it again the next day.

"If he's anything like his daddy," cooed Eve, "Baby Pete will latch on." Looking at Gerald, she said, "You better go home and get some rest. Tomorrow, I have a confession. I promised I wouldn't mention it until after our boy was born."

"Oh God, what now," said Gerald with an impulse of emotion.

"Oh, never mind," said Eve, "Go home and crash for a while. I'll be here tomorrow, same time, the same place; we'll talk about it then." The loving smile Eve gave to her husband suggested whatever she had to say couldn't be so bad. Breathing a long sigh, Gerald turned at the door and then came back to Eve's bedside and gathered her face in his hands.

"I don't care if you bark at the moon and dance like Elaine Bennis; I will love you anyway!" Then Gerald turned on his heel, departed the room, and drove home in a daze.

The following morning at 10:30, Gerald came with his parents trailing behind.

"They're not due to bring Peter-Henry in until a bit later," said Eve. "I'm glad you could all be here. I promised Gerald I had something to say, which all three of you need to hear. I don't mean to dampen the spirit of you meeting your new grandson, and If I'm right, you will take it in stride."

"Take what in stride?" asked Charles as his smile faded.

"Well, it's like this," Eve began. She sat up as Gerald raised the bed so his wife could sit erect. She had brushed her hair, and a pinafore covered her to the neck.

"Several months ago," she began, "Trish Hays told me that she had robbed your safety deposit box when she worked at your bank three years ago." There was a hush in the room, then Gerald and his parents started talking all at once.

Eve held up her left hand, saying, "Let me finish!" She was neither adamant nor challenging but wanted to get her story told without interruption.

"Trish, along with her husband Les and the bank president, started a recovery fund to make up for your loss. They have a portfolio set aside in Gerald's name that has accumulated about $55K."

Lynn Ingalls took a step forward, turned, and looked at her son and husband Charles.

"I knew there was something fishy when Trish left the bank; she was behind the robbery!"

Eve cleared her throat lightly and continued with her story.

"My Aunt Syl has deep pockets, and if I ask her, she would probably lay this matter to rest once and for all."

Then Charles had something to say.

"Lynn and I have earned that much in three or four home sales over the last few months." He didn't want his daughter-in-law to feel culpable over something that someone else had done.

Lynn spoke up again, saying, "Charles will not follow that financial loss with a personal loss on the family level. Just forget about it! We're not pointing fingers or filing charges!"

"So, it's all water under the bridge?" suggested Gerald.

"That's the way I see it said Charles, let sleeping dogs lie."

Looking around the room and finding seats, Eve's visitors took a few moments to digest their conversation.

About that time, a nurse brought little Peter-Henry into the room. "Do you want to hold him?" said Eve to her mother-in-law. Holding out her arms, Lynn Ingalls took her new grandson and gently rolled the nursery blankets away from his tiny face.

"You don't look anything like your pictures in vitro," she said with grace and humility. Studying his features, Lynn wiped a tear and looked up from the baby.

"This is all the compensation I need. Don't you agree, Charles?"

"It is," her husband said.

*   *   *

Six months later, things had settled down considerably. Eve, seated at her kitchen table, was attempting to spoon-feed Gerber green beans into the mouth of squirmy, six-month-old Peter-Henry. Wiping his entire face with a forearm, young Peter closed his eyes and mouth. Giving up on him for the moment, Eve wiped the boy down and placed him in his playpen. For the moment, it was quiet.

M.D. had gone to an art class, and Gerald was busy changing the oil in their new Nissan Murano. He was a freshman at Miami University balancing home life and classes. Eve leafed through her kitchen calendar to November, where, in large red letters, she had written, 'Anniversary.' She called Trish and opened the conversation by asking about her children. She wanted to know how Arielle was doing with tableware and if Dax still adored his little sister.

"They're getting along fine," replied Trish. "We have Storytime at the library in 45 minutes; I can't talk long." "Have you thought more about our Thanksgiving plans?" Eve asked.

"I have," said Trish. "Les and our kiddos are looking forward to seeing everyone!" When Gerald came into the kitchen, Eve was ready for her 11:00 class in the Juris degree program. She mastered the technical aspects of law, its theory, and its substance. It could be a grind, but Eve was thriving in her classes. Tenants' rights and environmental justice were of particular interest to her. They would apply in spades to the task ahead with Mildenhall Oil. She had maneuvered to graduate law school with the ease of milk to butter.

"Henry refused his green beans," Eve said. Picking their son from the playpen, Gerald held the toddler at eye level.

"We'll just see about that Prince Henry!" The little boy smiled at his father. The morning gave way to other pressing matters. Eve rode her bicycle to class and found her designated seat. On her computer screen, she cued the date and sat back to watch fellow students arrive. Her mind drifted. At that moment, she considered the comfort she tried to express to Aunt Syl on the death of Maria Sanchez. It was the first time she had seen the vulnerable side of her Aunt Syl.

"You lost a lifelong companion," she had said, "But we have new life in the family." Peter Henry Ingalls came along to assume his late uncle's name. Syl set about providing for young Pete's future; he was the apple of her eye. All parties would converge for a family milestone at the home of Eve's Great aunt and uncle in Colorado. Those in attendance would sit for a group photo of more than two dozen souls. Katie and Alfred celebrated their fifty-seventh wedding anniversary on Thanksgiving.

Their grand-niece Eve said, "If it weren't for you two, none of the rest of us would be here celebrating your special day, and I want you to know you had a hand in making me the person I am today; I feel so lucky. When my life was very bleak almost four years ago, you had my back, and I'm grateful to have you in our family. I love you both dearly!"

Katie and Alfred felt blessed by Eve's kind words, and they were proud of the choices she had made. A family guardian extraordinaire, she was the granddaughter they never had. Proposing a toast, Eve and Gerald surprised their family by announcing another baby would come in the new year. She took her husband's hand, saying, "If it's a girl, we have decided to name her Sylvia Katie Lynn."